"We're Going to Make Romeo and Juliet Look Like Casual Acquaintances..."

"This is really crazy! You and I don't even like each other. No one's going to believe we...we're romantically involved."

"It's up to us to make them believe it." Tristan's low, musical voice was evoking a picture that stirred Angelique's senses.

What was she thinking? "I'll go along with your wild scheme up to a point. We'll pretend that you're the one I came to visit, but only if we give the impression that our affair is in its early stages."

Tristan smiled mockingly. "Soulful glances and heavy breathing would make the whole thing much more credible."

"Go ahead, if you want your audience to see the shortest romance on record."

"I've never believed in brief encounters." His eyes flicked over her consideringly. "Real enjoyment comes from knowing a woman thoroughly."

Dear Reader:

Romance offers us all so much. It makes us "walk on sunshine." It gives us hope. It takes us out of our own lives, encouraging us to reach out to others. Janet Dailey is fond of saying that romance is a state of mind, that it could happen anywhere. Yet nowhere does romance seem to be as good as when it happens *here*.

Starting in February 1986, Silhouette Special Edition will feature the AMERICAN TRIBUTE—a tribute to America, where romance has never been so wonderful. For six consecutive months, one out of every six Special Editions will be an episode in the AMERICAN TRIBUTE, a portrait of the lives of six women, all from Oklahoma. Look for the first book, *Love's Haunting Refrain* by Ada Steward, as well as stories by other favorites—Jeanne Stephens, Gena Dalton, Elaine Camp and Renee Roszel. You'll know the AMERICAN TRIBUTE by its patriotic stripe under the Silhouette Special Edition border.

AMERICAN TRIBUTE—six women, six stories, starting in February.

AMERICAN TRIBUTE—one of the reasons Silhouette Special Edition is just that—Special.

The Editors at Silhouette Books

TRACY SINCLAIR
Dream Girl

Silhouette Special Edition

Published by Silhouette Books New York

America's Publisher of Contemporary Romance

SILHOUETTE BOOKS
300 E. 42nd St., New York, N.Y. 10017

Copyright © 1986 by Tracy Sinclair

Distributed by Pocket Books

ISBN: 0-373-09287-3

First Silhouette Books printing January 1986

10 9 8 7 6 5 4 3 2 1

America's Publisher of Contemporary Romance

Printed in the U.S.A.

Books by Tracy Sinclair

Silhouette Romance

Paradise Island #39
Holiday in Jamaica #123
Flight to Romance #174
Stars in Her Eyes #244
Catch a Rising Star #345

Silhouette Special Edition

Never Give Your Heart #12
Mixed Blessing #34
Designed for Love #52
Castles in the Air #68
Fair Exchange #105
Winter of Love #140
The Tangled Web #153
The Harvest Is Love #183
Pride's Folly #208
Intrigue in Venice #232
A Love So Tender #249
Dream Girl #287

TRACY SINCLAIR

has worked extensively as a photojournalist. She's traveled throughout North America, as well as to parts of the Caribbean, South America and Europe. Her name is very familiar in both Silhouette Romances and Silhouette Special Editions.

Chapter One

"Tilt your head to the side, Angel. I want to get a shot of your hair swinging loose. A little more. That's great." The photographer's staccato commands were accompanied by the rapid clicking of a high-speed camera.

Angelique Archer followed directions, turning gracefully while giving him the radiant smiles that were expected of Vendome Cosmetic Company's Dream Girl. After almost a year of being featured in their shampoo ads, her movements were effortless. She and Phil Nestor worked as a smoothly functioning team.

"Raise your chin slightly. Fantastic." He circled her, dropping to one knee for a different angle. "We'll have this campaign wrapped up in no time."

"Great!" Her smile widened to show perfect white teeth. "You wouldn't believe how tired I am of shampooing my hair every day."

"If you're looking for sympathy, forget it. Do you know how many models would like to be Vendome's Dream Girl—at your salary?"

"I know I'm lucky," she acknowledged, thinking of the hundreds of women who had applied for the job.

"Well, I wouldn't say it was all luck."

As Phil paused to reload he took a moment to look appraisingly at her. It was to be expected that a shampoo model would have beautiful hair, and Angelique's filled the requirement. It was a shade somewhere between blond and red, a tawny, glowing color that defied description. But the face it framed was even more exquisite. A curved, generous mouth, and a small straight nose were overshadowed by slightly tilted, deep blue eyes in an unexpected frame of sooty lashes.

Phil was accustomed to photographing beautiful women, yet he had never encountered one who had absolutely no bad angles. Angelique was truly blessed by nature. If she hadn't possessed that flawless face she could still have gotten by on her fantastic figure, he reflected. It was incredible that she was so completely unaffected. Top models were often difficult to work with, but Angelique was both cooperative and unimpressed by the multimillion dollar build-up that had made her face recognizable throughout the world.

"Of course it was luck." She was laughing now. "If I'd been born a brunette I'd probably be scrounging around for assignments advertising floor wax or paper towels."

Before Phil could refute the statement, the studio receptionist stuck her head in the door. "Got a message for you, Angel. The Vendome office just called; your secret admirer has struck again. They want to know if they should send the latest offering to your apartment, or would you rather stop by to pick it up?"

Angelique hesitated. For the past few weeks someone had been inundating her with flowers. Dozens of long-stemmed roses, gladioli, carnations, the whole gamut of the floral world, had been arriving anonymously. "I guess they'd better send them. The last basket was almost too big to fit in the cab."

"I should have such problems." The receptionist made a face before disappearing.

"The guy is still at it?" Phil raised a questioning eyebrow. "You don't know who he is yet?"

"The florist insists even he doesn't know—which is pretty hard to believe. At any rate, he won't tell me."

"I bet you'll find out soon. Long-stemmed roses don't exactly grow in the backyard. When the donor gets around to telling you his name, it will probably be accompanied by an invitation to spend the weekend on his yacht—just the two of you," Phil remarked cynically.

A slight frown marred Angelique's smooth forehead. "I don't think so."

"Come on, Angel! You've been in New York long enough to know the score."

"No, really, Phil. As you pointed out, he's spent a fortune on flowers without once trying to get in touch with me."

"That only proves he's a very clever gent. You're intrigued, aren't you?"

"Well, of course I am. Anyone would be. But I've come to a different conclusion."

"Which is?"

"I think my secret admirer is an older man," she remarked thoughtfully.

"It's entirely possible." Phil's smirk was faintly lascivious. "They used to call them sugar daddies in the old days."

"That's not what I meant," she answered impatiently. "I think it's someone very lonely." Ignoring Phil's snort of derision, she continued, "Maybe I remind him of his first love, or else a daughter he either lost, or never had."

"Dream on, kid. But when the guy makes his move, don't say I didn't warn you."

"We might never know which of us is right?" Angelique sighed. "He could disappear without a trace, as suddenly as he came into my life."

"I wouldn't worry about that. He has an investment in you now; he's going to want to collect a few dividends."

"Honestly, Phil! I'm glad I'm not a cynic like you. How can you look at roses and see only thorns? That takes all the fun out of life."

"Maybe, but it's better than getting stuck. The guy could be a real weirdo. If you're smart you'll nip this thing in the bud." He grinned at the outrageous pun. "Take my advice and have the florist tell his big spender that you suddenly developed an allergy."

Angelique would always wonder afterward, what would have happened if she'd taken Phil's advice. At the time she shrugged it off.

He was right about one thing—she *was* intrigued. Angelique was accustomed to a lot of male attention, but it had never been anonymous. After the first lavish gift of flowers arrived she had waited as cynically as Phil for a follow up. When it didn't come she was surprised, then puzzled, and eventually titillated.

It occurred to her, naturally, that it might be an elaborate build-up. But as time went on and the person made no attempt to contact her, Angelique began to look for something other than the obvious conclusion. That was when she formed her impression of the mystery man.

After weeks of splendid offerings without any strings, she started to feel quite fondly toward the unknown stranger.

The orchids that greeted Angelique when she let herself into her chic apartment were unbelievably beautiful. A huge ceramic bowl was filled with exotic blooms unlike any she had ever seen before. Long stalks of pink blossoms speckled with brown alternated with branches of tiny, feathery white flowers resembling butterflies. They provided a frame for the large bronze orchids with pale green centers that formed the middle of the arrangement.

As Angelique examined the bouquet with delight, something caught her eye. A small white envelope was tucked unobtrusively into the foliage. Excitement surged through her as she reached for it. Was the mystery about to be solved?

The enclosed message read: "I hope that my small offerings have not offended you. I wish only to pay tribute to your great beauty." It was signed, "Respectfully, Claude."

The stilted tone of the note reinforced her convictions. Only an older man would use such formal, old-fashioned language. Angelique felt a slight pang. In spite of her insistence to Phil, she had harbored a secret fantasy that her unknown admirer was actually someone young and exciting—a tall, dark stranger who would sweep her up in a fairy-tale romance.

Angelique's mouth curved in a rueful smile. Life wasn't like that. The fervent, impetuous man she dreamed of wouldn't worship her from afar. No, she had been right the first time. This was the next best thing, though. At least he hadn't turned out to be a lecher.

A feeling of depression filled Angelique at the thought of a person so lonely that he had to shower his affection on a woman known only from a picture. The man was obviously wealthy, yet he seemed to have no one. The sadness of it touched her. If he ever revealed his identity, she vowed to try to bring some color into his life.

After the first note there were others, all simply signed, "Claude," with no further identification. Then one day a letter arrived.

It was addressed to her, care of the Vendome Cosmetic Company, and rerouted by their office staff. She opened the square envelope indifferently, glancing at the unfamiliar signature, "Claude Dumont." Suddenly it rang a bell and she grabbed for the envelope. There it was—his return address!

Her mouth dropped open. Neatly printed in the upper left-hand corner were the words, "Number 1, Rue Royale, Kingdom of Souveraine." It had never occurred to her that the man might be from another country! Now that she thought of it though, it would account for the almost stylized form of English.

Where on earth was Souveraine? The name was only vaguely familiar to Angelique. After getting an atlas from the bookcase she looked it up, sitting cross-legged on the floor. "The kingdom of Souveraine has been a monarchy since the mid-fifteen hundreds," she read. "Its location on the Mediterranean Sea assures delightful weather much of the year. French is the official language, although the natives are conversant with a variety of languages because of the tiny kingdom's proximity to the other nations of Europe." There was a short paragraph about the customs and products of the country, but Angelique saved it for later. She hadn't read Claude's letter yet.

"If you feel that I am taking too great a liberty by addressing you directly, please inform me and I will not bother you again," he wrote. "I have admired you from afar for so long that I felt I must tell you. Never have I seen anyone so lovely. If you see fit to answer this letter with even one line, I will treasure it always."

Angelique had tears in her eyes when she finished reading. The poor sweet old man! She went immediately to her desk.

After that a letter arrived from Claude almost daily, although he assured Angelique that he didn't expect an equal response from her. It was as though a dam had burst once he had made the initial contact. She seemed to be the outlet for all of his frustrated yearning for companionship. During their exchange of letters Angelique became very fond of Claude.

It bothered her that he felt he had to compensate her for her friendship, which appeared to be the case because the floral tributes increased. Angelique gently tried to discourage them. "The flowers are lovely, but I don't have room for any more," she wrote.

Claude's answer to that left her gasping. It arrived along with a small package delivered by messenger. His note said, "I should have realized you were tiring of flowers. Please accept this token of my esteem instead."

Inside the square velvet box under the paper wrappings was the most magnificent necklace Angelique had ever seen. A complete circlet of diamonds with sapphires the size of her thumbnail suspended at intervals all the way around. Each sapphire was surrounded by more diamonds that glittered like cold fire.

Angelique could only stare in disbelief. The piece was worth a fortune! What on earth was Claude thinking of? For a moment Phil's warning surfaced, but she dismissed it as unworthy. There had been no hint that Claude wanted anything in return. Was it possible that he was a little dotty? He'd seemed perfectly lucid in his letters, but suppose he was slightly senile? Sending a gift this valuable to a woman he'd never met did seem to indicate as much.

Angelique put aside the disquieting thought for a more pressing one. How was she going to return it? It wasn't exactly the sort of thing you wrapped in brown paper and dropped in the corner mailbox. A necklace this expensive ought to be delivered by armed guard!

The frivolous idea sparked a genuine one. Why not return it in person? The advertising campaign had been wrapped up, and she had nothing to do for at least a month until they started a new one. Angelique was under exclusive contract to Vendome Cosmetics so she couldn't work for anyone else.

The more she thought about the plan, the more it appealed to her. She hadn't had a vacation in a long time, and what better place to take it than Europe? After a short visit to Souveraine she could go on to tour the Continent.

Claude would be so pleased. Angelique's eyes sparkled as she imagined the elderly man's surprise. It wouldn't do to tell him she was coming—that would spoil it. She would just take a taxi to his house and appear on the doorstep. He would know who *she* was immediately, but at long last she was going to find out if Claude Dumont fitted her mental picture of a sweet old man with courtly manners. As she looked up the travel agent's phone number, Angelique began to get quite excited.

From the air, Souveraine looked like a small piece of paradise. Pink and white houses clung to gentle hills half circling an aquamarine bay filled with tiny boats. As the plane swooped lower, the boats turned into sleek yachts, and the tiny houses became lovely villas surrounded by colorful flowers. It was the most enchanting spot Angelique had ever seen, almost unreal in its perfection.

She didn't even bother to unpack after being shown to her hotel room, not wanting to postpone her meeting with Claude another minute. After freshening up a little she went down to the desk in the lobby.

"Could you tell me where Number one, Rue Royale is?" she asked the clerk. "If it isn't too far I'd like to walk." There was more to see that way than driving by in a taxi.

"You wish to go to the palace?"

"Later perhaps. Right now I want to visit a friend," she explained.

The man looked puzzled. "I thought you wished Number one, Rue Royale."

"I do."

"That is the palace."

They looked at each other in frustration. "I don't think you understand." Angelique tried again. "I have a friend in Souveraine. His name is Claude Dumont. Do you know him by any chance?" It was such a small country that it was entirely possible. When the man shook his head she said, "He lives on Rue Royale."

"Not at Number one, *mademoiselle*," the clerk insisted. "That is where the palace is located."

Angelique was startled. Was it possible that Claude was some kind of functionary at the court? Did they still have dignitaries living in the compound the way the old royal families used to? Well, she was about to find out.

"Is it within walking distance?" she repeated.

"No, and it is not open to the public, *mademoiselle*, except designated apartments on certain days."

Angelique managed to repress her irritation. The man thought he was being helpful. She walked outside and hailed a taxi. The cabdriver gave her the same information about the palace that the clerk had, but Angelique was prepared. When she told him she had to see some-one there, he gave her a rather unpleasant leer.

Angelique's pleased anticipation was fading rapidly. What had she gotten herself into? Was there some secret connected with Claude, her gentle, respectful admirer? What if he turned out to be completely different from her mental image—closer to Phil Nestor's than her own? If that were the case it would be unfortunate, but there was nothing she could do about it. She was here now and the necklace had to be returned, especially if Claude wasn't the kindly gentleman he seemed.

The palace looked like a fairy-tale castle out of a chil-dren's book. The lovely old building was stately yet graceful, with long wings on either side of a crenellated tower. The blue and white flag of Souveraine flew from a battlement, rippling in the light breeze that carried the scent of roses from the gardens in back.

A soldier in an elaborate uniform marched back and forth in front of the main entrance to the palace. At one side of the wide courtyard that fronted it was a guard-house with another soldier keeping watch. It was like a scene out of a costume play, charming and unreal.

"We are here, *mademoiselle*." The driver's eyes ap-praised Angelique's delicate face and curved figure. "Give my regards to the grand duke."

What on earth was that all about, she wondered, after paying him and getting out of the cab. The man's smirk was distinctly lecherous. Putting it out of her mind, she approached the guardhouse.

"I'd like to see Claude Dumont. Would you please tell him that Angelique Archer is here." The surprise would be spoiled, but it couldn't be helped.

The young guard looked appreciatively at her before his eyes dropped reluctantly to a roster inside the booth.

After a moment he said, "I'm sorry but he's not in today."

Angelique had a sudden feeling of relief. At least Claude Dumont existed! For a time there she was beginning to think she had walked into a melodrama. "He does live here then?" she double-checked.

"Oh no, *mademoiselle*, this is the palace."

Angelique again felt as though she were Alice in Wonderland. "I know that, but I was told—never mind," she interrupted herself. "When will he be here?"

"I can't tell you exactly. Claude's wife is expecting a baby, and I believe he has requested some time off."

Angelique stared at him as the nightmare sensation closed in again. Her lonely, solitary, gentleman friend had a wife and family! He was neither alone nor old, not if they were young enough to have a baby. Was he even rich? He had to be to pay for all those flowers, not to mention the necklace. But the whole thing didn't make sense! Why would Claude spend time and money on a woman he didn't know and never expected to meet?

"Are you all right, *mademoiselle*?" The guard was looking at her anxiously.

"What? Oh yes, I...I'm fine." She pulled herself together hurriedly.

During the taxi ride back, Angelique's anger began to rise as the full implications hit her. Claude Dumont was a two-timing rat, even if he wasn't physically unfaithful to his wife. Those worshipful letters had been almost like declarations of love, and the money he spent was unconscionable. How could he justify it? The necklace alone was worth a king's ransom.

Suddenly a terrible suspicion entered her mind. Suppose she had been had from beginning to end? What if the necklace was a fake? It would be bitterly ironic if she had come all this way to return a priceless object that wasn't worth as much as the beige suit she had on.

Angelique's soft mouth set grimly as she paid off the cabdriver in front of the hotel. Instead of going inside, she walked down the block to a jewelry store she had seen from the taxi. When she noticed the discreet lettering announcing that Jacarde et Fils were purveyors to the royal family of Souveraine, Angelique knew she had come to the right place. They would know if the necklace was paste.

The elegantly dressed man in the shop looked at the diamond and sapphire circlet for a long time. After examining the stones with a glass in one eye, he inspected the whole thing again. His hands were trembling as he put it back on its bed of satin.

"Where did you get this, *mademoiselle*?" There was a faint quiver in his voice.

Angelique frowned. "That isn't really important. I just want to know whether it's genuine or not."

"I will have to subject it to further tests."

She wasn't mistaken, he *was* looking at her strangely. What was it about that wretched necklace? Before she could stop him, the man picked it up and took it into a back room. Was it conceivable that he meant to steal it? "*Monsieur*, I don't really have time for that now," she called a little desperately.

There was no answer, leaving her with a dilemma. Should she go after him and demand the return of her jewelry? It was a very posh store and she would feel like a complete idiot if she overreacted, but if the necklace *was* real, she had to get it back to that creep, Claude.

The minutes ticked by as Angelique agonized. The opulent surroundings reassured her, but the man's hasty retreat with her property canceled that out. Just as Angelique got to her feet, determined to go looking for him, the front door opened and four uniformed policemen entered.

Before she could open her mouth, the owner of the shop reappeared. Pointing dramatically, he said, "She is the one!"

As the policemen converged on her with expressionless faces, Angelique asked helplessly, "What's going on here?"

The officer with the most gold braid on his sleeve answered her. "Monsieur Jacarde says you have a very valuable piece of jewelry in your possession. May I ask where you got it?"

"No, you may not!" Angelique snapped. "I'd like to ask *you* what this is all about?"

"I am afraid I must insist that you answer my question." The policeman's tight jaw left no doubt about it.

Angelique's heart sank as she faced the possibility that the necklace was stolen. It had never occurred to her, but it was the obvious implication from this show of force. The owner of the store had recognized the piece. That was the problem, but what was the solution? She had no idea how to get in touch with Claude, and he wouldn't back her up anyway. Without his corroboration, would the police believe that he had given the necklace to her and she was bringing it back? Hardly. Angelique did the only thing she could under the circumstances; she tried to bluster it out.

"I happen to be an American citizen, a tourist in your country. I'm going to protest strongly to my embassy about this treatment," she declared firmly.

It got her exactly nowhere. The four officers took turns questioning her, with the store owner adding his bit from time to time. Finally Angelique's patience was exhausted. "Are you going to keep me here indefinitely? At least in my country the accused is allowed a lawyer while he's being given the third degree," she observed sarcastically, wondering who on earth she could call to get her out of this mess.

"You will be taken to the police station in due time," the chief officer informed her, which wasn't the news Angelique had been looking forward to.

Suddenly the door was flung open and the most dynamic man she had ever seen entered. He immediately dominated their little group, not by his superior height, but by the forcefulness of his personality. His gray eyes were stormy in a high-cheeked, patrician face that was all strong planes and angles. The only softening feature was a wide, sensuous mouth, but it was compressed now in anger. Fury seemed to radiate from his lean, powerful body as he strode up to them.

"Where is it?" he demanded.

When the owner produced the velvet box wordlessly, the newcomer stared down at it, his tanned face darkening. He turned to Angelique and for just a moment, whatever he had been about to say deserted him as he gazed at her flawless features. She stared back, feeling a strange thrill race through her veins. There was a magnetism about the man that made Angelique very aware of being a woman. Even while her mind was rejecting his domineering attitude, her body couldn't help responding to his overwhelming masculinity.

After the one instant of surprise, a curtain dropped and his bemused eyes became piercing. "Where did you get this?"

His return to arrogance made Angelique wonder how she had thought him attractive. "That isn't exactly original," she quipped, refusing to be intimidated. "I've been asked the same question quite a few times already."

"This time you will answer it," he assured him grimly.

He was dressed in riding breeches that were molded to his long muscular legs. His cream-colored silk shirt had several buttons unfastened, revealing a gold medallion nestled among the crisp dark hairs on his broad chest. He couldn't very well be a policeman, dressed like that, so Angelique didn't see any reason to oblige him.

She returned his scowl with one of her own. "Who are you anyway?"

"This is the grand duke, Tristan de Marchal," the owner informed her, shocked at the way she had put the question.

"Big deal," Angelique muttered under her breath.

For just a moment, a hint of amusement lightened the duke's face before it became stern again. "We can do this the hard way, or we can do it the easy way. But make no mistake, I shall receive my answer."

Angelique knew when she was beaten. The tall man confronting her radiated authority. "The necklace was given to me by Claude Dumont," she said.

Whatever answer he had been expecting, that wasn't it. She had succeeded in startling him, which wasn't easy, Angelique guessed.

"That is not possible!" he exclaimed.

She shrugged. "You asked and I told you."

The reaction of the others was equally strong. Their expressions ranged from embarrassment to a kind of discreet leer. Would the mystery of Claude Dumont ever be solved?

"Who is he anyway?" she burst out.

The duke's eyes narrowed dangerously. "I thought you said he was your lover."

"I never said any such thing!" Angelique gasped.

"I think you have quite a lot of explaining to do." He glanced briefly at the avidly listening men. "But not here." Taking her arm in a firm grip he led her toward the front door.

"I'm not going anywhere with you! What do you think you're doing?"

Her protests fell on deaf ears, just as her struggles to get away were useless. He pulled her to a low, racy Maserati parked at the curb and plunked her into the bucket seat, ignoring her indignant cries. When he buckled her seat belt, the feel of his strong, long-fingered hands brushing against her body was vaguely disturbing.

"You can't do this to me!" she stormed, trying to unfasten the belt.

He captured both her wrists in one hand, using the other to jerk her chin up. "I don't know what your game is, young woman, but when I get through with you, you're going to be sorry you ever heard of Souveraine."

With his face that close to hers, Angelique could see every black, spiky lash that framed his gray eyes. It occurred to her, irrelevantly, that they were much too long and luxurious for a man, yet strangely enough they didn't detract a bit from his virility. Even in his present state of towering rage, he radiated sexuality. With that strong, expressive face and athletic physique, the man could make a fortune in her business. The idea of the autocratic grand duke of Souveraine advertising men's jockey shorts made her smile involuntarily.

His dark brows drew together. "I'm glad you find this so amusing. Let's hope you continue to do so after I turn you over to the police."

Angelique realized that things had gotten way out of hand. "If you'll just calm down for a few minutes, I can explain everything," she began.

"Save it until we get to the palace." His terse tone didn't brook any arguments.

She didn't see why they had to go all the way there, but since the alternative was the police station, Angelique settled back with a sigh. A classic Monopoly game saying popped into her mind: "Proceed directly to jail. Do not pass go." It wasn't a comforting thought.

She couldn't have made her explanation on the way, in any case. The duke drove like a race-car driver. The lovely scenery went by in a blur as he took the sharp curves on screeching tires. It was only slightly comforting to know that he was in command of the powerful car at all times, mastering it like a superb rider taming a spirited horse.

It was evidently the way he treated women too, Angelique thought resentfully. And yet...that full lower lip indicated a sensuous side. Did he make love with tenderness as well as expertise? There was no doubt about the ecstasy that lithe body could bring, but did he take what he wanted without gentleness? Probably.

For one spine-chilling moment she imagined his dark, triumphant face poised over hers at the peak of passion. A shiver ran up Angelique's spine as she turned her head to look at the rushing countryside. It was madness to let her imagination run away with her. The duke was only a man, in spite of that fancy title, and she was more than a match for him.

When they reached the palace he parked in the courtyard in front of the door and hustled her inside without a word. She barely had time to appreciate the stately marble-floored reception hall dominated by a magnificent crystal chandelier, or the twin, curving staircases that led to an upper floor.

Never releasing her arm, he led her across the entry to an ornately paneled door. It opened into a room that appeared to be a small library. A comfortable couch flanked by down-cushioned chairs faced a fireplace with a carved mantel holding exquisite figurines.

"You will wait here," the duke ordered. After viewing her mutinous face he added, "Don't even think about escaping. The guards will not permit it."

"I have no intention of running away," Angelique answered indignantly. "I want this thing cleared up more than you do, if only to see your face when you hear the whole story."

"I can hardly wait to see yours when Claude gives his side of it," he replied, striding out the door before she could stop him.

Left alone in the gracious room, Angelique had to restrain herself from wringing her hands. The duke obviously didn't know that Claude wasn't in the palace that day. Would he believe her version of the story? Even to her own ears it sounded thin. Yet there was no way she could have stolen that necklace. Surely that would convince him.

Angelique stiffened as the door opened a few minutes later, but it wasn't the duke. A tall, gangly young man entered—a boy actually. He couldn't have been more than sixteen or seventeen. The resemblance to the duke was very marked. The boy had the same dark hair and acquiline features, but his were softened by youth.

His mouth dropped open as he saw her. "Angelique? Is it really you?"

"You know who I am?" She stared at him in equal shock.

"Of course! But I can't believe it. What are you doing here?"

"I came to see Claude Dumont. He sent me—" she broke off abruptly. "Never mind that now. Who are you? How do you know me?"

The boy seemed embarrassed. "You came to see Claude?"

"Yes, but he isn't here and I'm in a lot of trouble. Do you know him?" she asked urgently.

He hesitated. "Why don't you tell me about it?"

There didn't seem to be any reason not to. This was the first friendly face she had seen. Angelique started from the beginning with the flowers, but the young man cut her off.

"Claude didn't send them, I did."

"I don't understand! Why would—who are you?" she asked helplessly.

"My name is Alain de Marchal."

"But if you're not Claude Dumont, why did you sign his name?"

He looked like a small boy caught with his hand in the cookie jar. "When I saw your picture in the advertisements for Dream Girl shampoo I thought you were the most beautiful woman I had ever seen. I only wanted to express my admiration in the beginning, but then I began to hope that we could become friends. That was when I instructed the florist to put a card in the flowers."

"But why did you sign a phony name? Is there really a Claude Dumont?"

"Oh yes, he is my tutor."

"Did he know about this?"

"No," Alain admitted reluctantly.

Angelique's mind was reeling. Her lonely old gentleman had turned into an adolescent youth, Claude Dumont was really Alain de Marchal—she didn't dare even think about the necklace. Sinking down on the couch, she patted the place next to her. "I think you'd better tell me the whole story."

Alain sat beside her, his face puckered with dismay. "I never meant to cause you a moment's pain. All I wanted to do was make you happy."

"You did, Alain. The flowers were beautiful," she said gently. "But why didn't you just write to me? I would have been delighted to be your friend without all that extravagance."

"I was afraid it would make a difference if you knew who I really was."

"Because you're...uh...a bit younger?" she asked tactfully.

"I don't think age makes any difference when two people are truly fond of each other, do you?" His face was very earnest.

"No, of course not. But a good relationship isn't built on deception. Just look at what's happened. Everyone thinks poor Claude has been playing around, and that man who calls himself a duke—" Angelique stopped abruptly "—wait a minute? Did you say your name is de Marchal? Isn't that his name?"

"Tristan is my uncle. He is also my guardian until I am old enough to take over the reins of government."

"Then you are...?"

"Prince Alain Rupert Robaire de Marchal, head of the house of Charolais, ruler of Souveraine." His expression was resigned.

Angelique leaned back against the down-filled cushions, her mouth dropping open in amazement. "You're kidding!"

Alain shrugged. "You see? Already you feel differently about me."

"Oh no, Alain! I was just surprised. I've never met a prince before." He looked so crestfallen that she gave him a teasing smile. "They aren't too plentiful in America."

He sighed. "I would gladly bestow my title on someone else. It isn't much fun."

It didn't seem possible that he could be lonely, but all indications pointed to it. Why else would a handsome, privileged teenager pour out his heart to a stranger thousands of miles away? Of course there was always the chance that it was simply admiration for what he considered a glamorous older woman.

Angelique proceeded delicately. "It would seem to me that you're going to be the most eligible bachelor on the Continent in a few years. I'm surprised that you found time to write all those letters with the amount of girls who must be storming the palace gates."

"Is that what you think?" His laughter had a bitter sound. "The truth is that my social life is nonexistent, unless you count the state dinners Tristan forces me to attend. I get to dance with the wives of all our ministers. In the correct pecking order, naturally," he added mockingly.

Angelique was appalled. "Doesn't he allow you any time to see your friends?"

"I don't have any except for Claude, and Tristan of course. Tristan and I go riding together, and sometimes we spend a weekend at his hunting lodge when he has the time." Alain's face lit with enthusiasm. "Tristan is great fun to be with."

Angelique's teeth clicked together as she remembered the imperious man who had bullied her so unmercifully. He was even more of a monster than she suspected! Tristan de Marchal was keeping his nephew a virtual prisoner, cutting him off from everyone so his own influence would be absolute. He even had the boy brainwashed into admiring him. Did the duke covet the throne for himself? It certainly sounded like it. Everything about him pointed to it too. He was a cold, ruthless man. There was nothing Angelique could do about it either except be Alain's friend.

She reached for his hands impulsively. "I'm really glad that you wrote to me."

"Do you truly mean that?" he asked eagerly. "It doesn't matter that I'm a...a few years younger? I was afraid if you ever found out you'd think I was just a stupid kid, and you wouldn't want to be bothered with me."

She framed his face in her palms, looking at him fondly. "How could I possibly feel that way about such a charming, gallant young man? I consider it a privilege to be your friend."

He touched her hair very gently. "I knew when I saw your picture that you were someone special."

"You are quite correct, my dear nephew." Tristan de Marchal's mocking voice made them both jump. His footsteps hadn't made any sound on the thick carpeting. "International jewel thieves are indeed a breed apart."

Alain sprang to his feet, scowling. "That's a terrible thing to say! You will apologize to Miss Archer."

"I see that you have found yourself an ally, *mademoiselle*. It was foolish to let you out of my sight, but I didn't realize what an opportunist you were. An impressionable young boy must have been an easy target for someone of your...um...awesome attributes." Tristan's insolent gaze flickered over Angelique's slender figure, undressing her with his eyes.

"I am not a boy!" Alain stormed. "And you are being insufferably insulting. Angelique is my dear friend and confidante."

"Did she confide the details of how she came into possession of a diamond and sapphire necklace belonging to you?" his uncle asked derisively.

Triumph blazed from Alain's face. "It was unnecessary since I sent it to her myself."

Angelique derived deep satisfaction from the dumbfounded look on the duke's face, but it was urgent that she settle the matter once and for all. "I'm very flattered that you wanted to give me such a beautiful gift, Alain," she said gently. "But I couldn't possibly accept anything that valuable. It's a legacy that's supposed to be kept in your family."

"The necklace I sent you was not part of the crown jewels. It was a gift from my father to my mother. I think she would like you to have it because you are very much like her—sweet and beautiful."

Tristan waited for Angelique's response with a cynical expression that she itched to wipe off his dark, arrogant face. "That's the nicest compliment anyone has ever paid me," she told Alain. "But I still can't accept the necklace." Before he could argue the point she added, "I'd like to talk to your uncle alone for a moment if you don't mind." Her chin set grimly. "I think we both have a few things to say to each other."

"He owes me an apology too," Alain protested.

Angelique wanted to tell Alain not to hold his breath. Far from appearing repentant, the duke was regarding them with an enigmatic look in his gray eyes that made her vaguely uneasy. What devilment was he up to now?

It didn't matter because she intended to put distance between herself and the kingdom of Souveraine as speedily as possible. But first there was something she had to try to do for Alain. Perhaps things might improve for him if she pointed out to the duke that this whole incident would never have occurred if he allowed the boy a little more freedom. At least she could plant the idea.

Chapter Two

As soon as the door closed Angelique turned on Tristan angrily. "I'm not naive enough to expect an apology, but Alain is right—you do owe *him* one."

"For calling him a boy? Alain is only sixteen."

"All the more reason. Surely you must realize that he considers himself a man."

"Evidently." Tristan's appraising glance traveled over Angelique's lovely face and graceful figure. "But he's playing way out of his league. Leonardo da Vinci didn't start his career with the *Mona Lisa*."

"I suppose there's a compliment in there somewhere, although it's difficult to tell," Angelique remarked distastefully.

"Sorry. You're used to more conventional compliments, aren't you?" He sauntered over to stand very close. "I should have said that your skin has the texture of a camellia petal, and your mouth is as delicious as the nectar within, inviting a man to feast until he becomes drunk with it." Tiny lights smoldered in the depths of his gray eyes. "Is that poetic enough for you?"

Angelique was annoyed at the little shiver that ran down her spine, since she recognized the mockery under the sensual words. "Don't strain your imagination for me," she said coldly. "The only thing you and I have to talk about is Alain."

"There's something a little more pressing." When she looked at him with raised eyebrows he said, "The problem of what to do about you."

"What do you mean? Alain explained about the necklace! What more do you suspect me of?"

"My feelings don't enter into it. It's what the people of Souveraine will think."

She stared at him blankly. "I just arrived today. I don't know anyone here."

"But they'll know about you. In fact, I'll wager they do already." He lounged against a polished marquetry table, crossing his arms over his chest. Without wanting to, Angelique noticed the silken ripple of his biceps. "If we don't move quickly to defuse it, you're going to be the center of a most awkward scandal."

"I have no idea what you mean."

"Think about it. Four men besides myself heard you say that Claude Dumont gave you a very expensive present. It's widely known that Claude is a married man, and the whole kingdom knows that necklace was a gift to Alain's mother from his father. It leaves them a choice of two conclusions. Either Claude was cheating on his wife and stole the necklace to give to you, or Alain was using Claude as a front for a little precocious hanky-panky."

"But that's terrible!" Angelique was horrified.

"You're right. Claude's wife has no sense of humor," Tristan remarked dryly. "Also, I would prefer that Alain not be tagged as the youngest playboy on the Continent."

"All you have to do is tell everybody the truth!"

"That would be difficult since I don't know it myself. I only know what it *looks* like."

Angelique quickly explained the circumstances, starting with the first anonymous gift of flowers. "So you can see it was all perfectly innocent," she concluded. "Alain was merely looking for friendship in the only way he knew how."

"He just *happened* to pick a very glamorous woman as a pen pal." Tristan's voice was heavy with irony.

"It was all a fantasy, can't you see that? He never expected us to meet."

"But you had other ideas." His mouth thinned to a straight line. "Why accept a mere necklace when you can make a try for the crown that goes with it."

"Are you out of your mind?" Angelique gasped. "Alain is just a boy!"

"An extremely rich one," Tristan observed cynically. "He also has a title—something that is most attractive to certain American women."

"Not necessarily. A title doesn't automatically make a man palatable," she replied pointedly.

Tristan didn't pretend not to know what she meant. "Our opinion of each other isn't the important thing right now," he answered impatiently. "My main concern is protecting Alain. I can't allow him to appear irresponsible."

"If you were really that concerned about him this whole thing would never have happened," Angelique said angrily. "Why do you think he formed such an attachment to me, a total stranger? Because I represented all the romance that's missing from his life. At sixteen he should be writing love letters to girls his own age, but he doesn't know any. His entire social life consists of being dragged to state affairs with people twice his age.''

For the first time since they'd met, Tristan appeared slightly uncertain. He paced up and down the room, running long fingers through his thick dark hair. ''I know his life isn't ideal, but what can I do about it? In the normal course of things Alain wouldn't have had to assume the reins of government until he was well into his thirties. My brother was still a young man when he was taken so tragically.''

''Was it very recent?'' Angelique asked, gently. There were lines of pain in Tristan's strong face.

''Less than a year ago. It was a boating accident. A sudden storm came up and he and Celeste were washed overboard.'' His eyes were somber. ''If it weren't for Alain, I think they would have wanted to go together. They loved each other very much.''

''What a trauma for poor Alain!''

''Yes, he took it very hard, naturally. He was away at school in Scotland at the time, a sort of royal preparatory school where the heads of various countries send their crown princes for a thorough grounding in all phases of leadership. Unfortunately, Alain wasn't allowed time to grow into the job. He had to return to Souveraine and take over as titular head of state.''

That brought up Angelique's suspicions. ''But you actually run the country?''

''I am his legal guardian. Alain will take over when he is eighteen.''

As she watched the leashed vitality of the man pacing in front of her, an icy finger touched Angelique's spine. Surely palace intrigues died out with the Borgias? The duke wouldn't actually plot against his own nephew! Even as she tried to convince herself, the restless energy of the man provoked doubts. When the subject of the throne came up he was like a caged tiger, clawing at the bars.

"It's just an accident of birth that some people get to be rulers," she said uncertainly.

His face darkened. "How do you explain an accident?"

That could mean anything; either sorrow over his brother's death, or resentment at his own fate. Angelique proceeded carefully. "It's a great responsibility for a boy of eighteen. He'll probably rely heavily on you even after he takes the throne."

It didn't seem to comfort Tristan. His expression grew even more grim. "The thought has occurred to me."

"Being the power behind the throne doesn't interest you, I take it," she remarked dryly, her patience vanishing. Why couldn't he just accept things?

"Not in the slightest, *mademoiselle*. I don't look forward to years of getting a teenager out of scrapes while the whole country looks on. Which brings us back to the problem of what to do about you."

"You'll simply have to tell the truth," Angelique said firmly. "I'm sure people will understand."

"And Alain would become an object of derision. The story of his puppy love pursuit would follow him into manhood." Tristan shook his head very definitely. "Even scandal is preferable to ridicule."

"Not to me it isn't! I gather you've decided to throw poor Claude to the wolves. Well, I won't go along with it! I flatly refuse to say that he was my lover."

"That wasn't what I had in mind." The considering look in Tristan's eyes made Angelique uneasy. "I've been giving the matter some thought and I believe I have a solution. If everyone thought you were *my*...um...little friend, it would solve the whole problem."

"I suppose these little interludes are such a common occurrence with you that no one would take any notice," Angelique observed scornfully.

A person had only to look at him to know that. Tristan de Marchal's combination of an arrogant, interesting face and a lean male body would bowl some women over like ten pins. It annoyed her that he wouldn't even need the added attribute of great wealth and a title. Men like that were a menace!

A slight smile lurked around his firm mouth. "Let's say Souveraine is a romantic country, and I'm given a certain amount of leeway."

"I think the word is license," Angelique snapped. "At any rate you can forget the whole idea. I have no intention of posing as your latest conquest."

"You'd prefer to be perceived as a fortune hunter pursuing an inexperienced boy?"

"No one but you would believe such an idiotic story!" she flared.

In spite of her vehemence, Angelique wasn't so sure. Boys of sixteen had adult urges, and appearances were all against her. Who would believe that Alain would lavish so much attention and money on her without expecting some kind of relationship in return? Nor was it credible that she would travel across the ocean to see him, merely out of curiosity.

It was the sort of story the newspapers would love. "Internationally famous model and young prince of Souveraine an item, in spite of nine-year difference in their ages." The very term "model" would be damning, even though her reputation was spotless and she had never posed other than fully clothed.

Tristan watched the play of emotions over her mobile face. "I see the implications have occurred to you."

"Your solution doesn't make me look any better," she muttered. "Either way it's bad publicity."

"There wouldn't be any." The muscles in his broad shoulders shifted as he shrugged off her objection. "No one is interested in an obscure grand duke from a tiny country. Alain is the one who would make it newsworthy."

A hint of satisfaction lurked behind his matter-of-fact expression. He was like a hunter who had successfully baited a trap. Angelique was filled with a vague uneasiness. She didn't trust this man at all. "What about the necklace? How could you have given it to me when it belongs to Alain?"

"That's a little tricky," he admitted, staring at her thoughtfully. "Suppose we say that I asked you to take it in to have the clasp repaired. You were curious about its worth and asked the jeweler if it was genuine. The story is a little thin, but I think we can get away with it."

"Why not?" she asked bitterly. "It isn't any wilder than the truth. I must have been insane to come here in the first place!"

"It's a little late for that," he advised crisply. "I'll send someone to the hotel for your luggage."

"I'm not going to stay here with you!" she gasped.

"Don't worry, you'll be provided with adequate accommodations." Something kindled in his eyes as they wandered over her. "I doubt if I could keep my mind on the arduous affairs of state if we made our deception a reality."

Everything was moving too fast for Angelique. "This is really crazy! You and I don't even *like* each other. No one's going to believe we...we're romantically involved."

"It's up to us to make them believe it." He cupped her chin in his palm, tilting her face up to his. "We're going to make Romeo and Juliet look like casual acquaintances.'' His long fingers stroked the sensitive spot in back of her ear. ''We're going to look into each other's eyes and remember all the ways a man and woman can make love. The passion between us will tantalize, like a thirst we can't wait to quench.''

His low, musical voice was evoking a picture that stirred Angelique's senses. She could almost see a darkened room, a tumbled bed, the duke's taut body poised over hers for the ultimate experience.

Dear Lord, what was she thinking? ''No!'' She struggled to keep her voice even. ''I'll go along with your wild scheme up to a point. We'll pretend that you're the one I came to visit, but only if we also give the impression that our affair is in its early stages.''

Tristan smiled mockingly. ''Soulful glances and heavy breathing would make the whole thing more credible.''

''Go ahead, if you want your audience to see the shortest romance on record.''

''I've never believed in brief encounters.'' His eyes flicked over her consideringly. ''Real enjoyment comes from knowing a woman thoroughly.''

''*Your* enjoyment, naturally,'' she said sarcastically.

''There can be none unless it's mutual. Any man who would take his own satisfaction without first bringing extreme pleasure to his partner is not worthy of consideration.''

He didn't make a move toward her, yet his voice was a caress. Angelique knew she had been wrong in thinking this man would make love without tenderness. It would be an experience no woman would ever forget. Well, why not, she asked herself impatiently, annoyed at the rapid beating of her heart. He'd practiced long enough to become perfect.

"Kindly remember that I'm your partner in name only—and *then* only when other people are around. I don't like you and I don't trust you," she said bluntly.

His smile had the dangerous quality of a shark's. "Then I'll just have to change your opinion, won't I? In the interests of a convincing performance, that is."

Before she could deny the possibility, he was gone, leaving her extremely frustrated. How much clearer could she make herself? If the noble duke expected to exercise his royal prerogative he was in for a surprise, Angelique fumed.

Alain rejoined her, his expression eager. "Tristan says you're going to be staying with us. That's positively smashing!"

"I'm glad somebody thinks so," she replied crossly. "Do you know how many problems you've caused?"

"I'm sorry. I just wanted to get to know you."

He looked so crestfallen that Angelique regretted her moment of irritability. He was only a boy, and a very vulnerable one at that. "It's all right, Alain, I'm not really angry at you. I've just been working very hard and I was looking forward to a nice, uncomplicated vacation."

"You'll have it, Angelique, I promise! We'll go sailing and sightseeing—anything you'd like. All of Souveraine is yours for the asking."

She smiled at his extravagance. "How about starting with the grounds? The gardens out there look lovely."

Outside the tall French windows was a terrace bordered by rose bushes heavy with blooms of every color. The air was perfumed with them, drawing iridescent hummingbirds and brightly hued butterflies. Beyond the gardens were clipped yew hedges forming an intricate maze like the ones found in England.

"What fun!" Angelique exclaimed, looking over the precise planting that formed alleys and cul-de-sacs in a bewildering pattern. "I've heard about those but I've never seen one. Do you know your way through it?"

"Blindfolded." Alain laughed. "When I was small I used to hide in there at bath time."

Angelique's laughter mingled with his. "You were a little devil even then."

"Would you like me to take you through?"

"Later. First I'd like to see the rest of the grounds. What's down this path?"

"The stables. We have some of the finest horses on the Continent," Alain announced proudly. "Mainly due to Tristan. He has attended auctions all over the world, searching for the best bloodlines."

"A fitting occupation for an international playboy," Angelique muttered.

"Tristan? He's the hardest-working man I know."

"If you call what he does working."

"Souveraine is a very small country, but there are still many duties to running the government," Alain chided gently.

"I didn't mean to be rude. It's just that your uncle is a very infuriating man," she stated grimly.

Alain seemed surprised. "Most women find him irresistible."

Angelique didn't want to get sidetracked into a discussion of Tristan's dubious charms. Alain had given her the perfect opportunity to warn him. "Since you're the real head of the country, shouldn't you be taking some hand in running it?" she asked casually.

He made a face. "Now you sound like Tristan. He's always trying to get me to take an interest. He gets very impatient when I don't pay attention."

Angelique frowned. That didn't seem to fit, unless the duke was even more diabolical than she suspected. "Perhaps he only gives you the dull, routine things to do. You should be allowed to sit in on high level discussions. That could be fascinating."

"I don't like *any* of it—and neither does Tristan. But I figure since I can't take over for two years anyway, he's just stuck with it."

"What makes you think he doesn't like the job?"

"He never made any secret of it. Tristan always said the one thing he did right in life was being born the second son instead of the first."

Angelique filed away the information that the duke was a superb actor from an early age. It was something to remember. "It must be very difficult to be the second son in a royal family," she observed delicately. "Especially for a forceful man like your uncle. It would be understandable if he thought of the throne as rightfully his after his brother's death."

"I can see that you don't know anything about Tristan. He isn't a power broker, and there was never a hint of rivalry between the brothers. He and my father were very close in spite of being complete opposites. Father was the serious one, perhaps because he was groomed for the throne from infancy while Tristan got to do pretty much what he wanted."

"What your uncle did to occupy his time was a hobby," Angelique remarked tartly. "We're talking about a life's work."

"Tristan had his own career. He's a very talented artist."

That startled her. It didn't seem to fit the macho image of the man she knew. "Are you serious?"

Alain nodded. "He had already gotten quite a bit of critical acclaim. His nudes were especially admired."

The low, whitewashed building came into view when they rounded a bend in the path. Thoroughbred horses of every color, from pale fillies to sable stallions, stuck their heads out of the double Dutch doors. Most of the horses welcomed company, but one black stallion tossed his head, snorting disdainfully.

"That's Tristan's mount, Diavolo," Alain remarked admiringly. "No one else can ride him."

That figured. Tristan would ensure that anything he put his mark on belonged to him alone. It was vaguely disturbing for some reason. "Which one is yours?" Angelique asked.

Alain led her to a bay horse that was also typical. Its soft brown eyes were gentle, and it nuzzled her hand when she reached up to stroke its nose.

"I thought Anastasia would be fitting for you." Alain indicated a sleek palomino mare with a satiny caramel coat and a cream-colored mane and tail. "She is also blond, although not nearly as beautiful."

"She's lovely," Angelique exclaimed.

With her attention focused on the horse, she didn't notice the metal ring set in the concrete walk. Her high heel caught in it, pitching her forward against one of the Dutch doors, which she grabbed to keep from falling.

Alain was beside her in a moment. "Did you hurt yourself?" he asked anxiously.

"No, I just caught my heel." She lifted her foot, looking ruefully at her shoe. "I did a good job of it too; it's broken off."

Alain knelt and slipped the pump off her foot. After trying without success to force the heel back on, he had to give up. "I'm afraid it's hopeless, but don't worry. I will buy you a new pair."

"Don't be silly, it wasn't your fault. Besides, I brought plenty of shoes with me; the only problem is getting to

Wouldn't you know it, Angelique though.
edly. What Alain considered a vocation was real.
tension of Tristan's womanizing. With his conne.
the duke could get favorable reviews and have won.
beating down his door.

Alain laughed at her expression. "I can tell what
you're thinking, but you're wrong. Tristan doesn't need
a gimmick to attract women. *They* chase *him*."

Until he catches them, Angelique commented silently.
"I'm sure he was very dedicated, but sometimes unexpected events change our destinies. Power corrupts," she
said darkly.

"I can see you're determined to cast poor Tristan as a
villain," Alain teased. "How did he ruffle your feathers?"

"It isn't *my* feathers I'm worried about," she said
grimly. "I just don't like to see anyone stacking the deck
against you while making you think it's for your own
good."

Alain's laughter died. "Tristan isn't merely my uncle,
he's my friend. When I was growing up and father was
busy with affairs of state, Tristan was the one I went to
with my problems. He always helped me work them out
without lecturing me. He never talked down to me, and
I always knew he was there if I needed him. I don't think
I could have lived through the death of my parents without Tristan," Alain said simply.

Could she be wrong, Angelique wondered. The duke
must care about his nephew to have devoted that much
time to him. But there were so many nagging little dis-
crepancies. The chief one was the way he kept the boy
isolated in the palace. She didn't have time to pursue the
subject because the soft nickering of horses warned her
that they were nearing the stables.

them." She took an experimental step, seesawing on one high heel and one flat shoe.

"Let me help you." He took her arm.

After only a few paces, Angelique knew it wasn't going to work. The palace was too far away. She looked doubtfully at the gravel path. "I suppose I could go barefoot."

Alain shook his head. "You'd cut your feet on the pebbles." Suddenly he snapped his fingers. "How foolish of me! We will ride back."

Angelique glanced down at the straight skirt of her beige suit. It would be up around her thighs. "I'm afraid I'm not dressed for horseback riding."

"Sidesaddle you are," he replied confidently.

As Alain started to lead the big bay out of the stable, Angelique watched with a worried frown. "Maybe this isn't such a good idea. I've never ridden sidesaddle."

He laughed at her concerned expression. "Now that I have you here, would I let anything happen to you?" After urging her onto the wooden mounting block and then onto the horse's broad back, Alain swung himself up behind her. He put his arm securely around her waist. "Isn't this better than limping back?"

"Much. You're a very gallant young man." She turned a smiling face to him. "If I had a velvet riding habit and a plumed hat, I'd feel as though I were back in the days of elegance."

Fervent admiration shone out of his eyes. "Nothing could make you more elegant than you already are."

Angelique knew it was time to change the subject. "Tell me something about Claude Dumont. After all this mix-up I'm really curious about him."

Alain shrugged. "He's a good enough sort, when he isn't trying to cram irregular verbs down my throat, or correct my grammar."

"That's his job, isn't it?"

"With Claude it's an obsession," Alain complained. His expression turned mischievous. "I'll bet he even carries it into his personal life. If his wife ever said, *'Je vous aime, Claude,'* he would surely stop kissing her to say, 'No, no, Maryanne, *je t'aime, je t'aime!*'"

"He can't be that bad," Angelique protested, her mouth curving in amusement.

"Use the wrong pronoun and you'll find out."

"Between us we've gotten the poor man in enough trouble." She laughed. "I don't intend to tell him I love him in any language." Angelique was reminded of a question Alain had never answered. "Why did you sign Claude's name when you wrote to me?"

His young face sobered. "In the beginning I never meant to contact you directly, but as time went on it became almost an obsession to know you. There was always a chance that you wouldn't answer my note, but there was also a possibility that you would because you were as kind and beautiful as your photographs." He hesitated, searching for the right words. "If we did strike up a friendship, I wanted it to be because you liked me, not because I was Prince Alain of Souveraine."

"I understand," she said softly, her heart melting toward this boy who had so much and yet so little. "But why did you pick a real person?"

"I couldn't use a competely fictitious name or your letters wouldn't be delivered," he explained.

"You were lucky Claude didn't intercept them."

Alain threw back his head, shouting with laughter. "He would have gone into shock. Maryanne is the first woman he has been able to distinguish from a man."

As they approached the palace Angelique said dryly, "My letters didn't exactly contain purple prose."

"They were from a woman." His voice deepened to adulthood. "A very charming and generous one."

Angelique was in a quandary. She wouldn't hurt Alain for anything in the world, but something had to be done to discourage him. Before she could think of the right words, he slid down from the horse and held up his arms to her. There was nothing to do but put her hands on his shoulders and let him lift her down. It was while they were holding onto each other that Tristan strode across the terrace, a scowl on his dark face.

"Where have you been?" he demanded.

"I took Angelique to see the stables," Alain answered.

One peaked eyebrow lifted sardonically as Tristan looked pointedly at the big bay. "Have we run out of horses?"

Alain was puzzled by his uncle's sarcasm. "Angelique broke the heel off her shoe. We rode double so I could be sure no harm came to her."

"Very commendable." Tristan's tone indicated otherwise. "Since you've done your duty by Miss Archer, I suggest you get on with your lessons. Claude's vacation doesn't extend to you."

As Alain flushed painfully, Angelique was flooded with fury. How could Tristan embarrass the boy like that? She couldn't countermand his uncle's orders, but she could take some of the sting out of them.

Smiling up at Alain she said softly, "Thanks for bringing me back in one piece. It's certainly nice to have a man around when you need one."

He gave her a radiant smile. "The pleasure was entirely mine. I'll see you later, Angelique."

As soon as he rounded the corner Tristan said ominously, "I want to talk to you."

"And I want to talk to *you*!" It was time *somebody* did!

"Come with me." Clamping a hand around Angelique's wrist, he started to drag her toward the house, his long legs covering the ground rapidly. When she strumbled trying to keep up with him, he turned impatiently. "What's the matter?"

She glared at him. "Even if I were in the mood for a brisk gallop, it would be difficult on one heel."

He stared down at her feet. Muttering a few choice words under his breath, he swept her up in his arms.

"What do you think you're doing?" she gasped. "Put me down this instant!"

"Stop wriggling," he commanded, ignoring her protests as he started up the curving staircase. "Limping along at a snail's pace isn't going to postpone our little talk."

"Is that what you think I was doing?" Indignation almost choked her. "Well, for your information, I can't wait to tell you a few simple truths!"

"Good," he commented grimly. "Then we're both getting what we want."

As he unconsciously tightened his grip, Angelique was made uncomfortably aware of the power of Tristan's taut body. He carried her easily, the muscles of his thighs and upper torso taking her added weight without effort. She could feel the ripple across his broad shoulders, under her clutching hands.

"Where are you taking me?" she demanded.

"To your room." He turned his head to look at her, which brought his hawklike face within inches of hers. "Where did you think?"

"I...I didn't know," she answered, a little breathlessly.

Amusement warmed the stormy gray of his eyes. "Don't worry, I rarely ravish guests on their first night in the palace."

His slight unbending vanished when he dumped her to her feet inside an immense room that was almost like an apartment. The color scheme was all pink and cream with gold and crystal accents. At the far end of the room was a large bed with a graceful canopy overhead. The trailing folds of rose damask matched the rich draperies that covered the tall windows. Exquisitely crafted boule cabinets on either side of the bed held hand-painted china lamps and an enchanting assortment of antique ornaments.

The other end of the long chamber was a sitting room, complete with a fireplace faced in pink-veined, imported marble. Besides a delicate French desk, there was a quilted satin couch and several Louis Seize armchairs. Every comfort had been anticipated. There were even logs waiting to be lit on the hearth. Angelique was to discover all of this later because at the time her attention was centered on Tristan.

He wasted no time in getting to the point. "Just what kind of game do you think you're playing?" A muscle worked dangerously at the point of his square jaw.

"I don't play games," she stormed. "Unlike some people I could mention!"

"I'm in no mood for riddles. You were being very seductive to my nephew just now, and I don't intend to stand for it."

"It's just like you to mistake sympathy for seduction," she said disgustedly. "I was only trying to soothe his feelings because you made him look like a schoolboy in front of me."

"That's what he *is*!" Tristan practically shouted, running a hand through his thick sable hair.

"Weren't you ever sixteen?" she demanded. "Didn't you ever try to impress a girl? How would you have liked it if someone told you in front of her to run along and do your homework?"

"There's a very important difference here." Tristan's gray eyes were wintry as they traveled over Angelique's slim figure.

She sighed. "I realize as well as you do that he has an adolescent crush on me, but the way to cure it isn't by making fun of him."

"That's was never my intention." He glowered at her darkly. "Do you have any solution?"

It was a grudging plea for help which was most uncharacteristic. Angelique had a feeling that this autocratic man had rarely encountered a problem he couldn't solve alone. She answered his question with smug satisfaction. "I'm sure I could think of a better one than yours."

"Would it be too much to ask you to share it with me?"

"I'll have to give it some thought."

"That sounds suspiciously like a play for time."

"Time to do what? You can't honestly still think I have designs on Alain?"

"You haven't done anything to change my mind."

Angelique was suddenly very fed up with this autocratic man's outrageous suspicions. Since he was determined to think the worst, she decided to give him something to worry about.

"All right, you win." She heaved a theatrical sigh. "I suppose I *would* like to be the power behind the throne. We don't all have your ambition," she couldn't help adding.

His eyes narrowed as her barb struck home. An unreadable expression crossed his face. Annoyance? Derision? She couldn't tell. He seemed to be debating something. Finally his firm mouth curved in a mocking smile. "Did it ever occur to you that there's an easier way?"

"What do you mean?" she asked warily. This wasn't the reaction she expected.

He sauntered toward her to stand very close. "There's no point in our working at cross purposes. If we join forces we'll both achieve our goal. Of course I can't promise marriage, but I'll guarantee to make our relationship...rewarding."

The gaze that slid slowly over her was wholly male, penetrating her clothing with the certain knowledge of what was underneath. Swift color flooded her clear skin, as though she were actually nude in front of him. It was a terribly vulnerable feeling.

Angelique sought refuge in anger. "That's the most disgusting proposal I've ever heard!"

"Don't be too hasty—think of the benefits." His low, musical voice was like a caress. "You won't have to wait for me to grow up."

There was no doubt about that! Tristan de Marchal was a man in his prime, a man with the expertise to bring a woman untold ecstasy. Angelique's mind shuddered away from the thought of what it would be like to lie in his arms.

"I can't think of anything more loathsome than what you're suggesting," she said coldly.

"Are you sure?" His hand slid under the heavy weight of her fair hair, sensuously massaging her nape. "Let me show you how wrong you are."

Before she could back away, his arm circled her waist, drawing her against his hard body. When she started to protest, his mouth closed over hers. It was seduction by a master. At first his lips merely teased, trying to part hers. When she refused, he ran the tip of his tongue along the tightly closed line of her mouth, gently probing as his fingers traced an erotic path down her spine.

When his hand cupped her bottom, gently fitting her to the juncture of his thighs, Angelique gasped. It gave him the entry he wanted, and his tongue slipped into her mouth for a sensual exploration.

In spite of every resolve, her tense body relaxed as he wove his magic. She was invaded by him, enveloped by him, dragged into stormy waters that caused a rising tide inside her. The hands that had been warding him off now moved over Tristan's back, tracing the masculine cording of muscles under smooth skin.

When he drew away slightly she looked up in mute protest. His smiling eyes surveyed her softened face. "Are we in full agreement?" he murmured.

As sanity returned Angelique was appalled. How had she allowed him to provoke such a reaction? She pulled away, smoothing her hair with shaking hands. "No, we most certainly are not! If that macho display was a sample of your services, I'm not impressed." It would have been more convincing if her voice hadn't been so breathless.

Tristan chuckled, a deep male sound that rumbled in his chest. "Strange. I could have sworn that you were enjoying it. You'll have to show me where I went wrong."

"No!" As he moved toward her, Angelique took a step backward. "This whole farce has to stop right now. I wouldn't help you in your plot against Alain no matter what you offered, but that doesn't mean I want to be anything but his friend. I was only saying what you expected to hear."

"Perhaps I was too," he answered softly. "Did you ever think of that?" He watched her like a giant cat playing with a toy mouse.

Angelique's first reaction was disbelief, but then she remembered his past devotion to Alain. That, at least, appeared to be true. Had she let her personal feelings for the man color her judgment? At that point Angelique honestly didn't know.

She looked at him doubtfully. "If you really are on Alain's side, we aren't helping him by sniping away at each other."

"Exactly. And if you're as fond of him as you profess to be, you'll stop fighting me."

Tristan's turnabout was a little too pat. Angelique had the feeling that she was being manipulated by an expert, but she didn't have much choice other than staying on her guard. "I agreed to go along with your plan," she said grudgingly. "Just see that you don't get carried away with your role."

"I'll try to restrain myself." The promise would have carried more weight without the mocking light in his eyes.

She ignored it, making her voice purposely business-like. "When and where do we stage our little charade? I'd like to get this thing over with as soon as possible."

"Our first performance will be at the ambassador's reception this evening."

"This evening? I'm not going anywhere tonight!"

Tristan raised a dark eyebrow. "You're the one who's in a hurry."

"I didn't mean I wanted to start tonight! I just flew thousands of miles. I'm all mixed up from the jet lag, and this has been anything but a restful experience. All I want to do is go to sleep."

Tristan consulted a thin gold watch nestled among the springing hairs on his wrist. "It's early yet; you have time for a nap." He inspected the shadows on the delicate skin under her eyes. "You do look as though you could use some rest."

"Well, thanks! You certainly know how to make a woman feel good, don't you?"

The corners of his firm mouth twitched. "So I've been told," he murmured.

Angelique didn't know if she were more annoyed at herself for giving him an opening, or at Tristan for taking it. "Well, go fill someone else's life with joy," she muttered. "I've had more than my quota for today."

"Poor little Angelique." For once there was no derision in his tone. "I've given you a bad time, haven't I?"

This was a completely different Tristan. Angelique had a sudden glimpse of just how charming he could be. It was a little frightening. "I'll be fine once I've had some sleep," she assured him.

"There's plenty of time before the reception. I'll leave you now."

"Wait!" She stopped him as he was about to go out the door. "I can't go to this thing tonight after all. I just remembered that I don't have anything to wear. It's probably formal, isn't it?"

"No problem. I'll call one of the shops and have them send something over."

"You don't even know my size."

"I believe I can describe you accurately." His smile held remembered enjoyment.

Angelique stared at the closed door, her emotions in turmoil. The reminder that Tristan knew every contour of her body was bad enough. What made it much worse was the memory of her mindless surrender in his arms. It disturbed her greatly. What was it about this man? She had met men equally handsome, and certainly a lot more anxious to please, but never one who had been able to make her lose control. It was a sobering thought, especially since his motives were still questionable.

Was Tristan de Marchal a villain or a hero? And what part did she play in his plans? The only thing Angelique knew for certain was that he was a consummate lover. A funny little flutter started deep inside her at the memory of his firm mouth moving so sensually over hers, parting her lips for a male invasion she was helpless to resist. When he held her close, molding her body to his lean length, her response had been total. And he had known it.

She shivered suddenly. Any way you looked at it, the grand duke was a dangerous man. He must never be allowed to slip under her guard again. The next few days were certainly going to be trying, Angelique concluded, her slender shoulders drooping with fatigue.

After wearily removing her suit and blouse, she hung them in the cavernous closet. Her other things were already there, indicating that her luggage had arrived and someone had unpacked it. That meant her night things were either in the dresser or the armoire, but she was too tired to go looking for them. She removed her confining bra and got into bed wearing only her pair of lace panties.

The monogrammed satin sheets felt almost wickedly luxurious. Angelique wriggled contentedly in the soft bed, snuggling into a down pillow. These people might spend all of their time plotting and scheming, but they certainly did it in comfort. Her eyes closed and she was asleep in minutes.

The room was in semidarkness when Tristan returned much later. He put the large box he was carrying on a table before walking silently over to the bed. In the dim light Angelique's thick lashes were dark fans, and her glowing hair was a pale cloud on the pillow.

He stood there for a long moment, staring down at the gentle slope of her bare shoulders, and the small, peaked mounds her breasts made under the satin sheets. The expression on his face would have puzzled Angelique. For that matter, it would have surprised Tristan as well.

Chapter Three

Angelique awoke feeling wonderfully refreshed, until the events of the day returned. Then she wanted to turn over and hide her head under the pillows. Did she really have to go through a whole evening with Tristan de Marchal? It appeared unavoidable, unless he hadn't been able to get a dress for her.

The vain hope vanished when she turned on the bedside lamp and saw the large white box. It bothered her for a moment that Tristan had been in the room without her knowing it, but she dismissed the groundless apprehension immediately. He didn't need to take a woman by surprise. Angelique knew she wasn't in any danger while she was asleep; it was quite the opposite.

The big box intrigued her, dispelling other considerations. What had he selected? Knowing Tristan even this short a time, she had no doubt that he had issued explicit guidelines. What kind of taste did he have, good or bad? She removed the lid curiously, hoping for the best but resigned to the worst. It was probably something in red or purple that would make her fair skin look anemic.

When she parted the mounds of tissue paper, Angelique's stoic expression changed to one of pleasure. Inside was a pale yellow chiffon gown glistening with crystal beads on its intricately draped bodice. It was an exquisite creation—fragile and expensive. Angelique had modeled clothes long enough to recognize designing genius and the price tag that accompanied it. As she shook out the delicate folds she noticed something underneath. On closer inspection it proved to be a long velvet cloak in the same shade of pale yellow.

The rustle of tissue paper and her absorption in the stunning outfit prevented Angelique from hearing the soft knock at the door. She was examining the fine workmanship when Tristan entered.

For a moment they were both too startled to move. Then his eyes started to glow as they slid slowly over her slender, nearly naked body, lingering on her firm, pink tipped breasts. The increased beat of her heart released Angelique from her inertia, and she pulled the dress up to her chin.

"How dare you just walk in on me like that?" she raged.

"I knocked," he answered almost absently, his attention focused on the shimmering fabric draped so inadequately over her. "When you didn't answer I thought you might still be asleep and I didn't want to wake you."

"Since you can see that I'm up, the gentlemanly thing to do would be to leave!" Angelique was burningly aware that the filmy chiffon only veiled her body, making it more provocative.

"You're right, of course," he agreed meekly. "May I just ask if the gown is adequate?"

"It's fine," she answered impatiently.

"Just fine? That sounds as though you're not completely satisfied. I wouldn't want that. Is it the color you don't care for, or the style?"

Angelique knew exactly what he was doing under the guise of solicitude. He was baiting her, enjoying her embarrassment! "Will you kindly leave!" The demand was issued through clenched teeth.

"Anything to please a lady," he replied with exaggerated courtesy that didn't quite mask his amusement. After closing the door softly, he opened it a second later. "Your, er, charms drove everything else out of my mind. I came to tell you that the reception starts at eight."

Angelique was so furious that she wanted to throw something, but everything in the room was too precious. She paced the floor angrily, trying to think of some suitable revenge. None occurred to her, but she vowed that some day she would make Tristan de Marchal as miserable as he had made her ever since they'd met. Stalking into the pink marble bathroom, she turned on the shower full force.

She had just returned to the bedroom when there was a knock at the door. This time she was ready for him, Angelique thought grimly, belting her robe more securely. It wasn't Tristan, however. A servant stood there carrying a tray. It held a Limoges plate filled with tiny sandwiches and a delicate crystal flute brimming with champagne.

"The duke said you hadn't eaten all afternoon," the man explained.

Angelique was startled by the thoughtful gesture. It was kind of Tristan to realize that she'd had a hectic day. She hardened her heart almost immediately. He never did anything without a reason. She smiled cynically as one occurred to her. If she fainted from hunger before the assembled dignitaries, they might think she was pregnant.

As a professional model, Angelique knew how to make the best of her assets, which in her case were abundant to begin with. By the time she finished applying two shades of eye shadow, outlining her full mouth with peach-colored lip gloss, and shading her high cheekbones, her classic face was a work of art.

After that she started on her hair. Pulling a strand up from each temple, she fashioned a braid to cross over the top of her head, weaving a string of costume pearls into the gleaming coronet to give the illusion of a tiara. The rest of her thick hair was pinned at the crown and left to cascade down in a glorious golden mass of waves and curls.

The exquisite gown fit perfectly. It clung to her slender figure like a second skin before flaring out at the knees. The color flattered her delicate skin, showcasing its creamy texture. Angelique stared in the mirror critically, seeing exactly what she had hoped for, a woman who was both desirable and unattainable. She picked up the velvet cloak with a nod of satisfaction.

On the stroke of eight she walked down the long curving staircase, feeling as though she were taking part in a play. Tristan and Alain were waiting at the foot of it, looking like fellow actors. Their impeccable black and white evening clothes were augmented by red satin bands worn diagonally across their gleaming shirtfronts. The wide sashes were decorated with medals set with precious stones.

As they watched her glide gracefully down the stairs, the faces of both men expressed dazed admiration. For once Tristan was speechless, which delighted Angelique.

It was Alain who said, "You look magnificent, Angelique! Just like a princess."

"What a nice compliment. Too bad your uncle doesn't agree," she remarked lightly.

"Of course he does! Don't you, Tristan?" Alain asked.

Tristan had recovered his poise. "A princess sounds so unapproachable—and Miss Archer is anything but that." His firm mouth had a sardonic slant.

The ready color rose under her ivory skin as his insolent gaze roamed over her curved body. Angelique's jaw tightened. "You're quite wrong. I detest familiarity, especially when it's forced on me."

"That's understandable." The mischief in Tristan's eyes wasn't reflected in his solicitous tone. "Only a cad would force his attention on a lady."

"I'm glad we found something to agree on," she answered coldly.

"I think we're in agreement on more things than you'll admit," he murmured.

Alain was watching them with a slight frown. "Shouldn't we be going?" he asked abruptly.

"This is the first time I've seen you in such a hurry to get to a state affair," Tristan commented dryly.

"It's the first time I've had such a beautiful lady to escort." Alain offered Angelique his arm, leading her to the front door while Tristan followed with an enigmatic expression.

The ambassador's residence was a square, fortresslike building on top of a hill. A liveried butler met them at the door and escorted them to the head of a broad flight of stairs, after a maid had taken Angelique's cloak.

It was like an operetta, Angelique thought, as the man solemnly announced Alain to the assemblage below. "Prince Alain de Marchal."

The formally dressed people all looked up expectantly. For an instant Angelique expected them to burst into song. The thought made the corners of her mouth twitch. Alain gave her a rueful look before starting down the stairs at a stately pace.

"Grand Duke Tristan de Marchal and Miss Angelique Archer," the butler intoned next.

As they paused at the head of the staircase a murmur went through the crowd. Angelique was accustomed to being stared at; she had modeled in many fashion shows. But this was different. There was speculation on the faces of the people who were inspecting her from head to toe. It seemed incredible, but Tristan was right. Stories about her had spread already. Angelique was so tense that she stumbled slightly as she started forward.

Tristan's steadying hand was on her arm immediately. He bent his head to whisper in her ear. "Relax. You look like one of the early Christians being led to the lions."

"I hope the outcome is different this time," she whispered back. "Please don't leave me. I won't know what to say."

He smiled. "Don't worry. The men won't care and the women will be too busy examining your hairdo to listen."

A portly man in his mid-forties was waiting to greet them. "Good evening, Tristan. I don't believe I've had the pleasure of meeting your charming companion."

Tristan introduced her to the ambassador, then to his wife as a smartly gowned woman joined them. "And this is Madame Lamperre."

The woman looked at Angelique with lively curiosity under a mask of politeness. "We're so delighted that you could be with us this evening. I understand you just arrived in Souveraine. Is this your first visit?"

"Yes, and what I've seen has been charming," Angelique answered, knowing this was only the opening salvo in an interrogation.

"I'm so pleased. We've tried to preserve our old-world charm without stifling progress—like new hotels, for instance. Do you find your accommodations comparable to others on the Continent?" Madame Lamperre asked blandly.

"Angelique is my guest at the palace," Alain answered for her.

"She is *our* guest," Tristan corrected smoothly. Before Alain could take exception, he went on, "I believe everyone is waiting for you to lead off the dancing with Madame Lamperre."

For a moment Alain looked mutinous. He glanced longingly at Angelique, but Tristan's voice was implacable. "Don't let us keep you, the music has started."

The ambassador's wife wasn't any happier to leave them. She was bursting with unanswered questions, but a lifetime of diplomatic training couldn't be ignored. "We must have a long talk later," she told Angelique. "There are so many things I want to ask you—about your country, I mean."

"I'll look forward to it," Angelique replied with an outward serenity that masked her inner tension.

She had just realized that she and Tristan hadn't formulated any story. Pretending they were interested in each other opened up all kinds of pitfalls. People were bound to ask where they'd met, how long they'd known each other—a million snoopy little details. She and Tristan had better get together on a story fast.

Before she could alert Tristan, the ambassador took her hand. "Being host has its privileges. This is my dance, Miss Archer."

She couldn't very well refuse, but she tried to send Tristan a signal. "Will you wait for me?"

He lifted her hand to his lips. "I shall count the minutes, my dear." Something flared in his eyes as they held hers.

His act wasn't lost on the ambassador. As he led her onto the dance floor he said, "Tristan is a very possessive man, but tonight he will have to share your company. That is the price one pays for escorting the loveliest lady here."

"You're very kind," Angelique murmured, wondering how to change the subject. She decided not to waste time on subtleties. "You have a beautiful home; it's so spacious. Do you and Madame Lamperre have a large family?"

"Only two girls, fifteen and sixteen." He chuckled. "With teenage girls, however, there's always a houseful."

"That's Alain's age," Angelique remarked politely. "Do the young people see each other often?"

"They used to play together when they were children, but the prince has been away at school for the past few years. And now, of course, he's kept busy with palace affairs. Such a tragedy about his parents, poor boy."

"Yes, it must have been." Angelique's mind was very busy. She had asked the ambassador about his family merely to steer him away from awkward questions, but suddenly the germ of an idea was beginning to take shape.

Tristan was in the midst of a group of men when they rejoined him. Before she could have a word with him, someone led her back to the dance floor. As she went from one partner to another, Angelique caught frequent glimpses of Alain. He looked increasingly frustrated, and she couldn't blame him. This was no kind of evening for a teenager! Angelique decided right then that she was going to do something about it, with or without Tristan's blessing.

She questioned each of her partners the way she had the ambassador, finding out that many of them had children Alain's age. They all knew each other too, which made it more convenient. By the time she returned to Tristan much later, Angelique was filled with enthusiasm for her plan. It almost drove her current problems out of her mind, until Madame Lamperre rejoined them with determination written all over her face.

"You must tell me where you got that exquisite gown, Miss Archer. Everyone has been remarking on it. Lady Parnisse says she saw it at a shop in town, but I told her that couldn't be since you only arrived this afternoon."

Angelique waited with grim fatalism for Tristan to take credit for buying the gown. It would leave no doubt about how things stood between them if he were buying her clothes, and he couldn't care less what it did to her reputation. To her surprise, he passed up the opportunity.

Taking her hand he said, "That's correct, Angelique just arrived today and we've spent almost no time together. I'm sure you'll excuse me if I claim this dance."

"Thanks for the life preserver," she whispered as they walked away. "We have to talk."

"No, we have to give the impression that we're mad about each other," he answered, fitting her body against his and folding his arms around her.

The remembered feeling of his hard chest and broad shoulders made her heart beat faster. She looked up, examining his strong features. "You could have made your case by telling them you bought this dress. Why didn't you?"

He smiled, a melting smile that softened the hard angles of his face. "I'm not a complete scoundrel. I might indulge in a spot of throne stealing, but I would never embarrass a lady."

She frowned. "Will you stop putting me on?"

"About the throne or the lady?" He chuckled.

"Be serious," she said impatiently. "We really do have to talk."

"I can think of much better things to do." His warm mouth slid across her cheekbone to her ear. He blew in it softly while he fingered the bouncing curls at the nape of her neck.

"What do you think you're doing?" she demanded angrily.

"If you don't know, then I must be doing it wrong."

In an abrupt movement he released her. Taking Angelique's hand he led her through a pair of tall double doors to a broad terrace outside. Beyond the ornate stone balustrade, the hillside fell away steeply to a beach below. Moonlight cast a glittering path over the dark water, illuminating the foaming wavelets breaking in a cove between two cliffs.

The romantic setting made Angelique forget her annoyance. "How beautiful!" she exclaimed.

"Yes, it is," Tristan agreed. His eyes were on the pure line of her profile.

She sighed. "I wish I could just enjoy it instead of being mixed up in all this intrigue."

"You could if you'd let yourself." He smoothed the silken bangs off her forehead.

His gesture, although innocent, managed to be very sensuous. Especially coupled with the husky note in his deep voice.

Angelique felt her skin burning where he'd touched her. "We're not talking about the same kind of enjoyment," she said coldly.

"Appreciation of beauty is universal," he murmured, moving closer.

"Since there's no one here to impress, you can drop the act," Angelique said, retreating until her back was against the stone parapet.

He followed, grasping the railing on either side of her so she was hemmed in. "I like to live my part. It's more convincing that way."

"Then you admit to being an actor," she said scornfully.

"Absolutely." The moonlight on his face made Tristan's eyes glitter. "I only appear to be civilized. At night my fangs grow and I roam the halls of the palace, ravaging chambermaids."

Angelique raised a delicate eyebrow. "It must be easier to get help here than it is in America."

He laughed. "You don't believe me?"

"I don't know what to believe about you," she answered frankly. "The only conclusion I've formed is that you go after what you want without letting anything stand in your way."

"Is that bad?"

"It depends on what you want."

"What if I told you it was you?" A long forefinger traced the shape of her mouth.

"I'd tell you that you were wasting your time," she replied bluntly. "I'm as out of reach as that throne you yearn for so badly."

"Perhaps you could make me give it up. The love of a good woman might reform me."

"I'm sure you've had the love of a great many women, and it hasn't had much effect."

He linked his arms lightly around her waist. "Maybe I just never met the right one."

Angelique braced her palms against his chest to keep him from drawing her closer. The hard wall of muscle made her hands tingle. "Am I supposed to believe I'm the one? That line is older than this country," she scoffed, "and not very original."

"You don't think it could be true?"

"No, I don't."

"You won't admit there's at least some kind of chemistry between us that surfaced at our first meeting?"

"I suppose you could call it chemistry," she commented dryly. "It *was* rather like an explosion. You shouted at me and I shouted back. Is that your idea of a romantic encounter?"

His teeth gleamed white in the moonlight. "At least we weren't indifferent to each other."

"You're wrong there too." Angelique raised her chin disdainfully. "That expresses my feelings toward you exactly."

His fingers idly traced the outline of her spine. "Is that why you're trembling?"

She couldn't help herself. There was something very intimidating about his raw masculinity. Not that she was afraid of Tristan, at least not in the usual way. It was the powerful attraction he exerted. She had to be honest with herself; it would be so easy to let him make love to her. Angelique knew instinctively that it would be an experience she'd never forget, and perhaps never get over. His deeply stirring kiss had warned her of that. The thought of his full possession made her shiver involuntarily.

"I...it's chilly out here," she said hastily.

"I wouldn't want you to catch cold." His arms wrapped around her, gathering her close. "Do you want to go in?" he murmured.

His face was just inches from hers. With his breath feathering her cheek, and his body making her aware of his essential maleness, it was difficult to think clearly. "I...I think we should."

His mouth just barely grazed hers. "Because you know I'm going to kiss you if we stay here?"

The illusive contact was tantalizing. "Yes," she whispered, parting her lips helplessly.

Tristan's mouth covered hers, moving over it with slow enjoyment. His tongue traced a path along the inside of her lower lip, sliding over her teeth before plunging deeper. He explored the moist recess lazily, as though confident of his welcome.

Angelique's initial resistance was an instinctive act of self-preservation. It grew feebler as his hands caressed her body, gliding down her back to curve over her hips and draw them closer to his. Tristan's body heat ignited a blaze deep inside of her, destroying the last of Angelique's defenses. With a sigh of surrender, she clasped her arms around Tristan's neck.

His embrace tightened and he buried his face in her hair, inhaling the fragrance. "Sweet, passionate, Angelique. You were aptly named, little Angel."

Her heart was thundering as she clung to him. Angelique dimly realized that she was being very foolish, but it didn't seem to matter. Reality was this tall man who brought rapture with every touch.

Tristan feathered her face with kisses before raising her chin and gazing compellingly into her dazzled eyes. "It's going to be so good between us, sweetheart."

A loud burst of music suddenly intruded on the quiet night, making Angelique conscious of her surroundings. Reason returned slowly as the wild tide of passion began to recede. She removed her arms from around Tristan's neck. Smoothing her hair self-consciously, she murmured, "I don't know what you mean."

He framed her face in his palms, forcing her to look at him. "I'm going to make love to you. We both know it's inevitable." His husky voice was muted.

"I...that's ridiculous." Her words were more forceful than her tone of voice. She tried to summon up righteous indignation but it was impossible.

"You know better than that."

As the pressure of his hands increased, Angelique knew she wouldn't be able to withstand him. The interruption came as a mixed blessing.

"I should have known not to trust you." Alain's body was taut with fury as he came toward them. "Angelique even tried to warn me but I wouldn't listen. I didn't think you'd betray your own family."

Tristan's hands dropped to his sides. "I don't know what you're talking about."

"I've seen you with enough women to recognize all the moves," Alain answered bitterly. "I saw it in your eyes when Angelique came down the stairs tonight, but I told myself I was imagining things. It's true, though. You're trying to take her away from me!"

Tristan's jaw set grimly. "Listen to me, young man, it's time we—"

Angelique grabbed Tristan's arm. "No, wait! Let me handle this." From the anger both men were displaying, an ugly scene could ensue that would damage their relationship irreparably. Angelique knew she couldn't let that happen. "This isn't what it looks like, Alain. Your uncle and I were just pretending to...to be attracted to each other."

His young face set in cynical lines. "He was giving a very convincing performance."

"You don't understand. We're actually doing this for you." Before Alain could erupt she hurried on. "You and I know that age doesn't make any difference when two people are fond of each other, but some people are awfully narrow-minded. They could be very unkind about our relationship," she explained carefully.

"No one would dare say a word against you," Alain replied haughtily.

"Not openly perhaps, but you can bet there'd be talk. As the future ruler of Souveraine you can't afford a scandal. That's what Tristan and I were trying to avoid by seeming to be...uh...involved."

Alain was clearly skeptical. "Tristan is the *present* ruler of Souveraine," he pointed out.

Angelique forced a light laugh. "Everyone knows about his little flirtations. No one takes them seriously."

Alain scowled. "I won't let you do this for me. I won't have people thinking you're one of his women."

"You make it sound as though I have a harem." Tristan frowned.

Alain's set jaw resembled his uncle's. "That's close enough."

They were like an angry stallion and an outraged colt facing each other. Angelique cast a distracted look at the crowded ballroom only steps away. At any moment someone could walk out and join them. They had to get this thing settled now.

"Will you two stop it!" she demanded impatiently. "Before we go back in there we have to decide on some answers. That's why Tristan and I came out here in the first place."

"It looks as though he's already decided everything, as usual." His sulky glance at his uncle made Alain look like the sixteen-year-old he was, in spite of the elegant dinner jacket and chest full of medals.

Angelique had taken care not to injure his male pride, but she didn't have time to put up with temperament. "Since you created this situation, Alain, I suggest you be part of the solution."

Her crisp tone produced the desired result. In his effort to atone, Alain forgot his animosity toward his uncle. "I'll do anything you say, Angelique. Please don't be angry at me."

"I'm not angry, Alain, I just want to get this mess cleared up so I can get out of here."

"You're not thinking of leaving so soon? You just got here today!"

It didn't seem possible. The events of that day and night would have crammed an ordinary week!

"You can't leave yet," Alain insisted. "We've barely gotten to know each other. Besides, you haven't seen anything of Souveraine. There are so many places I want to take you."

He simply refused to understand. Angelique looked uncertainly at Tristan. "Maybe it would be better if I just left."

"We've been over all that." His firm manner left no room for argument. "Your sudden departure would only add fuel to the fire. People would speculate about what happened."

"I don't think they could speculate any more than they're already doing," Angelique muttered. "Madame Lamperre is wild with curiosity."

"Then let's go in and satisfy it," Tristan said decisively.

"Wait!" She grasped his arm. "What are we going to say?"

He smiled. "I thought we'd let our actions speak for us."

Angelique was conscious of Alain stiffening angrily. Before another scene could develop, she said, "In spite of what you think, you don't know much about women. Madame Lamperre has a lot of questions, and she's going to want some answers. Like where we met, and how long we've known each other, for starters."

Tristan looked thoughtful. "I see what you mean."

"We could say that you and I met when I was at school in Scotland, and I invited you to visit Souveraine," Alain offered helpfully, anxious to get back in Angelique's good graces.

She and Tristan exchanged a glance. "The idea is to direct attention away from you," Angelique explained delicately. "It would be better if the invitation came from your uncle." Her brow wrinkled. "Where could we have met? Have you been out of Souveraine lately?" she asked Tristan.

"You went skiing in Switzerland a couple of months ago with Marie Dupres," Alain answered for him. "And you took Anne Brissard to the Riviera."

Tristan looked annoyed. "I didn't know you kept a scorecard."

It would have to be a lengthy one, Angelique thought grimly. "Have you ever been out of the country *without* a female companion? It isn't very credible that we would have gotten chummy if you were...otherwise occupied."

His smile was sardonic. "Why not? The two of you have already decided that I'm a modern-day Don Juan. Don't you think I could satisfy two women?"

It was a question Angelique wouldn't touch with a poker. "Your romantic capabilities don't interest me," she said coldly. "Just stick to the subject."

"All right, I was in Paris recently. How's that?"

She shook her head. "I've never been there. What about London?"

Tristan nodded. "I went to the Council of European States on that same trip."

"That's it then! We met in London—where?"

"In Regent Park. Your horse was running away with you, I stopped it at great peril to myself, you fell into my arms gratefully, and it was the start of a beautiful friendship."

Tristan was being about as helpful as Alain. "Will you be serious?" Angelique asked crossly.

"I am being serious. What's wrong with my story? Madame Lamperre would love it."

"Only if she's addicted to soap operas," Angelique replied. "Think of something believable."

Alain had been looking consideringly at Angelique. "Your first name is French. Is your family from France by any chance?"

"My mother's family was. As a matter of fact, I have distant relatives in Paris. I had thought of looking them up when I left here."

"Then why not say you and Tristan met through your relatives?"

"Because I told you, I've never been to Paris."

"No one has to know."

"They will if we get into a conversation. I don't know the left bank from the right bank."

"Tristan and I can cover for you." Alain grinned boyishly. "This will be the first time I've ever had fun at one of these receptions."

"I wish I shared your expectations." She sighed. "Okay, no use putting it off. We might as well go in and get it over with."

Alain led the way, his good humor restored at the prospect of playing a game on the adults. Angelique was finding out that he had a quick temper like his uncle, but they both got over it fast, perhaps too rapidly in Tristan's case.

As she followed Alain, Angelique suddenly remembered a point they hadn't covered. She turned abruptly, colliding with Tristan. His hands came up to steady her.

"Quick! How long have we known each other?" she asked urgently.

His hands subtly caressed her arms, and his deep voice dropped a note. "That pleasure is still ahead of us."

Angelique's heartbeat accelerated in spite of her annoyance. Before she could set him straight, Alain turned a laughing face to them.

"Get ready. Here comes the head of the local spy ring."

Madame Lamperre bore down on them as soon as they entered the room. "Oh, there you are! I was beginning to think you'd spirited off *both* our royal young men," she told Angelique archly.

"Only as far as the terrace," Angelique replied serenely. "They were showing me your truly remarkable view."

"It's even lovelier by daylight. You must have... someone bring you over to see it." Madame Lamperre looked expectantly at the two men who flanked Angelique, waiting avidly to see which one would volunteer.

"That's very kind of you," Angelique answered, without actually taking her up on it. They all looked back at the older woman with blank faces, although the corners of Alain's mouth twitched.

"How long are you staying, Miss Archer?" she persisted.

When Angelique hesitated, Alain answered for her. "A long time, I hope."

She groaned inwardly, but Tristan saved the day. "Alain and Miss Archer have hit it off wonderfully ever since they met this afternoon," he said smoothly.

"That's right. And since my uncle is so busy, I've offered to entertain her," Alain said just as smoothly. The gleeful look in his eyes challenged Tristan to disagree.

Fortunately for Angelique's nerves, the ambassador joined them with welcome news. "Supper is being served, my dear. Will you come into the dining room?"

As he led his wife away, Tristan turned on Alain. "I suppose you thought that little performance was clever," he said glacially.

Alain laughed, not a bit intimidated. "You have to admit it kept her guessing."

Angelique realized it was all a joke to him. He enjoyed outwitting his elders, like any other sixteen-year-old. The main thing was to keep Tristan from blowing his cork and making the scene they were trying to avoid.

She sighed. "Come on, let's get something to eat. I have a feeling we're going to need all our strength before this evening is over."

Chapter Four

Angelique slept late the next morning. The difference in time and the traumatic events of the previous day and night had finally taken their toll.

When she returned from the ambassador's reception Angelique had climbed gratefully into bed, too tired to worry over all the unsolved problems that lay ahead. Tomorrow she would have to deal with them, though. Would her plan to divert Alain succeed? Had Madame Lamperre bought their story? What was actually behind Tristan's blatant seduction?

His dark, aristocratic face suddenly appeared inside her closed eyelids. His pewter eyes had the same molten glow they'd had in the moonlight, just before he'd kissed her. Angelique's lips parted automatically as she experienced again the touch of that firm mouth, that erotic tongue staking a confident male claim.

She could almost feel his hard body covering hers in the concealing darkness. Tristan's weight would mold her to him at every point, pressing her into the mattress. Angelique gave a tiny gasp as she realized that her body was arched tautly. In one swift movement she turned over and buried her face in the pillow.

It was almost ten o'clock when she awoke. The luxurious room was dim, but Angelique could hear birds singing outside. When she opened the heavy damask draperies a glorious blue and gold day was revealed.

After a quick shower in the marble enclosure that was too grand to be called a stall, she put on a sleeveless white piqué dress with a scooped neck and a red and white braided belt. Red sandals completed the outfit.

The previous night's elaborate hairdo was abandoned for a simple style that fell around her shoulders like a spill of sunshine. Her makeup was equally simple, just a touch of lip gloss and a flick of mascara on her thick lashes.

After she was dressed Angelique wasn't quite sure what to do next. Would it be all right to go into the kitchen and ask for a cup of coffee? Somehow it didn't seem quite the thing to do in a palace, besides the fact that she had no idea where the kitchen was. But she couldn't stay in her room all day, waiting for someone to remember she was there.

Angelique walked down a long corridor lined with richly detailed paintings that she assumed were de Marchal ancestors. They were a handsome lot. The air of authority, symmetrical features, and more than a hint of sensuality were evidently characteristics that went back many generations. She paused in front of a portrait depicting a dark-haired man with an ermine-trimmed cloak tied loosely at the base of his bronze throat. He was breathtakingly virile with a hint of savagery under his urbane mask. The clothes and hairstyle were from a different era, but it might have been Tristan staring boldly back at her. A tiny shiver ran up Angelique's spine at the thought of matching wits with a man like that. For the first time, little doubts about her ability began to surface.

Shaking them off she made her way to the sweeping staircase. At the bottom she paused irresolutely. There wasn't a soul around. Did all of these spotless rooms get cleaned by little elves in the middle of the night? She started down a corridor leading to the back of the palace, looking into the stately salons that opened off of it. For the most part they were vast reception rooms, furnished with exquisite antiques. Rich fabric drapes were tied back from eleven-foot-tall windows, and the morning light illuminated polished tables and museum-quality furniture.

Farther down the hall she finally heard the hum of male voices. When she reached their source Angelique stuck her head inside the door hesitantly, not wanting to disturb Tristan at work, but beginning to feel quite deserted. It wasn't Tristan, however.

Alain looked up with a pleased smile. "Angelique! Come in. Did you sleep well after that eventful party last night?" His smile broadened to a grin.

"When I was finally able to relax. Listening to you and Tristan fielding all those questions about Paris was nerve-racking. Madame Lamperre would have been a credit to the Spanish Inquisition."

"Oh, I don't know." Alain looked smug. "She didn't get anything out of us."

"Is that the way you see it?" Angelique asked dryly. "How about the inference that my French relatives were descended from royalty?"

Alain chuckled. "Since you've never met them you don't know that it isn't true."

The other man in the room cleared his throat with an impatient sound. He was a small man with light brown hair and a sparse mustache above a rather prim mouth. His tie was knotted precisely, and he kept his narrow shoulders squared, military fashion. The effect was one of competence, but not warmth.

"Sorry, Claude, I guess our next lesson will be on manners, won't it?" Alain's eyes were dancing as he turned to Angelique. "I'd like you to meet the elusive Claude Dumont. You see, he really does exist."

After acknowledging the introduction, Claude frowned at Alain. "Of course I exist. What a strange thing to say."

"There was a time when Angelique wasn't sure," Alain answered with elaborate innocence.

"Alain has told me a great deal about you," Angelique put in hurriedly.

"He's a fine young man." Pride and censure warred with each other in Claude's tone. "He could be a top student if he just applied himself."

Angelique had a feeling that her views on the subject wouldn't be welcome, but she voiced them anyway. "Perhaps he misses the challenge of competing with other students."

"It was his uncle's wish that he be tutored at home."

Claude was as disapproving as she'd known he would be, but Angelique persisted. "Where do Ambassador Lamperre's daughters go to school, and Sir Delain's son, and all the rest?"

"I believe they attend the Royal Academy," Claude replied distantly.

"They do." Alain looked wistful. "I saw Suzette Lamperre in town a while back and we had a chance to talk for a few minutes. I hadn't seen her in years."

"You were quite friendly when you were children, weren't you?" Angelique asked casually.

"Yes, a whole group of us used to play together and go to birthday parties and things. I guess they still do," he added matter-of-factly.

Alain's resignation broke Angelique's heart, and re-kindled her fury at Tristan.

Claude cleared his throat, sounding like a fussy hen. "I don't wish to be rude Miss Archer, but Alain does need to get on with his lessons. It wouldn't do to have him fall behind."

Behind what, Angelique wondered silently. She was taking a definite dislike to this prissy little man. If Alain had to spend every day with him, it was no wonder he escaped into a world of fantasy. Why couldn't Tristan see it? Or was it that he just didn't care? Perhaps the main thing was to keep Alain out of circulation. All of Angelique's suspicions returned in full force.

"You were the one who missed class the last few days, not me," Alain's aggrieved voice broke in on Angelique's thoughts.

"Not I," Claude corrected automatically.

Alain's frown dissolved into a grin as he shot Angelique a mischievous glance. "What did I tell you?"

"And it was only because of an unavoidable occurrence," Claude continued as though there had been no interruption.

"Your wife went into false labor, didn't she?" Alain asked.

Claude turned a dull red. "Yes, she…uh…we needn't discuss it."

The man was unreal! He acted as though pregnancy was a dirty word. Angelique covered her scorn with solicitude. "How disappointing for the poor thing. But how comforting to have her...co-producer...so to speak, there beside her."

"Yes, Claude has proved he's a good man." Alain's eyes sparkled with repressed mirth.

The tutor looked positively apoplectic. "I believe you have a test to complete." He turned to Angelique. "If you'll excuse us, *mademoiselle*." His tone brooked no argument.

"Of course, Monsieur Dumont, I've disrupted your class long enough. Besides, I want to talk to the grand duke." Her small chin set firmly.

"You'll find Tristan in his study," Alain volunteered. "Down the hall and to the left."

Tristan was sitting behind a cherrywood desk that curved around him in a vast semicircle. The gold-tooled leather top was almost obscured by papers. His dark head was bent and he wore a scowl as he scrawled his signature on a lengthy document.

In the moment before he noticed her, Angelique stared at him, feeling her pulse start its familiar tattoo. Tristan wore a white cotton T-shirt, but it didn't make him look any less authoritative than his ermine-clad ancestor. There was a leashed vitality about him, a barely submerged, savage impatience with the work at hand. As though he wanted to be riding a wild horse, or brandishing a saber, or subduing a woman?

Tristan's scowl changed to a smile as he saw Angelique standing in the doorway. He jumped up from the high-backed chair to greet her. When she saw that he was wearing white tennis shorts, Angelique began to laugh.

He glanced down swiftly. "What's so funny?"

"I was picturing a portrait of you dressed like that, among all your elegant forebears in the upstairs gallery."

Tristan chuckled. "It's a thought. I've always considered all that satin and lace slightly effeminate."

Glancing at his firm, muscled legs and broad-shouldered torso, Angelique could have told him that was something he'd never have to worry about. Annoyance at herself set in immediately. She hadn't come here to notice Tristan's physique, or let him charm her out of her indignation. What he was doing to Alain was unconscionable.

"I want to talk to you." Her delicate brows slanted down.

"Sounds ominous. What could I have done between last night and this morning?" He grinned wickedly. "Don't tell me I walked in my sleep. If I missed...an experience...with you, I'll never forgive myself."

Angelique's blue eyes sparkled angrily. "You and I are never going to have an experience, as you so euphemistically put it—asleep *or* awake!"

He wound a shining strand of hair around his forefinger, smiling into her flushed face. "You know better than that."

"What can I—ouch, that hurts!" When Angelique jerked her head away, Tristan's hand remained tangled in her hair.

"Only when you fight the inevitable." He slid his free arm around her waist, pulling her close while he gently unwound the springy curl. "See how easy it is when you don't struggle?"

Angelique's palms were flattened against Tristan's chest to keep him from drawing her any closer. Through the thin cotton T-shirt she could feel the measured beat of his heart. It was a lot steadier than her own.

She pushed her way out of his arms and smoothed her hair. "I thought we agreed that this amorous act was only going to be played before an audience."

"Every act needs a rehearsal," he murmured.

"You already have yours down pat," she commented witheringly.

"A little practice never hurt." He smiled. "You know the old saying—anything worth doing..."

Angelique regarded him coldly. "It seems to me that you're losing sight of the reason for this whole charade. It's all for Alain's welfare, not yours. Actually that's why I'm here."

"Not because you couldn't wait to see me this morning?" he teased. "I'm crushed."

"Will you be serious! I just saw Alain, and met Claude, incidentally."

"What did you think of him?"

"Not much."

Tristan chuckled. "I'll admit he wouldn't win any personality contests, but Claude is good at what he does."

"There's more to life than irregular verbs," Angelique observed tartly. "How would you like to spend every day with Claude Dumont?"

"No thanks. But he's a pussycat compared to some of the headmasters at the schools I went to."

"You weren't tutored at home?"

"No, I went to a succession of schools." Tristan's gray eyes lit with mischief. "It seemed only fair to spread the burden around."

"In that case, will you tell me why Alain isn't given the same opportunity, instead of being kept in this glorified jail under virtual house arrest?" Angelique's translucent skin was flushed with indignation.

"What are you talking about?"

"In plain words, why doesn't he go to school with his peers? You can't tell me it was Alain's idea to study at home, all alone except for that dried up little disciplinarian."

The tolerant amusement vanished from Tristan's face, leaving it bleak. "No, it was my idea. We didn't discuss it because at the time, he wasn't up to making any decisions. The loss of his parents pretty much destroyed Alain. For a long time he wandered around like a lost soul." Tristan thrust his fists into the pockets of his white shorts, tightening the fabric over his muscular thighs. "I wanted to be available whenever he needed me. If he couldn't sleep at night we went for a drive, sometimes all the way to the border. Or if the days closed in on him, we'd saddle our horses and ride in the hills above town. He couldn't very well go to school under those conditions, and I felt it was more important for him to have time to get over his first shattering grief."

There was a vulnerability about Tristan that touched Angelique unexpectedly. "You must have been suffering too," she murmured softly.

He gazed out the window without seeing the riotous flowers that bordered the green lawn. "I'll always miss my brother and his wife, but Alain's loss was much greater. He's only a boy, and this was his first brush with tragedy. My own sorrow had to take second place."

It was a statement of fact, not a plea for sympathy, yet Angelique's heart melted. Tristan's selfless devotion made Angelique ashamed of her suspicions. He didn't covet the throne of Souveraine. He had been telling the truth about disliking court life, which made his sacrifice all the more poignant. Tristan had given up his whole life for Alain in more ways than one.

"That must have made it even harder for you—having to keep his spirits up when yours were so low."

He shrugged. "The end result is all that matters. Alain weathered his storm. He's back to normal now." Tristan smiled wryly. "You're living proof of that."

His explanation had changed Angelique's opinion of him, but it hadn't altered her plans for Alain. She approached Tristan tentatively.

"I can imagine how difficult it was for both of you. But now that Alain has bounced back, don't you think it's time to, uh, reevaluate the situation?"

"What are you driving at?"

"I think he needs more...well...companionship. Living here in the palace with only you and Claude for company is rather an unnatural existence."

Tristan's eyes narrowed slightly. "What are you suggesting?"

Angelique was too intent on her purpose to notice his wary attitude. "I know it's none of my business, but Alain really does need to be with youngsters his own age. There's no longer any necessity for his being tutored at home. Couldn't he attend the Royal Academy?"

Tristan's tense body relaxed. "Is *that* what you've been leading up to?"

Angelique stared at him blankly. "What did you think?"

"Well, it occurred to me that you—never mind, it isn't important." He looked slightly sheepish.

Suddenly Tristan's suspicions became clear. In spite of everything she'd said and done, he still thought she had designs on Alain and was trying to insinuate herself into the household. Angelique's quick flash of anger died as she realized that she had been guilty of leaping to some pretty swift conclusions herself.

"Don't you think it's time we started to trust each other?" she asked quietly.

Tiny points of light flickered in his gray eyes. "Does that mean you've decided to trust *me*?"

Angelique looked at him doubtfully. She trusted him where Alain was concerned; Tristan's intentions toward her were a different matter. Angelique sidestepped the question.

"I'll admit that I let my imagination run away with me in the beginning, although you didn't go out of your way to set me straight," she couldn't help adding. "But I realize now you really do care for Alain."

Tristan moved closer, making her very aware of his powerful, slim-hipped body, so evident in the brief tennis outfit.

"Is that the only thing I told you that you believe?" His low voice held a vibrant note that set Angelique's nerve ends quivering.

She tried not to think about his conviction that they were destined to make love. "We were talking about Alain," she reminded him hurriedly. "Don't you think the Academy is a good idea? Alain told me all his friends go there—the kids he grew up with."

Mention of his nephew sobered Tristan as it always did. "That's true," he said slowly. "But conditions have changed. Alain is no longer heir to a distant throne, he's now the virtual ruler, even though I happen to be the interim one. Would he be accepted back into the fold? Or would he be a curiosity, someone they'd feel uncomfortable with? I wouldn't want to subject him to that."

"I don't think you have to worry. Kids are a lot more levelheaded than adults when it comes to pomp and ceremony. It doesn't impress them a lot."

"I wish I could be sure."

"Maybe there's a way to prove it. That's the other thing I wanted to talk to you about. I think it would be a good idea if Alain gave a party. He could invite all the young people he used to be friendly with. It would be a way of easing him back into the group."

Tristan looked doubtful. "What if the party was a bomb? They'd have to attend, but suppose they just sat around and looked at one another?" He rumpled his dark hair distractedly. "Who can figure what teenagers are likely to do?"

"You worry too much. Besides, I'm way ahead of you. From the minute those kids step through the front door, they're going to be too busy to be self-conscious."

"How do you plan to accomplish that?"

Angelique's lovely face lit with animation. "By sending them on a scavenger hunt in the maze. I'll hide a lot of little objects ahead of time, and we'll pair the youngsters off in couples. We'll have them draw for partners so there won't be any awkwardness about who chooses whom. At the end of a time limit—say an hour—the game is over and the couple that finds the most items gets a prize. I guarantee that the ice will be broken by the time they all get together again."

Tristan nodded thoughtfully. "It might work."

"It *will* work!" Angelique was filled with confidence. "When they come back we'll serve refreshments. They're bound to be hungry by then. After that we'll roll back the rugs for dancing. What we have to decide is the best place to hold it."

"No problem. There's a ballroom on the third floor."

"No, no, no! This isn't a state affair, it's a teenage party! We want something smaller and cozier, a place that feels like somebody's living room. Do you have anything like that?"

He sighed. "Not really, but we'll find something that will do."

"I can go ahead with it then?" Angelique asked eagerly.

Tristan's hand curved around the nape of her neck. His voice was husky as he said, "You've put a lot of thought into this, haven't you?"

The warmth in his eyes bathed her in a golden glow. "Alain is very special to me," she mumbled.

His fingers were caressing, moving sensuously over her sensitive skin. "He's a very lucky young man."

Little bubbles of excitement swelled and burst inside of Angelique. She tried valiantly to keep Tristan from knowing how he affected her. "Could I borrow a car for a little while? I need to get invitations and prizes. Oh, and decorations! It has to look festive; that sets the mood."

To her intense relief Tristan removed his hand. "I'll have a car and chauffeur waiting at the front entrance whenever you're ready. Get whatever you like and charge it to me."

"It won't come to that much," Angelique protested. "I'll take care of it."

"No, you've done more than enough. I'm already deeply in your debt." His firm mouth curved in a melting smile. "I'd like very much to repay you."

Ignoring his deepened tone she said, "Okay, you can help me blow up the balloons."

"Is that all I can do for you, angel?"

It was more of an endearment than a nickname. Tristan's muted voice made her name sound like a whisper of love. It was a caress, a prelude to something wonderful. When he moved closer Angelique started to tremble.

She knew it was a purely physical response. Their truce was too recent for there to be any real feeling between them. Not that there ever would be, no matter how long they knew each other. Tristan wanted the same thing from her that he wanted from any other presentable woman.

To be perfectly honest, Angelique had to admit that she was also powerfully drawn to him; their sexual attraction was electrifying. But a warning voice told her that she was getting into deep water.

There was no doubt that Tristan would be a magnificent lover, tender yet masterful. Angelique's stomach fluttered at the thought of what it would be like to lie in his arms. One thing she was afraid it would be, however, was habit forming—and that would be fatal. Tristan didn't have a lasting relationship in mind, and she wasn't interested in an affair.

His suggestive question hung in the air, inviting an answer that would bring them both untold pleasure. Angelique closed her mind to it firmly. "You can tell me how to get to the kitchen."

It was clearly the last thing he expected. "The kitchen?"

She almost laughed at his blank expression. "Yes, I'm lost without my morning coffee."

"Didn't you have any breakfast?" he demanded.

"No, I slept late this morning, and...well, I didn't know where to go."

"Alain and I have breakfast together early, but all you had to do was pick up the house phone and order whatever you wanted." He looked at the thin gold watch on his wrist and frowned. "It's almost eleven-thirty. You must be starved."

"No, coffee is all I ever have in the morning."

"That's not enough," he declared.

Angelique laughed. "Now you sound like my father."

Tristan's slow smile was faintly mocking. "I care a great deal about your welfare, but believe me, Angel, the resemblance stops there." Before she could answer he put his arm around her shoulders, guiding her toward the door. "Come on, let's get you something to eat."

He led her to a light and airy room filled with a profusion of flowering plants. The green and white wallpaper furthered the impression of an indoor garden. After seating her at a round glass table Tristan tugged at a velvet bell pull, then seated himself next to her.

"If you prefer to come downstairs in the morning, this is where breakfast is served," he said. "It's a little more intimate than the dining room."

"It's lovely, but now that I know where it is, you don't have to stay with me." She was torn between wanting Tristan's company, and having reservations about it. "I know you must have things to do."

"Nothing I'd *rather* do." The vibrant note in his voice told Angelique that her fears were justified. Before she could protest further, a servant entered. "Miss Archer will have orange juice, a mushroom omelet, toast, butter, and marmalade. And we'll both have coffee."

"I never have that much for breakfast!" she gasped as the servant left.

"That's because you live alone." He covered her hand where it rested on the table, and the warmth seemed to invade her body. "Breakfast can be very special if it's shared."

His meaning was quite clear. Angelique could almost see sunlight peeping through drawn drapes, highlighting a tumbled double bed. Tristan was incorrigible! He could take the most innocent subject and turn it into something erotic.

"I can't think of anything worse than having to make conversation in the morning," she said coolly.

"It isn't strictly necessary. There are all kinds of sharing," he murmured, managing to contain his laughter.

Angelique was annoyed to feel her cheeks growing warm. A welcome interruption came in the form of a young man with black-rimmed glasses who turned out to be Tristan's secretary.

He hovered uncertainly in the doorway. "I'm sorry to disturb you, sir, but the minister of finance is on the telephone. He says it's most urgent."

Tristan swore under his breath as he rose reluctantly to his feet. "All right, Charles, tell him I'm coming." He turned to Angelique. "I'm sorry, honey—*noblesse oblige.*" His chiseled mouth curved in a derisive smile. "For the next two years anyway."

She could almost feel Tristan's frustration as his long legs carried him to the door. Everything about him rejected the role he had been forced into. Once again Angelique wondered how she could have misread him so completely.

When she finished brunch the chauffeured limousine was waiting at the door as Tristan promised. It took her into the charming little town that was a harmonious blend of old and new. Quaint small shops, and even the newer hotels and office buildings, preserved the flavor of long ago. There were a lot of casement windows and shutters, and many carved stone friezes decorating rooftops. But the merchandise displayed was comparable to any in New York or Beverly Hills. Souveraine might be small, but it was rich. It was also incredibly clean and lovely. All of the buildings were painted white or pastel colors, and the leisurely atmosphere was that of a resort.

Angelique enjoyed browsing for a time in the shops before she buckled down to the business of selecting invitations, balloons, and large posters of current rock stars. After that she picked out trinkets to hide in the maze for the scavenger hunt.

Angelique was sure that the palace kitchen would take care of the food handsomely, but just in case their menu should lean too heavily toward gourmet fare, she bought large cans of popcorn, big bags of potato chips, and an assortment of candies. By the time she finished shopping, the back seat of the limousine was filled with a clutter of plebeian paper parcels.

The palace was deserted when she returned in the afternoon. Alain wasn't in the classroom, nor Tristan in his office. They had both escaped to parts unknown.

Angelique experienced a feeling of letdown. She was bubbling over with plans for the party and had no one to discuss them with. The invitations, which should go out immediately, couldn't even be addressed until she got the guest list.

After unpacking her purchases, Angelique looked at the trinkets thoughtfully. This might be a good time to scout the maze, since she had never been inside it. The items that the young people had to bring back should be hidden well enough to make it a challenge, but not too obscure to take the fun out of it.

She gathered up the coffee mug embossed with a funny saying, the silver whistle on a blue ribbon, the green rubber snake, and all the other things. Although the party wouldn't be until the following weekend, there was no reason why she couldn't place the things around now.

It was the first time Angelique had been inside a maze. She spent the first half hour wandering delightedly, feeling like Alice in Wonderland. The ancient yew hedges formed corridors twelve- or fourteen-feet high. They were as smooth as walls, and the tops were leveled off in a precise line. Angelique marveled at how the gardeners managed to get the tops so even.

At regular intervals the path made a geometric angle to the right or left. Usually other paths beckoned, but sometimes she found herself at a dead end, forced to retrace her steps to another intersection. It was like playing blindman's buff with her eyes open.

After indulging herself for a time, Angelique decided she'd better get down to work. There weren't really that many places to hide things. The paths were kept immacuately free of leaves, and the hedges formed smooth barriers, unbroken by shrubbery at the base. She couldn't push the trinkets too deeply into the thick hedges or they'd never be found.

Angelique finally decided that the maze itself would be enough of an obstacle. Any couple lucky enough to turn down the right corridor would be rewarded, and everyone should be able to find something.

The sun was sinking behind the mountains by the time she hid the last item to her satisfaction. It was still daylight out, but inside the maze it was growing dim, warning Angelique that it was time to leave. It had been such fun that she gathered up her paper bags reluctantly, starting back the way she had come.

At least she thought it was the way. When she ended up in a cul-de-sac, Angelique laughed. Yet when repeated turns led nowhere but to other dead ends, or to endless paths branching off to similar ones, she started to get uneasy. No one knew she was here, and it was the last place anyone would think to look for her. It was conceivable that she might have to spend the night in this place!

Forcing down the unreasonable panic that tightened her throat, she tried to think sensibly. Even if the worst happened, it wouldn't be the end of the world. It wasn't as though there were any wild animals about, and certainly no intruders could penetrate the palace security. But the nights turned cool, one of the blessings of Souveraine's climate. Already she could feel the breeze on her bare shoulders.

Taking a deep breath, Angelique called for help. "Hello! Is anyone out there?" Her only answer was the chirping of awakening crickets and a few distant bird calls. "I'm in the maze, can someone get me out?"

For all the response, she might as well have been on a desert island. The graceful bulk of the palace was so near and yet so far. The glittering windows looked blankly down on the spacious grounds. Angelique jumped and waved her arms, hoping someone would see her. When that proved futile she started shouting again.

She had just about resigned herself to spending the night when Tristan's astonished voice called, "Angelique? Is that you? Where are you?"

"I'm in the maze and I can't find my way out!"

"Stay where you are," he ordered. "Just keep calling and I'll come and get you."

When Tristan appeared, Angelique felt relief out of all proportion to her plight. She could barely restrain herself from rushing into his arms. Something about her expression communicated itself to him, and he put his hands on her shoulders.

"Are you all right?" His face was concerned.

"Yes, I...I'm fine. I just couldn't find the right path, and I guess I sort of panicked. I must have an atavistic fear of being trapped in an unfamiliar place." Her breathing was ragged.

When Tristan gathered her close she didn't resist. Angelique rested her forehead in the curve formed by his neck and shoulder, inhaling his reassuring male scent.

"What were you doing here all alone?" he asked.

All she wanted was for him to hold her close. His arms were a haven, and his hard body bolstered her confidence with its strength. She had to force out the words.

"I was hiding the tokens for the scavenger hunt. There wasn't anyone around when I got back from town so I thought it would be a good time to do it, but then I got all turned around."

"That was a foolish thing to do," he scolded gently. "Why do you think these things are sometimes called follies?"

She managed a tentative smile. "I believe I just found out."

"Well, no harm was done anyway."

"Except for my being scared to death," she said indignantly. "I pictured myself stuck here for the night."

His arms tightened slightly. "You must have known I'd come looking for you."

"I hoped *somebody* would."

Tristan's fingers traced a teasing pattern down her spine. "Just anyone?"

The sun had gone behind the mountains and darkness was falling rapidly inside the maze. Suddenly the atmopshere changed to one of intimacy. Tristan's arms became more than a haven. They were now an unmistakable embrace. Angelique was quiveringly aware of every contact point of their bodies—the tips of her breasts brushing tantalizingly against his chest, Tristan's firm thighs resting against hers, making her aware of his masculinity.

She felt her heart start to thunder. "It's getting dark, we'd better get out of here."

When she started to move away his clasp tightened, trapping her in his arms. "There's no hurry." The murky light didn't conceal the blaze in his smoky eyes.

Angelique moistened her lips nervously, drawing his attention to them. "Unless you have a flashlight in your pocket, we're both going to be trapped here for the night."

The statement was meant to urge him along, but as soon as the words were out Angelique knew they were a mistake. Tristan's head dipped lower until their lips just barely grazed. When she drew in her breath it was mingled with his.

"I'd like to spend the night with you, sweet Angelique, but I would never trap you into it. You will come to me willingly, and I'm going to make love to you in light, not in darkness." His hands slid down her back to cup gently around her bottom, guiding her to the juncture of his thighs. "I want to see every inch of your beautiful body as I remove your clothes, kiss every secret place and share your pleasure."

The sensuous words and the heat of his loins kindled dormant embers deep inside her. A fierce blaze raced through Angelique's veins, leaving her taut and aching. "Please, Tristan," she murmured, shaken by the intensity of the desire he had awakened so effortlessly.

"Yes, my darling, I will please you in every way I know how. You want that too, don't you, angel?"

As though sure of her response his mouth covered hers. When her lips parted helplessly, Tristan's tongue slipped inside for a sensual exploration of the warm depths. The seduction of her senses—the touch, taste, and feel of him were too much for Angelique to resist. With a soft sigh of surrender, her arms circled his neck.

Tristan groaned deep in his throat, gathering her even closer. He covered her face lightly with tiny kisses. "Tell me you want me, sweetheart. Let me hear you say it."

"I want you, Tristan." How could she deny it when every fiber of her body longed for his possession?

His mouth burned its way down her throat to glide over the rounded slopes above her scooped neckline. The exquisite sensation intensified as he slowly unfastened the tiny buttons of her sundress. Her bare breasts gleamed white in the near darkness, the pink tips curled into tight rosettes of excitement. When he touched one with a warm, moist tongue she cried out in delight.

"Do you like that, my love?" His eyes were like molten metal. "You have the breasts of the angel you were named for."

His mouth captured a hardened nipple, rolling it between his lips until she gasped and dug her fingers into the bunching muscles of his back. Tristan's hand cupped her other breast, stroking it with the tips of his fingers until her legs felt too boneless to support her. She clung to him mindlessly, moving against him in a silent plea for release from the tension that was building to a fever pitch.

"I wanted our first time to be on silken sheets, but you're irresistible," he muttered. "Forgive me, my love."

Forgive him? Angelique would never have forgiven him if he hadn't filled the aching void that was tearing her apart. Her hands were already tugging the shirt out of his slacks. But as Tristan was lowering her to the ground, Alain's voice ripped through their private paradise, calling their names.

"Angelique! Tristan! Are you in there?"

They looked at each other in disbelief, as though this couldn't be happening. Then as sanity returned, Tristan framed Angelique's face in his palms and gently kissed her trembling lips. "This is only a postponement. You know that, don't you?"

She couldn't reply. The enormity of what had almost happened overwhelmed Angelique. Her fingers were shaking so badly that she had trouble doing up her buttons. But when Tristan tried to help she pushed his hands away. Even though she was now fairly well in command of herself, his touch still had the power to disturb her.

"Hey, is anyone in the maze?" Alain's voice came again.

"We're coming out now," Tristan called.

He put his arms around her, but Angelique pulled away, holding herself stiffly. After a glance at her averted face Tristan led her silently through the twisting paths.

Alain was waiting for them with a quizzical expression. "What's going on? One of the gardeners said he thought he heard someone hollering, but before he could investigate he saw Tristan going into the maze."

"Angelique decided to do some exploring on her own and she got lost," Tristan explained.

"Just like my nurse when I was little." Alain laughed. "Didn't I warn you?"

Her answering laugh was shaky. "Next time I'll believe you."

"It's a good thing Tristan was there to rescue you."

Tristan's dancing eyes invited her to share his amusement. When she refused, he said dryly, "It was entirely my pleasure."

Angelique's cheeks flamed as she remembered her unbridled response to him. Unreasoning anger made her voice sharp. "If we're through examining my stupidity, can we go inside now? I'm getting chilly."

Alain's questioning eyes sought his uncle's over Angelique's head. Tristan merely shrugged and started toward the patio. When Alain went ahead to open the French doors, Tristan took her arm. He bent his dark head to murmur in her ear, "Will I see you after dinner?"

"No!" Her muted answer was nevertheless explosive. "Not tonight or any other night!"

Tristan wasn't in the least disconcerted. His well-formed mouth curved in a bewitching smile. "Foolish little Angelique. Don't you know you can't struggle against fate?"

As she preceded him through the double doors her mind was in turmoil. Was Tristan right? Angelique knew it wouldn't be fate that would betray her, it was his own fatal attraction. Could she manage to resist him? With a sinking sensation she realized that only putting distance between them would save her. And she was committed for an indefinite time.

Her fingernails made little crescent marks in her damp palms as Angelique followed Alain inside.

Chapter Five

Angelique's nerves were running a relay race through her body as she applied her makeup. Concern about the outcome of the party wasn't the only reason. It had been a difficult week.

After her traumatic encounter with Tristan in the maze, she had tried to avoid him, but he wouldn't permit it. Tristan had pressured her in subtle ways. He was much too expert at seduction to use obvious methods, yet the tug was always there.

She would glance up to find him gazing at her with an enigmatic look on his lean face. He was like a stalking tiger, patient because he was confident of ultimate victory. Angelique shuddered as she remembered how close he had come to it. That brought back all the memories she was trying so hard to suppress. Which was exactly what he intended. It was a further tightening of the silken trap.

If only the party that night were successful! If Alain got back with his own age group and began dating teenage girls, no one could possibly imagine he was interested in her. And as soon as he was busy with normal activities, Alain would get over his schoolboy crush. The party was the key to everything. With luck she could be out of Souveraine in a week. It promised to be seven days of ordeal, but at least there was light at the end of the tunnel.

She quickly finished applying her makeup. Angelique's blue eyes in their frame of long lashes were a rare shade of sapphire, and her flawless face was marred only by the tiny frown between her delicate brows. After brushing her hair until it shone like a length of pale silk, she let it drift around her shoulders in a casual style. Her appearance really didn't matter. She and Tristan were only chaperones, an unavoidable nuisance as far as the young people were concerned.

The dress she selected was festive nonetheless. The delicate chiffon was printed in muted shades of rose and blue, like a Monet watercolor. Its wide neckline exposed her creamy neck and shoulders, and the soft fabric clung lovingly to her small, firm breasts. High-heeled sandals called attention to her slender legs.

Angelique went downstairs early to check out the party site. The room they had finally settled on was a small—by palace standards—reception salon. Its formality was transformed to a great extent by the decorations, and especially by Tristan's inspired contribution. He had supplied sophisticated stereo equipment, complete with amplifiers. It was set up on prominent display, providing a disco atmosphere. While the youngsters were busy with their scavenger hunt, the rugs would be rolled up for dancing. There was something to be said for having unlimited servants at your disposal, Angelique reflected.

She had to admit that Tristan's help had been invaluable. He had taken time from his duty-packed days to confer with her on all sorts of details. His enthusiasm was only tinged by regret that he hadn't seen what was instantly evident to her. Tristan's concern for his nephew was truly touching. It showed how deeply he could care. It was too bad his capacity for love didn't extend to a woman, Angelique thought wistfully. She dismissed the fruitless thought.

"How are the young girls going to stand a chance tonight when you look like that?"

Tristan's husky voice startled Angelique. The undisguised admiration in his smoky eyes was so frankly sexual that it sent a little shiver down her spine. She had to force herself not to show how his blatant masculinity affected her. Tristan's superbly tailored dark suit didn't blur Angelique's memory of the powerful body underneath. She had felt its hard angles too intimately to forget easily.

Somehow she succeeded in keeping her voice casual. "Oh—hi. I was just making sure we have enough of everything. Didn't we figure on thirty-four people? That calls for seventeen flashlights. We wouldn't want any of them to get lost in the maze."

"It could be a memorable experience."

Angelique felt her color deepen. He might have the decency not to remind her when she had enough on her mind! "Will you be serious?" she asked crossly.

"I think you know the answer to that." He sauntered across the room to stand very close to her.

She frowned. "You don't have to go into your act. We aren't on display tonight."

"You never can tell. Kids are self-centered little brutes, but they just might go home and tell their parents that I couldn't stay away from you." Tristan's long fingers curled around Angelique's chin, tilting her face up to his. He bent his head until their lips were only inches apart. "And they would be right," he murmured.

It was useless to remind herself that was just one more step in Tristan's campaign to wear down her resistance. His magic was too potent. Her lips were starting to part when Alain's voice preceded him.

"Is there anything I can do to help?" He stood in the doorway, surveying the festive room. "You shouldn't have gone to so much trouble, Angelique. They probably won't stay long."

She wasn't fooled by his blasé observation. Angelique's heart melted as she realized how insecure Alain felt. This party meant a great deal to him, but he was plagued by a fear of rejection. He had been out of touch for so long. Could he achieve the old camaraderie, or would the evening be a stilted disaster?

Angelique knew better than to reassure him openly. Male egos were fragile at best, and teenage ones even more so. She matched his disinterested tone. "If they clear out early, the three of us can go to one of those swinging discos. This party is really an obligation on your part, but we don't have to spend all evening doing the juvenile bit."

"That's right." Alain brightened at being subtly declared an adult. "It's about time Tristan and I showed you some of Souveraine's nightlife."

When the guests started to arrive Angelique was as nervous as Alain. Especially since it seemed his fears were justified. The young people were clearly uneasy. They weren't quite sure how to treat Alain. He wasn't one of them anymore; he was now the imminent monarch of Souveraine.

Lacking the experience of adults at small talk, they closed ranks, clustering in whispering groups. Angelique's attempts to draw them out brought only polite responses. Without Tristan's assistance it could have been a calamity. Besides knowing all the young people, he seemed to be well liked. They relaxed when talking to him.

"I almost didn't recognize you, Suzette." Tristan was exerting his charm on a lovely blond girl with blue eyes and a peaches-and-cream complexion. "If you'll excuse the cliché—my how you've grown! It doesn't seem that long since you and Alain were playing hide-and-seek in my studio."

She responded flirtatiously, gazing up through long lashes. "That was ages ago."

"I suppose it must be since Alain is grown up now." He put his arm around his nephew's shoulders. "He's starting to teach *me* things."

Only someone very young would believe that, Angelique thought cynically. Alain gave promise of being a very handsome man, but there was something special about Tristan, a magnetic quality that set him apart from other men. Suzette, however, was dazzled by the implication of Alain's experience.

She looked at him with different eyes. "I guess it's a good thing we're too old to play hide-and-seek," she murmured.

Tristan chuckled. "You don't have anything to worry about—unless he catches you."

"You're a fine relative. How would you like it if I warned off *your* girlfriends?" Alain showed signs of following in his uncle's practiced footsteps.

"As long as you don't try to take them away from me." Tristan gave him a playful nudge. "You're getting to be formidable competition." He glanced over as two more couples came through the door. "Well, hello, look who's here."

When he left them, Alain and Suzette were making the first tentative overtures toward each other, and Alain looked a little less tense.

Tristan moved easily from one group to another, getting everyone to talk—at least while he was with them. The party was far from jelling, though. It wasn't until the last guest arrived and they were able to start the scavenger hunt that things started to look up.

Tristan passed out the lists and explained that they would be divided into pairs. After giving each girl a playing card with a red back, he held up a bowl filled with blue cards. The boys would pick a blue card, from the bowl and be the partner of the girl with the corresponding red card.

Angelique was content to let Tristan take over. She was mildly surprised when he reached into the bowl himself instead of letting the boys pick their own cards, but it didn't really matter. The important thing was to get them to loosen up.

It seemed to be working too. As each couple was paired off there was much laughing and teasing. Angelique gathered that some of the chance drawings were exactly what the lucky card holders were hoping for.

She was engaged in her own private wishing game. Alain had shown definite signs of being intrigued with Suzette. It would be wonderful if by some kind stroke of fate they could end up as partners. After an hour alone together, who knew what might develop? Suzette was adorable, and she seemed attracted to Alain also.

Since Alain was the host, Tristan saved him until last. Angelique held her breath every time he dipped into the bowl. When the cards were down to only a few and Suzette was still available, the suspense was unbearable. Angelique felt like cheering when the final card, a queen of hearts, paired Alain and Suzette. It seemed like a good omen.

The atmosphere in the room had changed drastically, which also boded well. The ice had definitely been broken. All the young people were laughing and chattering as they checked the time and gathered their flashlights and bright paper bags. When the front door closed behind them, Angelique breathed a sigh of relief.

She turned to Tristan for reassurance. "It was somewhat of a fiasco in the beginning, but I think everything will go well from now on, don't you?"

"They're having the time of their lives. The scavenger hunt was a brilliant inspiration."

"I'm glad it worked out that way. I was terrified that they might consider it a children's game on a par with pin the tail on the donkey."

"Or spin the bottle?"

Angelique laughed. "No, that would probably have been acceptable. But I didn't want them to get *that* friendly."

Tristan's chuckle had an amused male sound. "You don't think there's going to be any hanky-panky going on in the maze?"

A dimple appeared at the corner of her full mouth. "The sheer number of players is going to limit it severely."

"That's true," he conceded. "But it won't lessen the enjoyment. A stolen kiss can be tremendously satisfying to a teenager."

His tolerant amusement reminded Angelique of how far removed Tristan was from that state. His kisses weren't furtive, snatched little affairs. They were enflaming caresses that began slowly and built to almost unbearable heights.

Angelique decided it was time to change the subject. "You don't think they'll get self-conscious again once the scavenger hunt is over?"

"Not a chance! After the prizes are given out we'll start the music and the buffet—two things they thrive on. We probably won't sweep them out of here until the early hours."

"I hope you're right."

He raised a mocking eyebrow. "You can't think of anything better to do than spend a whole evening playing chaperone?"

"I'd put in a lot more time if it meant that Alain could go back to leading a normal life," she answered quietly.

Tristan's derision fled. He cupped her cheek in his palm, looking down at her with strong emotion. "Has anyone ever told you that you have a beautiful character?"

Angelique was touched. It was the sweetest thing he had ever said to her. She smiled tremulously. "I don't believe that's ever been mentioned."

His fingers caressed her cheek before gently tracing the shape of her soft mouth. "No, I suppose not. And I've been as guilty as the rest of my sex." His eyes wandered over her delicate face, cataloging each perfect feature. "You're so incredibly lovely that some insensitive clods never look beneath the surface."

"Are you admitting you're one of them?" she teased.

"Not anymore. You've humbled me completely." Tiny lights flickered in his eyes as he bent his head slowly.

He didn't look humble. Nor did she feel like a conqueror. Tristan was the one in command of the situation. His gratitude had changed rapidly to desire, and she felt threatened once more.

"Then perhaps we can be friends after all," Angelique remarked lightly.

"Just friends, Angel?" His husky voice curled around her like a caress.

She moved out of his reach. "Be thankful we accomplished that much before it was too late. I figure if all goes well tonight I should be able to leave here within a week at the latest."

Tristan's manner changed markedly. "What brought you to that conclusion?"

"Suzette Lamperre partly. If Alain acquired a girlfriend his own age, no one could ever suspect him of being interested in me. And he's very attracted to her."

"So I've noticed," Tristan observed dryly. "Has it occurred to you why?"

"Because she's adorable!"

"She also resembles you greatly—blond hair and big blue eyes. Although she's a long way from achieving your beauty." His voice deepened once more.

"Don't be ridiculous! The fact that we're both blondes is just a coincidence. I gathered that Alain has had a crush on her for a long time. I was watching his face when you were drawing the cards tonight. He was so anxious to get Suzette for his partner that he had everything crossed but his toes! Wasn't it a wonderful coincidence that they had matching cards?"

"Almost an act of God."

Something about his cynical tone alerted Angelique. "It *was* chance, wasn't it? But it must have been," she answered her own question.

"If you say so."

Tristan's self-satisfied expression told her there was more to it. "You rigged it so they'd be partners, didn't you? But how could you possibly be sure?"

He laughed. "You weren't the only one who saw how Alain felt. I knew what Suzette's card was, so I arranged for him to play king to her queen."

"How could you do that?"

"A slight dog-ear is wonderfully effective."

Angelique's eyes widened. "Talk about sneaky! Remind me never to play poker with you."

"It wasn't the game I had in mind." He bridged the distance between them and put his hands on her shoulders. "But I would never cheat you, Angel—and I don't want to play games. There's more between us than that. Surely you feel it, don't you?"

Angelique was too confused to know *what* she felt. Tristan played on her emotions until she couldn't distinguish between passion and love. The word startled her. Could she possibly be falling in love with Tristan?

That would be disastrous! Certainly he desired her, yet Angelique was under no illusions. She was only one more in a long line. It was different for her; she had never felt this way about another man. That was a distinct warning. Giving her heart to Tristan would be foolhardy enough, but giving her body would put his mark of possession on her forever. After experiencing the ecstasy he could bring, she would never be free.

But Tristan wouldn't want her forever. Angelique shuddered involuntarily as she imagined the bleak future after Tristan tired of her. She took a deep breath, vowing she would never put herself in a position for that to happen.

"You're feeling grateful," she told him matter-of-factly, "but it isn't necessary. Whatever I did was for Alain's sake. I'll stay around long enough to clear up the problems he created, but after I leave we'll never see each other again. It's as simple as that."

"You can't honestly believe that."

"I have a very successful career that's the most important thing in my life. Coming here was just a lark, a spur of the moment decision. I got more deeply involved than I expected, but when I go home all of this will just be a fantasy."

"Including me?" he asked evenly.

"Especially you. Handsome grand dukes are the stuff fairy tales are spun from. You're part of the fantasy. You aren't real."

"Shall I show you how real I can be?"

He moved close enough for her to feel the heat from his body, although he didn't touch her. He didn't need to. Angelique was quiveringly aware of every taut muscle, every hard contour. Her memory supplied the details only to convince her that her own treacherous body was in league with him.

Angelique's long lashes swept down as she fought the feeling. "Aren't you forgetting this is Alain's party, not yours?" She moved gracefully away.

Tristan watched silently, but when she started to gather up crumpled paper napkins and used soft drink glasses he stopped her. "You don't have to do that." He tugged on a tasseled bell pull, and minutes later a uniformed maid entered. "You can straighten up in here before the young people return," he told the woman.

An uncomfortable silence fell as the well-trained servant went deftly about her work. Angelique wanted desperately to make small talk, but she couldn't think of anything to say. When the maid edged around her with a murmured apology, Angelique remarked, "We seem to be in the way."

"I was thinking the same thing," Tristan answered. "There's really no reason for us to stay here. The kids won't be back for an hour."

"That's true," she agreed.

"Since there's no one here to chaperone, how would you like to see my studio?" he asked.

"I didn't know you had one."

He nodded. "I don't get to do much painting any-more, but I keep it as a monument to the future."

"Is it here in the palace?"

"No, it's in a separate building near the swimming pool. When I knew I'd be living here for the next couple of years I took over a small guest house and brought over my canvases and paints. Whenever I get really fed up with court life I retreat to my studio." His mouth twisted wryly. "And then I get even more frustrated."

"It must have been difficult to give up your career."

"I haven't given it up, just postponed it." His eyes sparkled with sudden devilry. "Come take a look. You might think it's the best thing that could have happened."

Angelique had always found it difficult to imagine Tristan as a painter. She had always thought of artists as dreamy, impractical people—traits that certainly didn't describe him. It was hard to picture this impeccable man in paint-stained jeans, and harder still to visualize all that pent-up energy confined in front of an easel for hours on end. Yet Alain said Tristan had received high praise for his work. It would be interesting to see if he won it by talent or influence.

"I'd love to see your studio," she told him.

"Just like that? Without any coaxing?"

"Why should I need coaxing?"

"Do you always accept this readily when a man asks you up to see his etchings?" he teased.

"Don't be ridiculous!" she said impatiently. "Since when have you needed an excuse to make a pass?"

"That sounds so unromantic," he protested.

"I notice you aren't denying it's true," she answered dryly.

"Would it do any good?"

"No."

He ran his palm down the length of her shining hair, then wound a curl around his forefinger. With a gentle tug he tilted her face to his and looked down at her with glowing eyes. "I won't pretend that I haven't made my share of passes, even at you in the beginning."

She gazed back at him steadily, refusing to buy what he was selling. "Am I supposed to think you've reformed?" Angelique braced herself for a very sensuous attempt to convince her.

But after staring at her for a long moment, he laughed and unwound the curl. "Can a leopard change its spots?"

No more readily than a tiger can stop stalking, she thought grimly. At least Tristan was finally being honest with her. "Now that we understand each other, let's go to your studio," she said coolly.

"I suppose I should have known you'd see through me sooner or later."

There was something subtly mocking about Tristan's voice, but when she looked at him sharply his expression was mildly rueful. Putting his arm lightly around Angelique's shoulders, he propelled her toward the door.

The guest house had been furnished luxuriously, judging by the few things Tristan had allowed to remain. It was actually a self-contained little house consisting of a living room, bedroom, small kitchen, and a large, elegant bathroom.

Through the open door leading into the bedroom, Angelique glimpsed a king-sized bed covered with a velvet spread monogrammed with the royal crest. The bathroom beyond appeared to be mirrored from floor to ceiling, although she could only get a tantalizing peek.

The living room couldn't have been in greater contrast. All the furniture had been removed except one long couch. A few costly scatter rugs were pushed carelessly aside, leaving a large area of bare floor under and surrounding a big wooden easel. Canvases were stacked untidily around the room, and sketches were fastened to the cream-colored walls with no regard for the damage the thumbtacks would cause.

"Well, what do you think?" Tristan was waiting for her reaction.

"It looks like an artist's studio," she admitted.

He chuckled. "What were you expecting? Fur rugs with naked models lolling about?"

Angelique's color deepened as she realized that it wouldn't have surprised her. "Alain did say you painted nudes," she observed primly.

"Not exclusively. If they're going to shock your sensibilities, I think I can manage to find a few landscapes lying around." His firm mouth twitched with the amusement he was trying to conceal.

Angelique raised her eyebrows in what she hoped was a disdainful look. "I imagine I can handle it. I *am* a model myself."

"I thought you didn't pose in the nude."

"Well, I...I don't."

"That's a pity."

Angelique could feel herself growing warm as his eyes went over her appraisingly. They seemed to penetrate the filmy folds of her chiffon gown, wandering over her breasts and hips as though she were completely naked.

"You have such a beautiful body, Angel. I'd love to paint you. Although I don't know if I could capture the exquisite quality of small, delicate bones under satin soft skin." His smoky voice indicated that he had a different goal in mind.

"Well, don't worry about it," she answered tartly. "You aren't going to get a chance to try."

"Why won't you pose for me?"

"Really, Tristan! I expected better from you than that tired old gambit," she remarked scornfully.

"You think this is another attempt to seduce you?"

"Is there any question about it?" she countered.

"I assure you that I really do want to paint you."

"Can you honestly say that if I took off my clothes right this minute, all you'd do would be to reach for a brush?"

His slow smile made her erratic pulse beat even faster. "It would be exceedingly difficult, but that's exactly what I'd do. Would you like to get undressed in here or the other room?"

"You're incredible! Knowing what's on your mind, how could I possibly stand here nude and let you stare at... I mean I'd feel..." she stumbled to a halt.

"It would make it easier on both of us if we made love first," he teased. "But I won't insist on it."

Angelique took a deep breath to compose herself. It was annoying to be so rattled when he was in such command of himself. Of course he had a lot more experience at this sort of thing!

"This whole conversation is tasteless," she said coldly. "Just for the record, I wouldn't pose for you with or without clothes."

"That's an idea." He stared at her speculatively. "We could make a compromise. Perhaps a chiffon scarf or two." He grinned. "Placed strategically of course."

"Didn't you hear a word I said?" Her slim figure was taut with outrage.

"Why do you find the idea so disturbing?" Tristan dropped his teasing manner. He cupped her chin in his palm, searching her angry face. "Surely you know I would never force myself on you?"

Angelique knew that was true, and not merely because he didn't have to force himself on any woman. Her anger died as she admitted that it was her own response that was troubling. The idea of posing for Tristan inflamed her senses. A tiny feather seemed to tickle the pit of her stomach as she imagined his smoldering eyes gliding over her body, lingering at each erotic spot until it was almost a tangible caress.

Long lashes swept down to veil her thoughts. "I have my reputation to think of, Tristan—my professional one, I mean."

His fingertips stroked the length of her neck before tracing the delicate protrusion of her collarbone. "I don't know if my talent is equal to your beauty, but whatever I managed to get down on canvas would be a tribute to your loveliness. It would never be an embarrassment."

His muted voice and sensuous touch made it difficult to refuse him anything. "I couldn't pose for anyone even if I wanted to," she said desperately. "I'm under exclusive contract to the Vendome Cosmetic Company."

"That only applies to professional modeling—pictures of you that are shown to the public." Tristan's slow smile threatened to melt her bones. "No one else would ever see my painting."

"Is...is that your usual practice?"

"No." His eyes held hers.

Angelique bit her lip. "I...I'll think about it." She turned away, needing to break his dominance. "I haven't even seen your work yet."

Tristan seemed to realize that she needed a breathing space. "Are you afraid I'll paint you with one eye in the middle of your forehead?" he joked.

"It's something to find out," she said, grateful to him for easing the pressure.

Angelique was impressed by the canvases he offered for her inspection. Tristan was indeed talented. Any acclaim he had won was deserved. His technique was completely professional, but it was the insight Tristan brought to his work that made it remarkable. His nudes weren't merely undraped women, they were living, breathing females with passion flowing through their veins and intelligence in their sometimes jaded eyes. Not all were beautiful, but each had an arresting quality.

As Angelique continued her fascinated inspection she began to notice that Tristan had used one model over and over. Not surprisingly, she was very lovely with a mass of auburn hair and big green eyes, coupled with a voluptuous figure. Besides her beauty, an intense sensuality seemed to leap from the canvas. This was a woman that most men would find irresistible.

"What a stunning woman!" Angelique exclaimed.

"Yes."

Tristan's noncommittal agreement piqued Angelique's curiosity. "Who is she?"

He seemed to hesitate a moment. "Lady Claremonte."

Angelique's eyebrows climbed. "She isn't a professional model?"

"No."

His reluctance spoke volumes. This woman had been Tristan's mistress. The very profusion of her canvases should have told Angelique that, in addition to the model's possessive look.

Although she knew that Tristan had had many mistresses, Angelique felt a sharp pain in her midsection. Was he still seeing the woman? He hadn't had much time with the crisis over Alain, but there had been many nights when Tristan either disappeared after dinner, or hadn't even shown up. Would he have been carrying on as usual while romancing her? It was entirely possible. Men like Tristan were capable of a need for variety that a woman would find repugnant.

"She seems to be your favorite model," she remarked lightly.

"Natalie was a good subject."

"Was?" Angelique seized on the operative word. "She doesn't pose for you anymore?"

"Not for quite a while."

"That's too bad. She has a remarkable...expressiveness."

Angelique looked at the profusion of canvases. Natalie being provocative, acting sulky, expressing anticipation. And most telling of all—Natalie looking deliciously sated, as though she had just made love with a man who had filled her to the brim with rapture.

Tristan's slight smile was reminiscent. "She's a very volatile woman."

Angelique hated herself for pursuing the subject, but she couldn't let it drop. "Did you capture all her moods? Is that why you stopped using her?"

He raised a faintly mocking eyebrow. "I wouldn't exactly put it that way."

No, Tristan hadn't used her. It was obvious that the woman was a willing—make that eager—participant. What had happened then? Who had gotten tired of whom? It suddenly became very important to know the answer.

"If she wasn't a professional, perhaps she got tired of sitting," Angelique remarked carelessly. "Modeling might sound glamorous, but it's a very grueling job."

"I'm sure it is," he answered politely. "Especially posing for an artist. I'm afraid I sometimes get so caught up in what I'm doing that I forget to be considerate."

"Is that the reason she left you?"

The question hung in the air between them, revealing in its intensity.

"Why do you want to know, Angelique?" he asked quietly.

She tried to cover up. "I just wanted to find out what I'd be letting myself in for if...if I decided to pose for you after all."

He was silent for a long moment. Then he said, "Natalie and I were good friends. She sat for me for a long time." His eyes were enigmatic as he gazed at one of her paintings. The full-figured redhead was sitting on the floor in a suggestive position. Her widespread elbows were resting on the couch, which displayed her outthrust breasts to full advantage. "Our...association...was mutually rewarding. It came to an end as these things often do, but we parted as friends."

"Do you still see her?" Angelique asked in a small voice.

"Every now and then when she's in town. Natalie and her husband travel a good deal."

"Her husband?"

"Yes, she married Lord Claremonte recently," Tristan said casually.

Now Angelique didn't know *what* to think! Knowing Tristan she had just assumed that he had been the one to tire of the relationship, but now it seemed that Natalie had left him for another man. Was all of this offhandedness hiding a broken heart? The signs seemed to point to it. Why else would he surround himself with her paintings?

"I suppose it must be a great comfort to have all these reminders of her," Angelique offered uncertainly.

"Actually, it's a great nuisance. They were promised to different galleries on the Continent, but Claremonte took a dim view of his wife being exposed to public scrutiny, as he put it." Tristan slanted an annoyed look at the stacked canvases. "He begged me not to exhibit them, and yet he doesn't want them himself. The man is a quivering mass of insecurity."

At last Angelique had her answer. Tristan's chilling disregard for the paintings told her that he no longer cared for Natalie. But he once had. Did he urge her to pose for him as he had Angelique? Did he imply that he would cherish her image forever and keep it only for his own enjoyment? Undoubtedly.

"Angelique? Is anything wrong?"

She realized that she had been staring. "Oh…no. I was just admiring your work. You're really amazingly good."

"Thank you. Coming from you that's high praise," he said dryly.

"It's true. You've captured her moods so perceptively that I can almost tell what she's feeling. No wonder her husband doesn't want these exhibited," she added with a touch of bitterness.

"I knew her long before she met Claremonte," Tristan said gently.

That was evident since these paintings would have revealed their affair. But how could she have married another man after Tristan?

Angelique's eyes returned to the canvas, examining the woman carefully. The bold eyes looked out confidently, challenging any viewer to make a judgment. There was no doubt that she had enjoyed Tristan. But when it was over? That was another story. Natalie was a survivor, but Angelique was afraid *she* wouldn't be.

"I think we'd better go back to the house," she said in a subdued voice. "The young people will be returning any minute."

"I suppose you're right." Tristan's reluctance was coupled with dissatisfaction. As she started toward the door he put his hand on her arm. "Perhaps it was a mistake to bring you here."

"No, I'm glad you did." Seeing the pictures of Natalie had clarified her thinking.

"I've never pretended to be a saint, Angelique. But I've never used my art to seduce women," he said quietly.

"I know that."

The moment was fraught with tension. Angelique could feel Tristan's frustration. He was right; it *had* been a mistake to bring her here. Was he going to try to repair the damage? He moved closer, and for a terrible instant she thought he was going to take her in his arms. Did he count on his considerable expertise to make her forget that she was just the latest quarry in his endless chase? She flinched unconsciously, bracing herself to resist a temptation that could destroy her if she gave in to it.

An unreadable expression crossed his face as he registered her reaction. Was it chagrin? Regret? Or was it the anger of a hungry male animal thwarted by his prey? The emotion was suppressed too swiftly for her to say.

Tristan opened the door and stood back for her to precede him, once more the civilized sophisticate. "Well, intermission is over. It's time to get back to children's games," he observed mockingly.

Chapter Six

The success of Alain's party exceeded Angelique's fondest hopes. The teenagers returned from the scavenger hunt filled with high spirits that continued through the evening.

After the prizes had been awarded to the winners, they greeted the food with vocal approval. Perhaps because of its novelty.

Angelique planned the menu along with the rest of the details, but she had run into trouble with the chef. He was horrified at the idea of "hero" sandwiches, pickles and potato salad, not to mention the "do-it-yourself" ice-cream buffet she requested with different toppings so the guests could make their own sundaes.

The buffet itself was a bone of contention. Chef Ducloix wanted a sit-down supper in the formal dining room. Angelique could imagine how much fun young people would have with uniformed footmen swarming around. Alain's guests might be forced to attend, but you could bet they'd leave at the first opportunity!

After being adamant about the buffet and its location, Angelique tried to placate him on the food. "Perhaps we can make a compromise or two on the menu." She gave him her most charming smile. "What did *you* have in mind?"

Chef Ducloix was immune to her wiles. He was too indignant at the barbarity of having His Royal Highness and his guests help themselves. There was no way they could have come to an agreement anyway, since his choices were mousse of wild duck, lobster in aspic, and ox tongue served in a red wine sauce, along with a lot of other dishes whose names she couldn't even pronounce. In the end, Angelique was forced to dig in her heels and insist on having her own way.

On the morning of the party she had checked with him to be sure he had everything necessary to make the hearty sandwiches. Just to be sure he wouldn't improvise or claim he misunderstood, Angelique cut off a section of a long loaf of French bread and made up a sample sandwich. She was almost sorry for the elegant chef as he shuddered, watching her spread one side of the bread with mayonnaise and the other with mustard before layering it with several kinds of meats and cheeses. It must have been equally galling when two of his assistants seized it hungrily and divided it between them as she went out the door.

It was worth all the hassle, however, when the youngsters devoured the food as though they hadn't eaten in weeks. Their enthusiasm wasn't lost on Tristan.

"It seems Chef Ducloix has something to learn," he remarked dryly.

Angelique looked at him uncertainly. "He's a fine chef," she said tentatively.

"Even though he doesn't know how to make a hero sandwich?" Tristan teased.

"You knew about our...um...difference of opinion?" Angelique hadn't wanted to appeal to Tristan, feeling it was unfair tactics. But Chef Ducloix evidently wasn't bothered by similar scruples. "I wouldn't have insisted if I hadn't known I was right," she said defensively. "The menu he had planned was bad enough, but on top of that he wanted to herd everyone into the dining room like a bunch of visiting dignitaries!"

Tristan chuckled. "No one is more dedicated to pomp and ceremony than a family retainer."

"I'm glad you could make him listen to reason. For a while I was terrified that he was going to quit."

"In that case you'd have been obligated to take over the job and stay on here indefinitely."

There was an underlying challenge in the joking words that Angelique ignored. "You would have eaten out a lot. I'm not the world's greatest cook."

"Man doesn't live by bread alone," he murmured.

There was no mistaking the suggestiveness now. Angelique indicated the teenagers going back for seconds. "They might give you an argument," she answered lightly.

Fortunately for Angelique's peace of mind, she and Tristan didn't have many such moments alone. When the music started it was too noisy for intimate conversation. They were also coaxed to dance over Tristan's objections.

"This is more like exercise," he complained. "I can get that on the tennis court. Whatever happened to real dancing, where you held the girl in your arms?"

"He's been watching old Fred Astaire movies again," Alain remarked in mock disgust.

"Don't knock it until you've tried it, young man." Tristan held out his arms to Angelique. "Shall we show them what real dancing is like, Ginger?"

It was the last thing she wanted, but there was no way to decline. The teenagers were all clapping and shouting encouragement.

Angelique's nerves were quivering as she went into Tristan's arms. He couldn't help but feel the tremor that went through her when their bodies made contact, but she hoped he would attribute it to self-consciousness. Part of it was just that, and part was apprehension. Could Tristan guess that liquid fire seemed to be racing through her veins? When she tried to put a small space between them, his arms tightened, molding her so closely that she was aware of every sinew and muscle in his lithe body.

The exquisite torture ended when one of the boys called, "That's not the way they did it. You're supposed to twirl her around in fancy circles."

"That's right," Alain agreed. "Their routines weren't that much different from our dancing—only slower, and he held onto her hand."

Tristan's slow smile was devastating. "Fred had his technique and I have mine."

A pretty little brunette gave him a flirtatious look. "If you're giving lessons, I wouldn't mind enrolling in your class."

Everyone laughed but her date. "If we're through taking a stroll through the Dark Ages, how about putting on some real music?" he commented with a frown.

Angelique could hardly blame him. Tristan would have been formidable competition for Casanova! She gave a sigh of relief when he laughed and released her.

The party lasted very late, a sure sign of success. When Alain came back from escorting the last guest to the door, his eyes were shining with pleasure.

"It was a great party, Angelique! Everyone had a super time."

"I'm glad to hear they didn't stay this long out of a sense of duty," Tristan remarked dryly, glancing at his watch. "You'd better turn in."

"Not yet." Alain was too keyed up to sit down, much less go to bed. He strode up and down the room, picking things up and putting them down. "It was really great getting together again. Like old times."

"This is the way it's going to be from now on," Tristan said gently.

"I hope so. That's what I want to talk to you about." Alain pulled up a chair next to his uncle's. "I know I have obligations to Souveraine, but that doesn't mean I have to live in an ivory tower."

"What are you driving at?"

"I don't want to be tutored at home anymore." Alain stuck out his jaw pugnaciously. "I want to go to the Royal Academy with my friends."

Tristan nodded. "That sounds like a sensible idea."

Alain sprang to his feet, his face filled with incredulous joy. "You mean I can go? Just like that—with no argument?"

"It's already been suggested to me by someone whose judgment I value more than my own." Tristan smiled at Angelique. "Yes, you can go."

"Angelique, you're a wonder!" Alain scooped her up from the chair and whirled her around. Planting a resounding kiss on her cheek, he said, "I'll love you forever and ever for this."

"I think Suzette would take a dim view of that," she responded, laughing as she sat down again.

"Did you like her?" he asked eagerly.

"She's lovely." Angelique gave full approval.

"That's what she said about you. I want you to get to know her."

"I'm sure we'll see each other again before I leave."

Angelique was sure of just the opposite. The success of the party, and Alain's interest in Suzette made her continued stay unnecessary. From now on the people of Souveraine would see him go through dozens of crushes on one teenage girl after another. They would quickly forget the mystery that surrounded her own arrival at Souveraine.

Alain was upset by the idea of her leaving. "You can't go yet, Angelique! You haven't seen anything of Souveraine."

"I've had a very exciting visit," she assured him without looking at Tristan.

"But we were going sightseeing!"

"I imagine Angelique can stay long enough for that," Tristan put in smoothly. "Why don't you run along to bed and let me convince her."

"I think I'll go to bed too." She got up from the chair swiftly. Angelique knew how convincing Tristan could be, and she didn't intend to give him the opportunity. "It's been an eventful day and I'm a little tired."

"I won't keep you long." Tristan's fingers imprisoned her slender wrist. "We'll see you tomorrow, Alain."

"I won't be here." He turned at the door with a beatific smile. "A bunch of us are going swimming at Suzette's."

As soon as the door closed after him, Angelique pulled her hand away. "I really am tired, Tristan."

"I don't doubt it. You put on a fantastic party." He cupped her cheek in his palm. "Do you know how grateful I am?"

"It isn't necessary," she insisted, feeling the blood rush to the spot where he was touching her.

"Yes, it is," Tristan answered quietly. "You turned Alain's life around by seeing something I should have seen long ago."

Angelique was touched by the self-condemnation in his voice. "Sometimes it's easier for a stranger to see things. You would have gotten around to it sooner or later."

"You're very sweet, but Alain and I will always be in your debt." His fingertips stroked her cheek. "Isn't there some way I can repay you?"

She drew away from his inflaming touch. "You can invite me to the wedding. Yours or Alain's—whichever takes place first."

A curtain dropped behind his gray eyes. "I was thinking of something more immediate."

"A ride to the airport would do it," she answered brightly. "In that plush limousine."

"You can't leave yet, Angelique."

"There's no longer any necessity for me to stay." She enumerated all the reasons.

"I agree that we're on our way to defusing the situation, but your abrupt departure could ruin all the good work you've put in."

"I don't follow you."

"Suppose everyone thought Alain brought you here and then dismissed you when he happened to be thrown together again with Suzette?"

"That's the most ridiculous thing I've ever heard!"

"It would seem to be." His glowing eyes wandered over her flushed face. "But scandalmongers aren't always troubled by logic. They believe what's most sensational. Alain isn't out of the woods yet."

"You can't be serious!"

"Is it worth taking a chance? Why not stay on for another week? We'll make a point of being highly visible—Alain and Suzette, you and I. Surely a week won't upset your schedule too greatly," he coaxed.

"Well, no. I...I guess I could manage another week."

Angelique had a feeling that she was being manipulated, but she wasn't sure. Madame Lamperre's avid face rose in her memory. If there was even a chance that she wasn't convinced, it would be worth another week. Or was she rationalizing because she didn't really want to leave? Angelique pushed the troubling thought out of her mind.

"Good. Then it's all settled." Tristan was suddenly matter-of-fact. His seductive wiles vanished as soon as he had her assurance that she would stay.

Angelique puzzled over it as she got ready for bed. What exactly did Tristan want from her? It had seemed glaringly obvious, but now she wasn't so sure. Was he just using his charm on Alain's behalf? A man like Tristan wouldn't turn down any fringe benefits, but was it possible that his real interest was the one he stated—safeguarding Alain's reputation?

It was a repugnant thought. It meant that all of his apparent attraction to her, all of the passionate kisses and caresses were merely staged. She felt chilled, remembering her own abandoned response to him. Tristan was a master at seduction—he knew how to turn any woman on. Was the deeper feeling only on her part, Angelique asked herself. Knowing it was a dangerous subject to pursue, she turned over in bed and buried her head in the pillow.

Even though the following day was Sunday, Angelique found the small salon in perfect order when she made her way downstairs that morning. There were no signs of the previous night's party. The frivolous decorations had been removed, and throw rugs once more covered the parquet floor. All of the priceless ornaments had been put back in place, restoring the elegant room to its austere formality.

Angelique thought ruefully of her own apartment after a much smaller gathering. Chaos always greeted her the next morning. She decided it wouldn't be difficult to get used to the pampering that the de Marchal family took for granted.

Tristan was having breakfast in the airy garden room. He stood up to hold her chair. "I didn't expect you down this morning. Why didn't you ring for breakfast?"

"I don't want to get used to too much luxury." Angelique covered her self-consciousness with a little laugh. "It would be a shock to my nervous system when I get home."

Tristan's hands rested on her shoulders. "Since that won't be for a while yet, why don't you let me spoil you?"

She gave all her attention to unfolding her napkin. "I don't think that's a very good idea."

"Why not?"

"It just isn't, that's all," she insisted.

"It's not fair to put people in your debt and then deny them the privilege of repaying you."

"We settled all that last night. Do sit down, Tristan! I'm getting a crick in my neck trying to talk to you," which wasn't strictly accurate. After the first glance Angelique had avoided looking at him.

Tristan took the chair beside her with suppressed amusement, as though he knew how he affected her. "If you won't let me reward you with services, I'll have to give you a gift."

"No thanks. That's the way this whole thing started."

"I wasn't proposing anything that would compromise you." He drew a small velvet box out of his pocket. "This is something we award for exceptional service to the House of Charolais."

Angelique took the box gingerly, unable to tell by his expression if he were joking. Her eyes widened as she saw the jeweled medallion inside on its bed of white satin. It was shaped like a star, completely covered with diamonds and rubies set in an intricate design of interlocking circles.

"Tristan, it's gorgeous, but I can't accept this!" Angelique gasped.

"It's very bad form to turn down a medal."

"Is that what it is really?" she asked doubtfully.

"Of course. What does it look like?"

"Well, I...it looks like a piece of jewelry." She touched the faceted rubies that glowed with inner fire.

"I suppose it could be used for that." He lifted it out of the box, and Angelique saw that it was suspended from a narrow red velvet ribbon. Before she could stop him, Tristan slipped it over her head.

Angelique had worn tight-fitting jeans that morning, topped by a wide-necked white blouse that just skimmed her shoulders. The beautiful medallion nestled against her ivory skin, just above the cleft between her breasts.

Framing her face in his palms, he kissed her on both cheeks. "Souveraine thanks you, Alain thanks you...and most of all, *I* thank you."

His husky voice was like a tuning fork, evoking answering vibrations deep inside her. What was behind this fabulous gift? It certainly wasn't a little merit badge, given out for casual favors. Tristan must know she wouldn't buy that. Was it really gratitude? Or did it indicate a deeper feeling for her, besides the obvious one?

A small voice of caution warned her against wishful thinking.

"I'm overwhelmed," she said brightly. "I certainly must thank Alain too. Is he up yet?"

Tristan watched her reaction with enigmatic gray eyes. If he was disappointed he didn't show it. "He was up and out early this morning. I think he was too excited to sleep."

Angelique's mouth curved in a tender smile. "Something tells me you're not going to see too much of him around here from now on."

"Certainly not today." Tristan chuckled. "Those kids have enough plans to last all week. Which leaves us on our own. What would you like to do?"

"You don't have to entertain me," she assured him. "You probably have plans for today."

"I do." His hand covered hers where it rested on the table. The tiny lights flickering in the depths of his eyes left no doubt about Tristan's meaning, but when her fingers curled into a fist he said, "I thought we'd go sightseeing."

It sounded harmless, and she really did want to see something of Souveraine before she left. If Tristan's day didn't turn out as he planned, that was his problem.

"I'd love to go sightseeing," she said. "Just give me a couple of minutes to change and I'll be right with you."

His admiring glance traveled from her chic linen blouse down to the skintight jeans that molded around her small, curved bottom. "You're fine just the way you are."

Tristan wore jeans also. They rode low on his narrow hips and outlined his long, muscular legs. The cuffs of his navy shirt were rolled to below his elbows, and the front was unbuttoned to show a good deal of his tanned chest.

Angelique shrugged. If it was all right with Tristan, it was okay with her.

She half expected the limousine to be waiting, but the Maserati was parked in the curved driveway. The one Tristan had been driving at the time of their first, tumultuous meeting.

It was a beautiful day for sightseeing. The sun shone brilliantly, yet a light breeze cooled the air, bringing the scent of flowers mixed with salt from the sea. At the foot of the curving mounting road, the blue water sparkled like a bowl of sapphires.

Tristan drove up into the hills above the palace where pastel-colored villas framed in greenery clung to the cliffs. At the summit he turned into a small parking area and stopped the car.

They got out and strolled over to the low brick wall that formed a protective barrier. From that height the whole city was spread out for their enjoyment. The tiny cars darting far below could have been wind-up toys, and the elegant yachts moored in the bay were reduced to toy models.

"It's like an enchanted village!" Angelique exclaimed. "I feel as though I'm looking at a page out of Grimm's fairy tales."

"There were ogres and wicked witches in Grimm's," he reminded her.

"But they always got their comeuppance." She took a deep breath of the clear air. "It's heavenly up here—so peaceful and quiet."

"I'm glad you like it. It's one of my favorite spots." Tristan gazed out over the monarchy with quiet pride. "Souveraine is small, but it's a pleasant place to live."

"That's like describing paradise as an upwardly mobile neighborhood," Angelique declared indignantly.

An inner excitement suddenly kindled in his gray eyes as they narrowed on her rapt face, but he kept his voice carefully casual. "That's high praise coming from a city girl."

"It's precisely because I *do* come from a big city that I can appreciate all this."

One corner of Tristan's mouth lifted mockingly. "What's that thing tourists say? It's a nice place to visit, but I wouldn't want to live here."

"I don't know what kind of tourists you get, but they must be crazy."

"Could *you* live here, Angelique?" His eyes held hers with great intensity, making her aware that it wasn't a casual question.

Why would he ask such a thing? Was it possible that Tristan wanted her to stay and be his mistress? He certainly had enough money to set her up in style, and there was ample precedent for monarchs doing just that. It was viewed tolerantly. Angelique wanted to tell him how insulting she found it, but she couldn't very well do that until he made the proposition.

"It's different for me," she said coolly. "My work is in New York."

"And your job is important to you." It was a cross between a question and a statement.

"The most important thing in the world," she assured him.

"You're very dedicated," he remarked dryly.

"I suppose you think being a model is something faintly disreputable," she flared. "Just a cut above being a...a dance-hall hostess!"

"Do they still have such things?" He grinned.

"I don't know, and don't change the subject! I happen to be at the top of my profession," she stormed. "If

I told you how much money I make, even *you* would be impressed!''

"It doesn't take money to impress me where you're concerned," he replied softly. "You would be a success at anything you chose to do."

His generous answer sounded sincere. It made Angelique feel rather foolish for her impassioned speech. Damn Tristan anyway! He was always provoking a heated response of one kind or another from her. Soon he was going to wonder why.

She slanted him a sulky look. "I just wanted you to know that I take my career very seriously."

"Yes, I gathered as much." He seemed to lose interest in the subject. "If you've seen enough here, would you like to go down and walk along the beach?"

His tone verged on boredom, and Angelique bit her lip. Had she spoiled the day with her temper? If Tristan was going to be distantly polite there was no point in continuing.

"We don't really have to if you had other plans," she said diffidently.

"A leading statement if I ever heard one." The brilliant smile he gave her chased away all of Angelique's apprehensions and made her heart sing at the same time. "But let's walk on the sand first and see what develops," he teased.

The beach was crowded, which wasn't surprising on such a beautiful Sunday. What Angelique wasn't expecting was the sprinkling of topless sunbathers.

Tristan laughed at her expression. "You don't approve?"

She didn't answer directly. "I'd heard it was the custom on the Continent."

"You have nude beaches in your country," he pointed out mildly.

"I suppose so."

"But you don't approve?" he persisted.

She shrugged. "It's not up to me to judge. I just don't understand why a woman would want to display herself publicly."

"A woman's breasts are exceedingly beautiful."

"I'd expect that viewpoint from you—you're an artist."

"And therefore an unprincipled lecher." Tristan's white teeth gleamed in his tanned face.

"I didn't say that!"

"You didn't have to." He laughed as he took her hand and brought it to his lips. "You have a very conventional mind. But I'm going to get rid of those inhibitions of yours if it's the last thing I do."

That was the very thing she was afraid of! Angelique had no intention of going topless on a public beach, but being talked into disrobing in front of Tristan was a disturbing possibility. Or having him take off her clothes for her. She could just picture how he would do it—slowly, his long fingers lingering over every button, his warm mouth touching each inch of exposed skin. She snatched her hand back, appalled at his ability to inflame her imagination.

Fortunately there was an unexpected interruption. A small girl ran across their path so suddenly that Tristan almost tripped over her. When he reached out to steady the child, she dropped the scoop of ice cream out of her cone.

"My ice cream!" she wailed, reaching for the sand-covered glob.

Tristan stopped her. "I think that one's had it."

"You made me drop it." The little girl's outthrust lower lip quivered.

"I'm sure there's more where that came from." He reached in his pocket and brought out some change. "Let's go and get another one."

"Margaux! Stop bothering the duke this minute!" A young woman wearing a harried expression rushed over to them.

"I'm not bothering him. He's going to buy me another ice cream." The child held up the empty cone as proof of Tristan's obligation.

"Certainly not! I'm sorry, Your Highness." The woman whisked her daughter away, ignoring both protests and tears.

Tristan scowled after them. "I wish they wouldn't call me that."

Angelique was amused by the whole thing. "I guess 'Your Grand Dukeship' sounds rather awkward."

"Very funny," he muttered.

She thought he was overreacting, but the small incident set off a chain reaction that threatened to ruin their carefree outing. A couple of tourists who had heard the exchange suddenly scrambled for their cameras.

"That's him...what's his name...the grand duke!" a plump woman in a flowered bathing suit exclaimed in a loud voice.

"Who's that with him, his girlfriend, you think? I hear he's a very eligible bachelor." Her friend had the decency to lower her voice at least, but it carried clearly to Tristan and Angelique.

"I don't know, but he's the one I want to get a picture of. Run and call Agnes out of the water. She'll die if she misses this!"

After exchanging a glance, Angelique and Tristan started down the beach at a trot. When they were a safe distance away they slowed to a walk again, but it didn't help. Tristan was recognized and greeted with the title he disliked so much.

It was the same in the small snack shop where they went to get a soft drink. People stared at them and whispered to one another. Angelique knew that she was partially responsible. In a place this small, Tristan's subjects must see him frequently. When he was alone it was probably no big deal, but accompanied by an unknown woman, he became an object of speculation.

Tristan's face got darker and darker. Finally he said, "Let's get out of here."

He drove at breakneck speed up the hill to the palace. Angelique was sorry to see the day end before it had hardly gotten started, yet she understood how difficult it must be for him. It wasn't a great deal of fun for her to be stared at either.

She was surprised when they entered the palace and he pulled her after him up the broad staircase. "Where are we going?" she asked blankly.

"To my room." His grim voice told her it wasn't what it sounded like.

Tristan's "room" was a suite even grander than her own. It was an apartment actually, with cleanly styled furniture filling the sitting area, and a huge bed on a raised platform. All of the delicate little ornaments that graced the other rooms had been cleared away, leaving an intensely masculine atmosphere. Tristan's living accommodations resembled him—elegant, large, and unmistakably male.

While she was looking around, he disappeared into the dressing room. He returned with a checked shirt over his arm, two fisherman-style caps in one hand, and something she couldn't make out clutched in the other. Angelique was too speechless to stop him when he guided her arms into the sleeves of the oversized shirt and rolled up the cuffs. As if that weren't strange enough, he put one of the caps on her head and started stuffing her long hair under it.

"It's a shame to hide this beautiful hair, but it can't be helped," he remarked, viewing the result with satisfaction.

"What are you doing?" she gasped.

He grinned. "Transforming us into two everyday Souverainians out for a pleasant Sunday." After putting the other cap on his own head, he showed her what was in his closed hand. It was a false mustache.

"You're not going to wear that!"

"Watch me."

Angelique laughed helplessly when she saw the result. With his cap at a jaunty angle, and the thick mustache blurring the clean line of his upper lip, Tristan looked faintly sinister, like someone you wouldn't want to tangle with in a dark alley. His lean, whipcord body reinforced the warning.

Angelique looked at herself in the mirror and laughed even harder. "All we need are a couple of motorcycles," she joked.

"Well, maybe we'll have to skip lunch at the Coq d'Or, but I don't think anyone will bother us now," he observed complacently.

He was entirely correct. No one gave them a second glance as they strolled along the charming twisted streets, or mingled with the crowds in the public parks.

"I gather this isn't the first time you've done this, since you had all the props," Angelique commented when they were seated in a small café, surrounded by young people dressed much like themselves.

"It was a case of survival." He smiled. "It's difficult to romance a pretty girl with people watching your every move."

Suddenly it didn't seem as much of a lark when she thought of the other women with whom he had shared the experience. Angelique put down her menu. "I've decided what I'm going to have."

"Right." Tristan summoned the waitress with an imperious gesture.

She acknowledged it with the merest nod of her head and proceeded to another table. Tristan looked faintly astonished, then annoyed.

When she passed within earshot he said in a carefully controlled voice, "Will you kindly take our order, or send over someone who will?"

"I'll get to you as soon as I can. We're shorthanded today." Her annoyance was as evident as his.

Angelique burst out laughing at the expression on Tristan's face. "Welcome to the world of the common folk."

After a moment his scowl disappeared. "Was I being autocratic?"

"Well, you did stop short of calling out the guards and having her thrown in the dungeon," she teased.

"That's the worst of living in a rarified atmosphere." He reached for her hands across the table. "I need someone to bring me down to earth."

Angelique met his eyes steadily. "Someone like me?"

"If you'd care to take the job."

She shook her head, withdrawing her hands. "Your life is too rich for me."

"I don't imagine you lead such a simple one in New York City," he said dryly.

"It isn't as glamorous as people think," she protested.

"Tell me about your life, Angelique. Describe a typical week."

"A whole week? You'd be yawning before the first day was over!"

"Try me." He settled back in his chair, watching her enigmatically.

Tristan couldn't possibly be interested. He was only making polite conversation, but it seemed a safe enough subject. Better than a lot she could think of. "Well, you know about my work. I'm under exclusive contract to Vendome Cosmetics."

"How long does your contract have to run?"

"It's over in December, but I've been assured that they're going to renew it."

His eyes narrowed on her faintly discontented expression. "You'll sign, won't you?"

"I'd be out of my mind not to. The money's fantastic, and it's the top of the heap professionally." She hesitated. "The only thing that bothers me is all the free time between campaigns. I know that would appeal to some people, but after a while it gets boring. I like to keep busy, and I'm not permitted to work for anyone else."

Their order had finally been taken, and the waitress arrived with the food. Angelique hoped the subject would be dropped, but after the woman left, Tristan returned to it.

"Your career would seem to leave you time for other...um...projects. Have you ever considered getting married? Perhaps even having children? That would keep you busy."

His casual, almost mocking suggestion hurt badly. Also his indifferent way of wishing her off on just any man. Angelique raised her head high, giving him a look as derisive as his own. "Don't you think that's a rather drastic way of solving a minor problem?"

"You consider marriage such a dire fate?"

"I have about the same opinion of it as you do."

"What makes you think I don't intend to marry?"

"Really, Tristan! I thought we were speaking openly."

He was silent for a long moment. "I wonder if we ever do."

"Well, *you* don't anyway. Not if you expect me to buy that fiction."

"We make a good pair, don't we?" he asked lightly, although his eyes were watchful. "Both of us are career oriented, and opposed to marriage. It's a shame in your case, though." His gaze wandered over her delicate features. "You'd have such beautiful children."

They both would. Angelique stared at him, trying to picture the children they'd have together. Would the boys have their father's dark hair and aristocratic features, while the girls had her golden hair? Or would it be the other way around? Angelique found it hard to visualize a son of Tristan's being other than darkly handsome. It was silly to feel such a sharp pang that they would never be born, at least not to her.

"Who knows, I might get around to them," she said carelessly. "Some time in the far distant future. But first it would be nice to fall in love."

"Is that something else you've never done?"

"We really are quite similar in many ways, aren't we?" she answered noncommittally.

Tristan seemed suddenly tired. Little lines appeared around his firm mouth. "If you don't want anything more, we can go now."

As Angelique preceded him out the door her heart felt like a cold little knot in her chest. There was a great deal more that she wanted, but it was something he wouldn't, or couldn't, give her. For the first time, Angelique acknowledged her love for Tristan. She had finally met the man of her dreams, the man she wanted to spend the rest of her life with, and he only wanted a casual affair.

Chapter Seven

Angelique was self-conscious about seeing Tristan the following day. Their Sunday together hadn't been an unqualified success. After lunch he had seemed withdrawn.

Was he starting to give up on her? That would make him the more sensible of the two. Tristan knew enough to cut his losses, something she would be wise to do. She was committed to one more week, and after that it was back to reality. This whole romantic episode would take on a dreamlike quality. Men like Tristan were people you read about. You weren't ever supposed to meet them. In time she wouldn't be able to remember his dark, intense face, or the husky voice that flowed over her like liquid honey.

Angelique took a deep breath. That's what she hoped for anyway.

The garden room was empty that morning. The maid who brought Angelique's breakfast told her that Tristan and Alain had eaten earlier. Angelique was sorry to have missed Alain. She wanted to know how his day with Suzette had gone, although there wasn't a lot of doubt. Their attraction to each other was mutual.

Angelique knew better than to risk Claude's wrath by invading the classroom again, and she certainly wasn't going to visit Tristan's office. It left her rather at loose ends. She wandered outside and strolled through the beautiful gardens, feeling utterly useless. What did royal ladies do with their time?

Angelique's mouth curved in a smile as she remembered an interviewer on television asking a group of British children what the queen did all day. One little girl looked disdainful at the foolish question. "She cleans the castle!" Anyone knew that!

Angelique laughed out loud at the thought of asking the very proper palace servants if they needed any help polishing the silver.

Seriously though, how would she occupy herself if she lived here? There were many worthwhile charities for anyone with the time and money to devote to them. Angelique had always thought she'd be good at fund-raising. There were so many innovative things one could do besides those same dull dinner dances. It would be interesting to learn a foreign language too, almost a necessity here. Then, of course, there was Tristan...

She pulled herself up short as she realized where her fantasizing was leading.

It promised to be a very long day. Angelique had trouble filling up the morning. When neither Tristan nor Alain appeared at lunch, the afternoon stretched ahead endlessly. When the temperature began to climb she decided to go swimming.

The brilliant orange bikini that had seemed so skimpy at home, looked downright tame here. The kind of suits women wore on the beach here weren't even available in New York. What would it feel like to go topless she wondered for one brief instant. The thought of Tristan's smoldering eyes traveling slowly over the rounded full-ness of her breasts made the nipples harden involuntar-ily. Angelique slipped quickly into the cool water and swam the length of the pool.

She was asleep on a padded chaise when the sound of voices in the distance disturbed, but didn't awaken her. It was the unconscious feeling a few moments later of someone staring down at her, or maybe it was the cool-ing shade after the sun's brilliance.

Angelique opened sleepy eyes to find that Tristan had tilted an umbrella to cover her. He was standing over her, gazing down with a tender expression that vanished as soon as he saw she was awake. Or perhaps she imagined it. The look in his eyes now was one she recognized— frank desire. His avid inspection covered every inch of exposed skin and substituted an experienced guess at the small amount of her body that was covered. The warmth that raced through Angelique had nothing to do with the brilliant sunshine.

"Don't you know that you shouldn't fall asleep in the sun?" he asked. "It would be criminal to damage that beautiful skin."

"Not to mention what Phil Nestor will do to me if I get burned," she answered lightly, wondering if it would be too obvious to put on her cover-up. "He's the photog-rapher for Vendome, and they frown on peeling noses."

Tristan's mouth curved in a sardonic smile. "It cer-tainly wouldn't do to endanger your career."

Why was her career such a stumbling block between them? Every time it came up they were on the verge of an argument. Angelique couldn't understand it. With his keen intelligence, Tristan would have seemed the last man to be attracted to an empty-headed, clinging vine. But maybe that didn't apply when the only attraction was sex. It angered and saddened Angelique at the same time. That was all he wanted from her, and she wanted so much more.

"Where have you been all day?" she asked, changing the subject. What was the use? She was always the one to get hurt during their mocking exchanges. "Alain wasn't around either."

Tristan's manner underwent a change, as it always did when it was something concerning Alain. "We went over to the Royal Academy quite early in the morning."

"So soon!" They had only discussed it a couple of days before.

"I'm a fast worker, haven't you noticed? Especially once I've decided on a course of action."

Angelique was well aware of the double meaning in his words, but she ignored it. "That must have pleased Alain."

Tristan chuckled. "After he got over the shock of finding out he had to take entrance exams like everyone else. This is going to be good for him in more ways than one."

"There won't be any problem, will there?" she asked anxiously.

"I'm sure there won't. Claude might not be anyone's first choice for a dinner partner, but he *is* a good teacher. I expect Alain to come through with flying colors. And if he's weak in any area, there's still a month to work on it before school starts."

"That's true. The timing is certainly right."

"Angelique, did you hear? I'm enrolled at the Academy!" Alain came running down the broad terrace steps to the pool.

"I know, and I think it's great." She smiled fondly at his excitement.

"I can't wait for school to start." He grinned at his uncle. "Did you ever think you'd hear that coming from me?"

"No, but I can understand it in this case," Tristan said indulgently.

"Now the only thing I need is a car and then I'll be all set."

Tristan raised a dark eyebrow. "You don't have to be *quite* such a normal teenager."

"But I really need one, Tristan. How am I going to get to school?"

"You've never had to hitchhike before," his uncle remarked dryly.

"You don't expect me to go in the limousine?" Alain was horrified.

"No, I can see that wouldn't do."

"Then what did you have in mind? Can we share the Maserati?" Alain asked hopefully.

"No, we cannot!" Tristan was very definite on that point.

"I'd take extra special care of it," Alain coaxed. He winked at Angelique. "Can you imagine how I'd make out with the girls?"

"You'll just have to resort to charm," Tristan advised callously. "A Maserati is much too high-powered for a youngster."

"Okay, I'll settle for my own Alpha Romeo," Alain compromised promptly. "A little red one. I can score almost as well in one of those sporty little buggies."

"I haven't agreed yet to let you have a car. The idea of going to the Academy is not merely to 'score,' as you put it. Perhaps we'd better wait and see what your grades are like."

"You're joking, aren't you?"

"I'm not laughing, am I?" Tristan was unmoved by Alain's outrage.

"Boy! A lot of good it does to be a prince." Alain's face was like a thundercloud. "No one lets you do anything you want."

Angelique didn't know if Tristan was serious about the car, but she was impressed by the way he handled his nephew. Alain was a dear, but without guidance he had the makings of a spoiled teenager, especially with his rank. Tristan had shown he loved him, now he was demonstrating that he cared about his welfare. Alain would realize it in later years.

"If you think you're being restricted now, wait till you take over this job full time," Tristan warned.

"I already have to do all the rotten parts, like going to those dumb state functions." Alain's scowl deepened. "Well, I'll tell you something—I'm not going to that one tonight."

"Tonight!" Angelique had stayed out of the exchange between uncle and nephew, but now she was startled into speech. "There's another reception this evening?"

Tristan sighed. "It wouldn't surprise me if there was one *every* night. We don't go to all of them, but an important official from the French government is here so we have to put in an appearance."

Angelique's sigh echoed his. "Where is it this time?"

"At the Lamperre's again."

"Don't they do anything but give parties?"

"He does, she doesn't," Tristan replied tersely.

"You can tell me about it when you get home." Alain's outthrust lower lip made him look like a sulky child.

Angelique studied him thoughtfully. "Didn't you say you wanted me to get better acquainted with Suzette? Since the party's at her house, why don't you ask her to join us?"

Alain's face cleared as if by magic. "What a smashing idea! Can I, Tristan?"

"You can do anything you like, Your Royal Highness. As you just reminded me, you're the prince."

It was exactly the right touch. Alain looked thoroughly miserable. "Come on, Tristan! You know I didn't mean it that way."

"I know." Tristan laughed and ruffled his hair. "It's the famous de Marchal temper. We both need someone to keep us in line."

Angelique ignored his glance in her direction. Her hand went to the tumbled coppery curls pinned to the crown of her head. "I wish you'd told me about the reception sooner. I have to do something about my hair. Is it all right if I wear the same dress?"

"I thought women considered that a fate worse than dishonor."

"It doesn't bother me. Besides, I have nothing else to wear."

Tristan looked at his watch. "There's still time to call the dress shop. Or we can go down there and you can choose something if you'd rather."

"On one condition—that I pay for it myself."

"I'm going to call Suzette." Alain had lost interest in the conversation. He loped off toward the house.

"I couldn't let you do that when you're doing *us* a favor." Tristan sat down on the edge of her chaise and leaned over her in what looked like a casual pose.

Angelique was acutely aware of him. Every sense responded to the lithe body poised over hers. She was afraid to move a muscle. "It isn't a favor if I'm paid for it."

"I never for a moment considered it payment. Aren't you making a big deal out of nothing?"

"If there's one thing I know something about, it's clothes. That last outfit cost a fortune."

"You made it look like one." His husky voice teased her nerves.

"*Anyone* would have looked good in it," she insisted. "But that's not the point. I can afford to buy my own clothes."

Tristan straightened. "Yes, I know. You've told me."

"Well...okay then. If you really think I need a different dress tonight you can call that shop and order something just as long as I get the bill."

His square jaw set grimly. "Perhaps you'd better make your own selection. I wouldn't want you to feel compromised in any way."

"*Now* who's overreacting? You're being as sulky as Alain with just as little excuse."

He smiled unwillingly. "I guess you're right. I told you I needed someone to put me in my place."

"It's keeping you there that would be the hard part," she told him disparagingly.

"Don't you like challenges?" he teased.

"Not when I know the odds are all against me."

"You underestimate your potency, little angel." Tristan toyed with a bright curl that nestled in the curve of her neck. "You could get a man to do almost anything to win your approval."

His long fingers brushing against her skin made Angelique want to close her eyes and savor the sensation. She brushed his hand away. "Until someone else came along who told you that you were perfect just the way you were."

"Is that what you think I want?"

"It's what *every* man wants."

"How about women?" His gray eyes were opaque as he waited for her answer. "How about you, Angelique?"

What would he say if she told him the truth? That she wanted his love, not merely his desire. Although she had to admit that was one thing they shared. Angelique turned liquid inside when she thought of what it would be like to have Tristan make love to her. In the private darkness of the night she had imagined his taut body covering hers, his hands and mouth caressing her, driving her through the gates of paradise.

Angelique's fingernails curled into her palms. In her fantasies Tristan's face was worshipful with love; in reality it would be swollen with passion. It should be enough that they both wanted each other, but Angelique knew it wasn't. He would go on to other loves, she couldn't.

"If Freud couldn't figure out what women want, I certainly can't. Especially not when I have to wash my hair." Her bored tone dismissed the whole subject.

Angelique slid off the chaise, being careful to avoid any contact with Tristan. Not that he was apt to get physical in broad daylight, in full view of the palace. Still, she wasn't so sure. Tristan wasn't overly troubled by conventionality.

As she walked gracefully up the terrace steps, Angelique was very conscious of his enigmatic gray eyes on her long legs and gently swaying hips.

She spent a long time in the luxurious pink marble bathroom, washing her hair, blowing it dry and applying makeup. A chipped nail also needed repairing. That took additional time, so it was quite a bit later that she went into the bedroom and found a large dress box exactly like the first one. Had Tristan delivered it himself, expecting a replay of the time before? Her generous mouth thinned to a straight line as she tightened the belt of her robe. She wouldn't put it past him! He never gave up.

Her interest in his current selection drove away the momentary annoyance. When the layers of tissue paper parted to reveal sapphire-blue silk jersey, Angelique made a small sound of appreciation. Tristan certainly had the perception of an artist. The deep blue was the exact color of her eyes.

The Grecian-style gown was long and fluid. When she slipped into it the softly draped bodice molded to her body perfectly. It flared out as she walked, returning to swirl around her ankles with a soft whisper. Angelique didn't like to think about the price tag, but whatever it cost, it was worth it. She could wear this classic gown for years. Perhaps she would think of Tristan every time.

She put the troubling thought out of her mind.

"You look fabulous, Angelique!" Alain exclaimed when she joined the men in the den.

There was open admiration in his eyes, but it was subtly different from his former attitude. She was happy to note that Alain was expressing approval now, not possessiveness. He was making a swift adjustment, with help from Suzette.

"You can compliment your uncle," she said lightly. "He has marvelous taste in clothes."

"The obvious answer is that you'd look good in a paper bag." Tristan's sensual gaze traveled over every gentle curve, trailing a path of pleasure.

"You ought to paint her in that dress," Alain advised. "The color's a knockout with her bright hair."

Tristan's smile was amused. "I've asked Angelique to pose for me, but she turned me down."

"You ought to reconsider," Alain told her. "Tristan paid you a big honor. He won't paint just anyone."

Only the women he sleeps with—or hopes to, she felt like telling him. She shook her head instead. "Posing is hard work, and I'm on vacation. Shouldn't we be leaving for the reception?"

The procedure at the Lamperre residence was the same as before. Angelique took her place next to Tristan, feeling like an old hand at this sort of thing. She informed Tristan of this in a whisper as they waited for the uniformed butler to announce Alain.

His mouth twisted with distaste as he watched the man's stately tread to the head of the stairs. "Poor Alain. Can you imagine being sentenced to a lifetime of this?"

Angelique looked out over the spacious room decorated with flowers and filled with formally clad guests sipping champagne. "A lot of people would think they'd died and gone to heaven."

"Not if they had to attend more than one of these wretched affairs."

"You're just being an old grouch," she said impatiently. "If you'd stop saying things like that, Alain would too."

"You can't pin *that* one on me. He's bored silly at these functions."

"I'll admit he's too young to appreciate them," she conceded.

Tristan looked at her with sudden awareness. "You mean you don't find court life deadly?"

"Not at all." Angelique was glancing over the crowd, so she didn't see the excitement that flared in his eyes. "It's really quite glamorous."

"You're only saying that because you don't have to do this for the rest of your life."

"I would survive," she assured him, too engrossed in the colorful scene to register the odd note in his voice.

"Grand Duke Tristan de Marchal and Miss Angelique Archer." The butler had waited until Alain descended the stairs.

"That's our cue." Angelique placed her hand on Tristan's forearm, grinning impishly up at him. "Try to look suitably regal for your subjects."

"How would you like it if I picked you up in my arms and carried you down?" he murmured in her ear.

She dug her long nails into his elegantly tailored arm, whispering back, "Behave yourself! Tonight you're a monarch, not a man."

"Don't count on it," he answered, leering in a most unroyal fashion.

Angelique knew that their behavior was less than correct, but she didn't care. Let everyone think she was Tristan's mistress—that was the idea, wasn't it? She had found it difficult to act the part before, but that was all changed now. It could so easily be true.

Tristan's barely restrained desire gave her a heady sense of power. Part of his resentment over this evening was because he wanted to be alone with her. And yet, would he have this burning impatience if he'd already made love to her? Or was he one of those men who enjoyed the chase almost more than the conquest?

Angelique's speculations came to an end as they reached the foot of the staircase and were greeted by the ambassador and his wife. During their short descent Madame Lamperre had taken in every detail of Angelique's gown, her hairdo, and her whispered exchange with Tristan. The older woman's rather sharp face was set in lines of disapproval. She wasn't aware of how much she was revealing, but Angelique would have sensed it anyway by her opening salvo.

"It's so nice to see you again, Miss Archer. I didn't know if you'd still be here or not."

On the surface it was a polite observation, but Angelique recognized the malice behind the seemingly innocent statement. Tristan was noted for his affairs, and she was just one more in a lengthy procession. Angelique wondered briefly if Madame Lamperre disliked her personally, or merely resented her as an outsider. It didn't matter because she didn't intend to put up with her snipping.

"I have remarkable staying power," she answered coolly.

The woman's face reddened unbecomingly as she realized that Angelique was the kind who fought back.

It irritated her further when Tristan put his arm around Angelique's waist and said, "We're trying to persuade Angel to stay indefinitely. She was responsible for the success of Alain's party the other evening."

"Yes, Suzette said they all seemed to enjoy it." Madame Lamperre managed to turn it into a statement rather than a compliment.

"I think they had a good time," Angelique commented mildly.

"If they'd enjoyed themselves any more we'd *never* have gotten rid of them!" Tristan exclaimed.

"It was a great treat for them to spend an evening at the palace." Madame Lamperre's face wore a pinched look.

Tristan stopped just short of snorting. "Come on, Martine! You know they had to be blackmailed into coming. It was Angelique's planning that made it such a success."

"I certainly didn't mean to take any credit away from Miss Archer," the ambassador's wife hastened to say. "Or you, either, Tristan." Her smile was subtly sly. "You have a talent for getting attractive young women to do things for you."

"In this case her efforts were on Alain's behalf," he said stiffly.

Why didn't he just let it be, Angelique wondered. That was what they wanted her to believe.

"He's a fortunate young man to have all of your...um...friends looking out for him," Madame Lamperre replied smoothly. "Natalie Caron was very fond of our young prince too, wasn't she?"

Angelique experienced a moment of intense anger. That was really hitting below the belt! Tristan's involvement with Natalie was yesterday's news. If he were truly having an affair with Angelique as Madame Lamperre believed, why try to spoil it through sheer malice? She was really a defective human being, the kind of person who told people wounding things "for their own good."

Tristan had stiffened warily at the woman's tactless reference to Natalie, waiting uneasily for Angelique's reaction. She leaned her head against his shoulder, taking his arm and putting it around her waist once more.

"She's a stunning woman, isn't she?" Angelique purred. "Tristan showed me the oils he did of her, and I only hope he'll do as well by me."

Madame Lamperre looked like a cat who found the mouse trap empty. "You're very understanding, my dear."

Angelique opened her big blue eyes very wide. "Is there something you're trying to tell me?"

The woman retreated in panic after a quick glimpse at Tristan's grim face. "No, certainly not! I was just...I... If you'll excuse me, I must speak to the servants."

Tristan watched her hasty escape with baleful eyes, muttering something under his breath that Angelique was glad she didn't quite hear. When he turned back to her his face softened. "I thought you'd be angry."

"I was. I was furious!"

"I mean at me—about Natalie."

"Look, Tristan, I know you were in love with her." When he would have interrupted, Angelique didn't let him. "But that human barracuda wanted to be *sure* I knew. If we'd really been in love the way we're pretending to be, it could have caused a rift between us for no good reason. Females like that give our whole sex a bad name!"

He touched her flushed cheek with a gentle forefinger. "You more than make up for her, Angel."

She gave a self-conscious little laugh. "I think I shook her up some anyway. Maybe she'll think twice before she tries to break up your next romance."

"Has she succeeded with this one?" He drew her into his arms, moving just enough to give the semblance of dancing.

The slow swaying of his body against hers was very sensuous. Angelique felt herself relaxing in Tristan's embrace, inhaling his heady masculine aroma. She put her arm around his neck, tilting her head to fit in the crook of his shoulder.

He kissed her on the temple. "You haven't answered my question."

"We don't have a romance going." She ran her fingers lingeringly through the dark hair above his collar, knowing this was one of the few times she could safely indulge herself.

"You could have fooled me," he murmured huskily.

"That was the idea, wasn't it? To fool everyone?"

"Except that somewhere along the line it became a reality." He wrapped her so close that her breasts were crushed against the hard wall of his chest. "Do you have any idea how much I want you?"

"Yes," she whispered. It would be hard to deny at that moment.

"You want me too, Angel. Why won't you admit it?"

Why didn't she? He already knew the answer. When she was in Tristan's arms like this, it was difficult to remember the reasons why she had to resist him. Angelique raised drugged eyes to his, her lips softly parted.

He drew in his breath sharply. "My beautiful little love! It's going to be so good between us."

"We've been looking for you." Alain's cheerful voice was a rude intrusion on their private world. They looked at him blankly, but he didn't seem to notice. "Let's go sit down. Suzette wants to get acquainted."

Tristan frowned. "We'll join you in a few minutes."

Angelique drew away from him self-consciously, now that her head was out of the clouds. "No, it's all right...I...I'd like to talk to Suzette." She gave the young girl a shaky smile.

Angelique was very conscious of Tristan following her, his long body taut with frustration. He was like a black panther robbed of its prey once too often. How many more times could she count on being rescued from herself? When Tristan turned up the voltage she was powerless to resist him.

He waited until she was seated in a corner before stalking off with a muttered excuse. The young people didn't seem to notice his annoyance.

"I love your dress," Suzette said.

"Thank you," Angelique replied absently, watching Tristan's stiff back disappear in the crowd. "Yours is nice too."

"You don't have to be tactful. It's awful." Suzette groaned.

Angelique took a good look at her for the first time. The dress really *was* awful. It was pink taffeta with tiny puffed sleeves and a little ruffle around the neck, the kind of formal young girls used to wear to proms in the fifties. Angelique hadn't known dresses like that still existed. It simply had to have been Madame Lamperre's choice.

"It...um...it's a pretty color," she said tentatively.

"I look like one of those pink sugar Easter eggs," Suzette answered scornfully.

"Nice and sweet," Alain told her loyally.

She made a face. "You're both just being polite. Do you think it would help at all if I tucked the ruffle inside and wore a belt instead of this dumb sash?" she asked Angelique.

"I get the feeling I'm not needed here," Alain remarked. "I'll be back in a few minutes."

As he strolled away Suzette looked after him with shining eyes. "Isn't he dreamy?"

"Yes, Alain is a very handsome young man," Angelique agreed.

"It's more than just looks," Suzette said earnestly. "He's a wonderful *person*. Take tonight, for instance. I wouldn't have blamed him if he'd pretended not to know me in this ghastly dress. I would never have heard the end of it from the other kids, but Alain told me I looked beautiful. Can you imagine?"

It didn't surprise Angelique and she told the girl so. "But if you dislike your dress so much, why did you wear it? You must have things you like better."

"That's for sure! This...*thing*...was my mother's idea. She wouldn't let me come tonight unless I wore it."

Angelique's surmise was correct. There was only one thing she couldn't figure out. "Where did she ever...uh...where did she buy it?"

Suzette gave Angelique an understanding look. "It's something she's had put away in a trunk forever. She said she's been saving it for me. I guess in Mother's day this was considered foxy." Suzette fingered the ruffle disdainfully.

"Alain seems to think so," Angelique consoled her.

The young girl's discontent fled like magic. "Isn't he the most? We were all so surprised when we got that invitation to the palace. Of course we all knew Alain when we were little, but he went away to school ages ago and we sort of lost track. And then that terrible thing happened to his parents and suddenly Alain was the prince. I mean, he was always a prince, but we never thought about it when we were kids."

"That's understandable." Angelique smiled at the tumble of words erupting from the teenager.

"And then when he came back he was so grown up and gorgeous. Most of the girls had a crush on him, but he seemed so mysterious and distant." She shivered with delight. "I met him in town once and I didn't know what to say to him."

"You must have done all right. Alain mentioned it to me."

"I think he really likes me, don't you?" Suzette asked eagerly.

"I'm sure you can tell that." Angelique hesitated. If Alain turned out to be the local teenage heartthrob it could create problems. "How about the boys in your crowd?" she asked casually. "I suppose their interests are different from Alain's after all this time."

"Are you kidding? The guys are always talking soccer and tennis together. Or else they want Alain's uncle to take them all up to his hunting lodge. Tristan was always a big favorite of everyone's. He never talked down to any of us, and even now that he's actually the head of state, he's still like a real person." Suzette gave a little laugh. "But I guess you know that."

Angelique did indeed know. She wasn't surprised at Tristan's popularity; he liked youngsters. What pleased Angelique and quieted her fears was Alain's popularity.

The subject of their conversation rejoined them with a hopeful look on his face. "All through with your 'girl talk'?" Alain asked.

"Yes, it's safe to come back now," Angelique teased. "Have you ever noticed how men suddenly find somewhere to go when women start discussing clothes?" she asked Suzette.

As Alain was about to answer he spied Suzette's father bearing down on them with a distinguished-looking man in tow. "Uh oh," he muttered under his breath.

Before Angelique could ask any questions, the ambassador introduced his guest as the French minister. "Monsieur Ribeau is a compatriot of yours, Miss Archer."

"I could hardly wait to meet you after Monsieur Lamperre informed me of that fact." The slender, elegant man was regarding her with true Gallic appreciation.

"I'm afraid he's misinformed." Angelique smiled charmingly at both men. "I'm an American."

"But you have family in Paris," the French minister said. "That makes you one of us."

"They...uh...I don't see much of them. They're rather distant relatives."

"You must maintain ties, Miss Archer. Didn't you say you met Tristan while visiting them?" the ambassador reminded her.

"That's true." Angelique exchanged a glance with Alain, belatedly understanding his muffled exclamation.

"What is the name of your family?" Monsieur Ribeau asked.

That at least she could answer. "Monsieur and Madame Tatine."

"Do they reside in the city?" The Frenchman was only expressing interest. He couldn't know that Angelique's nerves were on red alert.

"Didn't you say it was somewhere in the fifteenth *arrondissement*?" Alain put in smoothly.

"Yes, that's it!" She threw him a grateful look. "I can't for the life of me remember the street name though. I have such a dreadful memory." She turned the full power of her blue eyes on the other man.

The Frenchman looked dazzled. "Any lapse would be forgiven in such a lovely lady."

"You're so kind, *monsieur*." Under cover of her lowered lashes, Angelique shot Alain an urgent S.O.S.

"Hold the fort, I'll be back with reinforcements," he murmured in her ear.

Left on her own, Angelique felt like a tightrope walker wearing skis. The French minister was so fascinated by her that he asked one question after another, and she was having trouble parrying them. How long could she plead forgetfulness without sounding as though her elevator didn't go to the top floor? It was a relief when Alain appeared with Tristan in tow.

"Forgive me for neglecting you, my dear." Tristan put his arm possessively around Angelique's waist. The anger that had made him stalk off seemed to have dissipated. "I trust everyone has been taking care of you."

"With a lady as lovely as Mademoiselle Archer, you need have no fear," the French minister said gallantly. "Any man would be delighted to take your place."

"I'm well aware of that," Tristan replied smoothly. "I'll just have to stay closer to her side."

That's what he should have done in the first place! Angelique was extremely annoyed at Tristan for throwing her to the wolves in a fit of temper.

"I was hoping you came back to dance with me," she said sweetly, although she had to force the words through gritted teeth.

"I can think of few things I'd rather do," Tristan replied mockingly.

"A Frenchman would not make qualifications," the minister chided.

"Only love of country comes first," Tristan answered blandly.

Angelique's eyes narrowed dangerously. "Do you think Souveraine would survive for one more day if we had this dance?"

Her back was stiff with fury as she preceded him onto the dance floor. As soon as Tristan took her in his arms she erupted.

"How could you do a thing like that to me? Monsieur Ribeau asked me all kinds of questions about my family in Paris. If it hadn't been for Alain I'd have been tripped up on the first question! When I agreed to this insane situation, you were supposed to help! Where were you when I needed you?"

Tristan heard her out with an amused look on his face. "I'm glad to hear you admit that you need me."

"I believe it's the other way around," she answered coldly.

"You're so right." He tightened his arms around her, burying his face in the softness of her hair. "That's what I've been trying to tell you."

"Don't try to get around me," she stormed. "Madame Lamperre's questions are bad enough, but how am I going to fool a Frenchman? If you don't keep him away from me, he's going to find out that I've never been to Paris."

"It isn't easy to keep *any* man away from you, let alone a Frenchman."

"Will you be serious? This is probably the worst thing that could happen, but it's going to come up again with someone or other. We'll have to formulate a game plan—maybe a set of signals."

Tristan drew back to look at her consideringly. "I've been thinking about that. All you really need is a rudimentary knowledge of Paris."

"Which I don't have!"

"That could be easily remedied. I have to fly there tomorrow for a meeting. I was going to come right back, but if you came with me we could stay for a couple of days, and you could take a crash course on the city."

"You have to be joking!" She looked at him incredulously. "What makes you think I'm going to be any more willing in a different locale?"

"That wasn't what I had in mind," he replied evenly. "This is strictly a business proposition. You'll have your own room—in a different hotel if you like. After my meeting we'll spend the time soaking up Paris. We'll go to all the places anyone could possibly ask you about so you don't feel so vulnerable."

"But that's crazy," she answered slowly. "I'll only be here another week. There can't be more than one or two of these things. We can sort of wing it."

His broad shoulders shifted in a shrug. "We can, but it would be infinitely easier if we didn't have to. Besides, it would be a little bonus for you." He smiled warmly. "This trip hasn't turned out to be the vacation you expected. A guided tour of Paris might make up for it a little bit."

Angelique was annoyed that he thought her that naive. "I'd like to see Paris, but I have a feeling that if I accepted your generous offer, the only thing I'd see would be the inside of a hotel room."

"I'm sorry you feel that way, Angelique. I made you a straightforward offer." His eyes held hers compellingly. "I promise that nothing will happen that you don't want to happen."

She was filled with confusion. Every instinct told her that Tristan was setting a trap. But he had offered to get her a room at a different hotel. That didn't mean he wasn't planning on sharing it with her. Still, she could always say no, and there wouldn't be much he could do about it. Angelique had to admit that it would be wonderful to see Paris with Tristan. Wouldn't she be foolish to pass up this opportunity?

"What's your decision?" His deep voice cut into her thoughts.

Angelique looked up at him uncertainly, the darkened color of her sapphire eyes expressing her doubts. "Okay, I'll go, but I think you're in for a disappointment."

He buried her face in his shoulder, so she didn't see the flare of excitement that lit up his countenance. Sensuously massaging the nape of her neck under her long silky hair, he murmured, "I'm a big boy, I can take it."

Chapter Eight

When they arrived at the posh hotel in Paris where Tristan always stayed, Angelique found out the true meaning of the words "visiting royalty." Their luggage was whisked away, and they were greeted by the manager who bowed from the waist as they stepped out of the limousine. It was almost as though he had been standing at the plate-glass doors waiting for them.

Angelique found out that royalty didn't bother with anything so plebeian as registering. The manager led them directly to a bank of elevators, fawning genteelly on the way.

"Your usual suite has been prepared, Your Highness. I trust everything will be to your satisfaction."

Tristan's brief nod expressed indifference. He was more interested in Angelique's accommodations. "Has Miss Archer's suite been taken care of?"

"Certainly, Your Highness. On a different floor as you instructed." The man's brief, sidelong glance at Angelique contained a flash of incredulity.

As he turned away for a moment to speak to a bellman, Tristan murmured in her ear, "I don't know if bringing you here was such a good idea. He's going to spread rumors about either my sanity, or my virility."

Angelique knew there was no danger of the latter. Tristan exuded masculinity, whether faultlessly tailored as he was now, or wearing an old pair of jeans. She had noticed all the female heads that turned to follow his progress through the airport, and this was attention from women who didn't know, and wouldn't have cared, that he was a duke. What they were admiring was a superb male. Most of them would have thought she was crazy not to share his bed.

Angelique had turned down Tristan's offer to put her in another hotel. It was the height of hypocrisy. If she didn't trust him, or herself, separate hotels wouldn't be any safeguard. It was equally silly for them to be on different floors, but it showed his good intentions.

After Angelique was shown to her suite, Tristan went on to his own. The first thing that greeted her was a living room full of flowers. Not just one arrangement on the coffee table in front of the satin-striped couch, but vases and bowls of roses, carnations, and gladioli placed around the spacious room. The bedroom behind a gold and white paneled door contained more flowers in the color scheme of the pink and white bedspread and drapes. Instead of a canopy over the wide bed there was a floor to ceiling panel attached to the wall, framed in gilt and padded with fabric that matched the bed.

It looked like the chambers of a favorite courtesan in the days of French royalty. But closer inspection showed that modern improvements had been incorporated. A delicate gold and white armoire was fitted with a television set behind its double doors, and the large bathroom had a stall shower, makeup lights around the mirror, and a hairdryer in a basket filled with perfumes and soaps. Every comfort a woman might wish for had been anticipated and provided. If this was a suite given to the common people, Angelique couldn't begin to imagine what the royal one looked like! She had to find out.

When Tristan called a short time later, the first thing she said was, "Can I come up to your suite?"

After a short, stunned silence he asked, "Is that a proposition?"

"Of course not! I just want to see what your room looks like. Mine is so gorgeous that I don't see how they could top it."

"You're pleased then?"

"Pleased? I could live here the rest of my life."

"That could be arranged," he murmured in a throaty voice.

"Don't be silly, Tristan. Can I come up?"

"Sure, I'll get out the champagne."

The royal suite turned out to be a complete apartment. Entrance was through a square foyer that had twin lighted cabinets against the wall facing the door. Behind their beveled glass doors were priceless objects—an eclectic collection of Chinese vases, Dresden figurines and Swedish cut crystal.

Angelique was speechless as Tristan led her into a huge living room that was big enough to host a reception. Couches and chairs were scattered around, and large mirrors in baroque gilt frames were interspersed among costly paintings on the flocked maroon wallpaper. A broad terrace that ran the length of the apartment was furnished like an outdoor living room with chaises and chairs and big tubs of blooming plants.

"This is unreal! I've *got* to see the bedroom!" Angelique exclaimed.

Tristan chuckled. "I should have brought you to Paris sooner."

She barely heard him. The bedroom was equal in magnificence to what she had already seen. It resembled Tristan's bedroom in Souveraine, except that it was more ornate. There were many touches that he would have dispensed with immediately—like the crown-shaped canopy suspended from the high ceiling, and the cream velvet draperies that descended from it to shield both sides of the bed. The effect was terribly regal, which was exactly what Tristan hated.

The dressing room that opened off the bedroom dazzled Angelique with its alcoves for shirts, slanted shoe shelves, and acres of hanging space.

But the bathroom totally blew her mind. The sunken bathrub in the middle of the room looked big enough to accommodate several people. A bench nearby was piled with thick, fluffy towels bearing a crest embroidered in gold thread. Mirrored walls reflected Angelique's incredulous expression.

"It looks like the setting for a Roman orgy!"

Tristan was watching her reaction with amusement. "I've never really liked crowds. Why don't we limit the party to two?"

She turned to gaze at him disapprovingly. "You've been behaving very well up to now. Don't spoil it."

Tristan grinned. "Not the response I'd like, but the one I expected."

He led the way back to the living room where a bottle of champagne was nestled in a silver wine cooler. Next to it on the cocktail table was a large tray of hors d'oeuvres. Caviar, smoked salmon, paté, and cheeses were arranged in a picture perfect display.

Once more Angelique was amazed. "Do you mean they delivered all those in just the time it took me to get up here?"

"No, they were in the refrigerator." He indicated a kitchen behind the dining room that held a long mahogany table and twelve chairs upholstered in wine velvet.

Angelique shook her head. "You kings sure know how to live."

"I'm not a king," Tristan answered sharply.

"Well, I'll settle for whatever you are."

"Will you, Angelique?" The testiness in his voice changed to a low purr.

She was suddenly very much aware of him again. Tristan had removed his jacket and tie, and unbuttoned his shirt. The stark white broadcloth accentuated the dark curling hair on his tanned chest, making him look lean and macho. It wasn't an illusion either. Angelique had good reason to remember every taut muscle in that hard chest.

"Who wouldn't want to live like this?" she answered lightly.

Tristan didn't press the point. "This is nothing. You should see how kings used to live." He looked at his watch. "How would you like to drive out to Versailles, Louis XIV's summer palace? A cozy little pad of a few hundred rooms."

"I'd love it! If you have time, that is. How about your meeting?"

"It isn't until tomorrow morning. I'll probably be all through before you're even up."

"Are you kidding? I didn't come to Paris to sleep. I'll be up and out early too."

"Are you going to look up your family?"

"I suppose I really should, for my mother's sake anyway."

"If you wait till I'm through I'll go with you."

"Oh..." Angelique hesitated. "I don't think that's such a good idea."

"Why not? Wait until I phone downstairs for a car, and we'll talk about it on the way."

By the time they reached the lobby, a Rolls-Royce convertible was parked outside the front door.

"Damn!" Tristan muttered. "I forgot to tell them I wanted something small."

"It's a wonder they didn't provide a police escort," Angelique teased. "That funny little man probably just realized his oversight and is inside this minute phoning for one."

"You could be right. Get in quick!"

As Tristan eased into traffic, Angelique examined the rosewood paneling and elegant appointments. "I think this car is smashing. What are you complaining about?"

"It's a little attention getting." He put his hand over hers and squeezed her fingers. "How can I park by the side of the road and kiss you?"

The tingle that went up Angelique's arm traveled throughout her entire body. She was seeing Paris with the man she loved! What more could any woman ask? The only flaw in her happiness was that she couldn't show it.

They were driving down the famed Rue de la Paix when Angelique dragged her attention away from Tristan. She didn't know what to look at first, the lush merchandise displayed in posh shops, or the stylishly dressed people strolling down the boulevard.

When they were out of the city Tristan returned to the subject of Angelique's family. "Why don't you want me to meet them?"

"I didn't say that," she protested.

"Okay, then why don't you want them to meet *me*?"

"That's too silly to talk about."

Tristan had hit on the truth, though. Her mother had been out of touch with this distant cousin, but if Angelique looked her up it was bound to prompt an exchange of letters. If she brought along just any man, Madame Tatine might not think to mention it. But Tristan was another story. How could you forget about a grand duke who was also the ruler of a country?

He had brought her to Paris, they were staying at the same hotel, and he apparently accompanied her everywhere. What would her mother think? What anyone else would, naturally. Angelique could just hear herself trying to explain. "He paid for my trip, Mother, but we're just good friends."

"Did you know that your nose twitches when you tell a lie?" Tristan teased. "You *don't* want them to meet me, do you?"

She explained haltingly. "I know it sounds silly to you," she began, "but my parents live in a small town in Vermont where people are very conventional. They didn't even approve of my having a career if it meant moving to New York. They still believe girls should marry their college sweethearts and stay married all their lives. It might not be too realistic these days, but at least I don't want them to think I'm having a flaming affair with a notorious grand duke."

"Ah, if it only were so!" He raised her hand to his lips and kissed the palm. "I'd still like to meet your family. Why do you have to tell them who I am? You can introduce me as Tristan Charolais—that's my family name."

"You don't think there's a tiny chance they might recognize you?" she asked dryly.

"Not necessarily. When someone is in a place where there's no valid reason for him to be, people simply don't make the connection. They might remark that I look like the grand duke from Souveraine, in which case I'd reply that people have told me that and the subject would be dropped.''

"I don't know," she said doubtfully.

"There's an alternative," he said with a mischievous grin. "I could wear my false mustache."

Angelique barely heard him. She was trying to decide if Tristan's argument that he wouldn't be recognized was valid. It was true that people tended to see what they were told they saw. That was the principle of magic tricks. Also, no one expected to find a celebrity in their living room.

Her preoccupation wasn't lost on Tristan. "It's all right, honey," he said gently. "I won't go if you'd rather I didn't."

"It isn't that," she answered slowly. "It's just that we always have to watch every word and action in Souveraine, and now here." She sighed. "I wish just once we could tell the truth." Angelique was pleating her skirt aimlessly so she didn't see his expression.

"I'll go along with you there."

She glanced up at the odd note in his voice, but Tristan was staring straight ahead. She gazed at his classic profile, feeling a rush of emotion. If only she could curl up next to him and rest her head on his solid shoulder. There was so little time left to touch him, to listen to his deep voice, to inhale the wonderful male aroma of him. He gratified all her senses. Angelique knew that her memories of this man would never dim, making it a dubious blessing.

The knowledge that time was running out was the deciding factor. She couldn't bear to lose a minute with Tristan, no matter what the consequences. "What the heck! We fooled Madame Lamperre so that makes us pros. I'd love to have you come with me tomorrow."

Their arrival at Versailles drove everything else out of Angelique's mind. The sprawling bulk of the palace, built in the seventeenth century, was awesome. Angelique tried to take in everything at once, knowing it was impossible. There were life-size statues and busts, arches and balconies decorated with urns and friezes, cornices and cupolas and chimneys. The craftsmanship was exquisite, but it was the sheer quantity of everything that was mind-boggling.

"It isn't a palace, it's a whole city!" Angelique gasped.

"That's exactly what it was in Louis's day," Tristan told her. "When he was in residence here he took the entire Court of France with him. Anywhere between two thousand and five thousand people lived in the compound at one time. Some of the accommodations, even in the noble's wing, weren't much more than cubbyholes, but it was an honor to live at the chateau."

Her eyes traveled over the seemingly endless wings that jutted out in different directions. "They must have needed a road map to get from one place to another."

"Would you believe they took sedan chairs when they had to go to a distant part of the palace?"

"Now I know you're putting me on!"

"Not at all. As you pointed out, the place is huge. And the nobles of that time were used to a lot of service. They called for a sedan chair the way we call for a cab. Actually, there's a similarity. No one but the royal family was allowed to own their own sedan chairs, so everyone else rented theirs from a private company. See, there was free enterprise even in those days." Tristan began to chuckle. "Although it wouldn't surprise me if Louis took his cut. He was pretty savvy about money."

Angelique turned to look at him. "You know a great deal about French history."

"It was crammed into me, and some of it stuck. Louis XIV was one of the more interesting kings." Tristan gazed out over the vast wooded acres. "One of the reasons that he built Versailles way out in the country was that he was a great outdoorsman."

Angelique's eyebrows rose. "From what I've read, he was a great *in*doorsman too."

"And practical besides. He knew how to conserve energy." Tristan's eyes glinted with amusement. "He put his wife's apartments on one side of his, and his mistress's on the other."

"He kept his mistress right here in the palace? I thought they always ended up with a big chateau of their own."

"Some did. His 'favorites,' as they were called, were rewarded with their own private estates. But Madame de Montespan, the reigning mistress for much of his life, lived at court and was regarded almost as an alternate queen."

"Didn't Louis's wife object?"

"It wouldn't have done any good. She tried refusing him her bed once to punish him, and he didn't come near her for two months. It took the intervention of his mother to patch things up. As a matter of fact, the queen got on quite well with the other woman. I guess she figured if it wasn't that *madame* it would be another one."

When they walked inside Angelique was dazzled all over again. The inlaid floors and pillars were a marvel of subtle shading. Blues, greens, and tans blended together in muted harmony. The gleam of gold on doors and ceilings was everywhere, and a magnificent crystal chandelier topped the head of the broad white stairs that formed the queen's staircase.

Tristan could barely drag her away. "Save some of your enthusiasm for the hall of mirrors," he advised.

Angelique didn't think anything could possibly top what she had already seen, but one glimpse had her entranced. The long corridor was lined with endless mirrored arches under a domed ceiling painted with religious themes, portraits, and hunting scenes. Gold and marble pedestals held tall candelabra, and gilt swags of carved wood were looped over the curve of each arch. Everywhere she looked there was another fresco, another tapestry, another detail she had overlooked.

"I can't believe it," Angelique said in awe. "This was a hallway?"

"Only during the day. At night it was used for dancing and entertainment." Tristan's eyes narrowed, as though looking into the past. "It must have been quite spectacular, all lit up with thousands of candles."

"And filled with beautiful people in satin and velvet." Angelique's face was dreamy. "Wouldn't you love to have seen it in those days?"

"Seen it, yes. Lived through it, no."

"Why not? Court life must have been exciting."

He looked at her quizzically. "You like intrigue?"

"I seem to have a talent for it." She laughed. "Maybe it's my French blood. Come on, let's go see the gardens."

As they wandered through the beautiful grounds Tristan took her hand. He told her about the arguments Louis had had with Le Notre, his director of the royal gardens. The king loved flowers and the gardener hated them, preferring long sweeps of lawn.

"Louis also had a passion for orange trees. He imported thousands of them. Eight of the original ones are supposed to exist to this day in the Orangerie."

Angelique gazed up at Tristan, appearing to give him her whole attention, but his fascination was much more potent that the Sun King's. She was filled with happiness that was all the more poignant because she knew it was fleeting.

On the way back to Paris, Tristan asked if she'd mind not going to a three-star restaurant. "I know it's selfish of me, but I'm known in all of them. I can't get away with being Tristan Charolais, and I don't want people pestering us. I want you all to myself," he said in a throaty voice.

Angelique's heart threatened to burst. "Any place is fine with me."

"Are you sure, Angel?" He frowned slightly. "Maybe I'm not being fair to you."

After she assured him that she wasn't any more interested than he in being fawned over, Tristan took her to a gypsy restaurant. It had beaded curtains over the doorways, and was lit mainly by the dripping candles on each red checked tablecloth. Not exactly three-star decor, but the food was delicious and nobody bothered them. Except for a swarthy violinist who may or may not have been a gypsy. In any case, he put on a good show. While they were having coffee he serenaded them with wistful music and soulful looks.

After Tristan handed him a bill, the man was extravagant with praise. "Many lovers come here, but none so perfect for each other. You are a beautiful couple. Your love lights up the room."

Was it that obvious on her part, Angelique worried. When the man left she tried to make a joke of it. "I'll bet he tells that to everyone so they won't realize they're economizing on electricity."

Tristan didn't join in her laughter. His husky voice tugged at something deep inside her. "He was right about one thing—you *are* beautiful. Did I happen to mention it?"

"Not since we got to Paris."

"I can hardly believe that."

"Tell me now," she said urgently, needing to hear the words.

He touched her cheek, stroking it with exquisite tenderness. "How can I describe the color of your eyes? They're like blue diamonds set in a precious frame." His fingers brushed lightly over her lips. "And this mouth— it's a gateway to heaven, delivering paradise here on earth."

Tristan's feathery touch was melting Angelique's very bones. She tried to laugh, but it came out as a breathy sound. "You should have been a poet instead of a painter."

His dark head bent so close that their lips were only a whisper apart. Their breath mingled as he said, "I want you so much, sweet angel. I want to make love to you. Will you let me make you part of me?"

Angelique was torn between sense and sensuality. It would be madness to give in now when temptation was almost at an end. But how could she give up the love of her life without ever experiencing the fulfillment she knew he could bring? As Tristan lifted her long silken hair so he could stroke the back of her neck, Angelique knew there could only be one answer. A long sigh shook her slender body. She closed her eyes and parted her lips to surrender, but incredibly, Tristan sat back in his chair with a groan.

"I'm sorry, sweetheart. I promised that everything would be strictly legitimate on this trip, and I meant it." He gave her a lopsided smile. "You do make it hard for a man to keep his word, though."

Angelique stared at him in confusion. Didn't he knew what her answer was going to be? Her long lashes swept down as she realized that he obviously didn't. Perhaps it was a sign. Maybe someone was determined to save her from herself.

Fortunately the evening was almost over because Angelique would surely have weakened. But when Tristan walked her to her door, she didn't want it to end. "Would...would you like to come in for a nightcap?"

Her guardian angel saw to it that Tristan shook his head. "No thanks, honey." His smile was rueful. "There's a limit to my willpower."

After he had gone Angelique tried to be grateful. She knew it was for the best, but her heated body refused to agree. What would prevent her from going upstairs to Tristan's suite? She stood very still in the center of the room as the thought tantalized her. After a long moment her slender shoulders drooped. It just wasn't the sort of thing she was capable of.

Angelique had trouble getting to sleep that night. She kept picturing Tristan alone in that princely bed. Did he wear pajamas? Or did only a sheet cover the hard angles of that superb body? Letting out her breath in a puff of frustration, she buried her head in a pillow to blot out the image.

After chasing sleep half the night Angelique overslept the next morning. By the time she finished bathing and dressing, Tristan was back from his meeting. She was uncomfortable with him at first. He had figured very graphically in her dreams! But since he didn't know about it, he was completely natural.

He was the same way with her cousins; they adored him immediately. Roselle Tatine was a chic woman with fashionably styled dark hair and a still-slender figure. She was overjoyed to meet Angelique, and completely captivated by Tristan.

Her husband, Paul, was a tall, spare man with receding hair and a quiet sense of humor. He let his wife do most of the talking while he smoked his pipe and watched her with quiet affection.

At first Angelique had been tense, waiting for some indication that they recognized Tristan. When they accepted him in good faith, she began to relax and enjoy herself. Tristan was evidently right. Who would expect to find the grand duke of Souveraine slouching on someone's couch? He was completely at ease, grasping his ankle, crossed over one knee, while he asked questions about the influence of computers on the way math was taught. Paul was a college professor.

Tristan didn't look very ducal either. His cream-colored slacks were faultlessly tailored, but he hadn't worn a jacket over the matching silk shirt. A crew-necked cotton sweater was knotted around his tanned throat instead. He looked utterly masculine and extremely handsome.

When Madame Tatine went into the kitchen to make coffee and Angelique went along to help, the older woman commented on it. "Your young man is very *sympathique*...very—" she waved one hand in the air "—attractive."

"Yes, he is, isn't he?" Angelique busied herself putting the cookies Roselle had handed her on a plate. "But he isn't my young man. We're just friends."

"Nonsense! A man and a woman are never friends. They are lovers, or they are indifferent to each other."

"Maybe it's that way in France, but American women have a lot of male friends."

"Not that one." Madame Tatine jerked her head toward the living room. "He was made for love, no?"

"I wouldn't know," Angelique answered carefully. "We haven't known each other very long."

"Long enough to fall in love," her cousin remarked calmly.

"You mustn't go writing things like that to my mother because it just isn't so!" Angelique said anxiously.

"I have seen the way you look at him, my dear. Your heart is in your eyes."

Angelique was stricken enough to give up the pretense. "Is it that obvious?"

"To a Frenchwoman, *oui*. But why are you so afraid to show your feelings?"

Angelique looked down at the cookie she was reducing to crumbs. "Because Tristan doesn't love *me*."

"What nonsense is this? The man adores you! His eyes follow you everywhere."

Angelique's lips twisted in an attempt to smile. "I thought we were talking about love."

"Love and passion are two faces of the same coin. If you love someone, you want them in your bed," Roselle stated matter-of-factly. "So don't tell me Tristan doesn't love you because he desires you as well."

Angelique laughed helplessly. "Are you sure you and my mother are related?"

"Don't change the subject." Madame Tatine frowned. "I cannot believe that you would let this splendid man get away."

"I don't know how to explain this without sounding like a prude, but I couldn't have an affair with a man when there was no future in it."

"He is married." The older woman's voice was sad, but accepting.

"No, of course not!"

"Then what is the problem?" She brightened up considerably.

"Well, there's my career. My job is in New York, and Tristan is...his is here."

Madame Tatine was clearly impatient. "We have models in France. You would not have to give up your career."

"It isn't only that." Angelique separated the cookie crumbs into little piles. "There have been so many other women. As you said yourself, Tristan is a very handsome man. But he has a short attention span, and I think the chase is more important than the prize. He's fascinated by me because so far I've held out. If I give in I'll join the ranks of all those other women, and I don't think I could bear that."

"So you won't play the game because you're afraid of losing. I'm really disappointed in you, Angelique."

"I was lost the day I met him." Unshed tears made Angelique's eyes very bright. "I was Tristan's just as surely as if he'd put his brand on me."

"Then enjoy him, my dear," Madame Tatine said urgently. "Life is so short, and true love is a precious thing. Store up memories and enjoy them without regret." Her dark eyes began to twinkle. "You might even find that your love story has a surprise ending."

Tristan pushed open the swinging door to the kitchen. "Can I do anything for you?"

The older woman looked consideringly at the long, relaxed length of him. "Where were you twenty years ago?"

He laughed, white teeth gleaming in his tanned face. He put his arm around Angelique, hugging her close. "Why aren't you more like your cousin?"

"I'm trying to teach her," Roselle commented dryly.

After her traumatic conversation with Madame Tatine, Angelique felt self-conscious. She was sure Tristan had picked up on her cousin's suggestive remarks. But they both behaved so naturally that after a while she began to breathe easier. The day hadn't been spoiled after all. Roselle had certainly surprised her though by her liberal attitude.

"They're great people. I'm glad I got a chance to meet them," Tristan said on the way home.

"You made quite a conquest out of Roselle."

Tristan chuckled. "She's a great gal."

"Yes, she's a lot of fun. But I never realized that the French are really different."

"In what way?"

"Well, she...they just are."

They arrived at the hotel and Tristan turned the car over to the doorman. He checked for messages at the desk before they took the elevator to Angelique's floor. As they walked down the corridor to her suite he returned to the subject they were discussing in the car.

"You didn't explain why you think the French are different."

Angelique was sorry she had started the whole thing. "Their views on, um, things...are more relaxed."

If she thought that would end it, she was mistaken. Tristan unlocked the door and followed her inside. "Like the relationship between men and women?"

"Yes," she admitted grudgingly.

"What's wrong with treating sex as a normal, healthy part of life?"

"I didn't say there was anything wrong with it," she muttered. "I was merely surprised that my own cousin..."

"Made it clear that we had her blessing," Tristan finished as Angelique's voice trailed off.

"That doesn't change anything," she murmured, her cheeks very pink.

"No, it doesn't. If I can't convince you myself, I don't deserve to have you. I'm no—what was the name of that fellow in your history books who sent someone else to plead his case?''

"John Alden." Silently she added that John Alden didn't ask his true love to have an affair, he wanted to marry her.

"That's the one. I'm no John Alden, but it's nice to know that someone in your family is on my side," he teased.

Angelique smiled reluctantly. "She couldn't have been more approving if she'd known who you really are."

"Why is it everyone finds me irresistible but you?" he complained.

"I'm surprised you haven't lost interest by now," she remarked lightly.

"That's a provocative statement if I ever heard one. Don't push your luck, young woman. I could easily forget my promise and show you just how interested I really am."

Tristan had slipped one arm around her waist and gathered her bright hair in his other hand. He tugged gently, tilting her face up to his own laughing one. Suddenly the laughter died as their eyes met. He pulled her nearer, wrapping his arm around her shoulders so she was held in a close embrace.

Angelique stood very still, staring up at him as his head slowly descended. When his features were too close to focus on, she closed her eyes, trembling with an urgent need that swept through her like wildfire.

After a quivering moment Tristan released her, groaning deep in his chest. "I'd better go."

Angelique felt chilled without his arms around her. She opened her eyes. Tristan was starting for the door; in another moment he would be gone. Her numbed brain started to race. Could she let him go again? Echoes of her conversation with Roselle rang in Angelique's ears. "Store up memories and enjoy them without regret."

That was the key! Without regret. She had been so busy worrying about the future that she was turning down a chance for present happiness. Yes, it would hurt when Tristan tired of her, but nothing would ever take away the memories. Bless Roselle Tatine! Without her there wouldn't have been any.

Tristan had a hand on the doorknob. "Wait!" Angelique cried. "Don't go."

"I have to, sweetheart."

"I don't want you to go." She walked slowly toward him.

He hesitated, looking at her uncertainly. "You don't know what you're asking, Angel. If I stay I'm going to try to make love to you again."

She put both her palms on his shirtfront, moving them over the hard wall of his chest. "You haven't made love to me for the first time yet."

He captured both her hands, none too gently. "Do you know what you're doing to me? You've never been a tease, Angelique."

She stood on tiptoe to kiss the tip of his nose. "Tell me the definition of a tease."

"You know perfectly well." A nerve pulsed at his temple.

"Someone who promises and doesn't deliver?"

"That's exactly right," he agreed grimly.

"Then I'm not a tease." She pulled her hands free so she could slide her arms around his neck.

Tristan gripped her waist, holding her slightly away so he could stare down at her. Excitement blazed in his eyes, but his words were cautious. "Are you sure this is what you want?"

"Now who needs convincing?" She untied the sleeves of his sweater and pushed it slowly off his shoulders. "I never thought *I'd* have to seduce *you*."

"My sweet, beautiful angel." He clasped her so tightly that she could hardly breathe. "I've wanted you for so long," he muttered into the silken cloud of her hair.

"I wanted you too," she whispered. "Last night I could hardly bear it when you left me."

"Then why—no, never mind. I'm going to make love to you now." His eyes held hers for a burning moment. "Slowly and repeatedly."

A wave of fire swept through Angelique at the promise she knew he could fulfill. When he picked her up in his arms she buried her face in his shoulder, trembling with anticipation.

Tristan carried her into the bedroom and stood her on her feet by the wide bed. He framed her face in his palms and kissed her tenderly, tasting her lips in a slow prelude. When her lips parted, he circled the moist interior with his tongue before thrusting deeper. Angelique gripped his shoulders, uttering a tiny moan as the sensuous male exploration aroused all her senses.

Her delight drew an answering sound from Tristan. Urgency built as he unfastened the long zipper of her dress. He let it slither to the floor, looking at her with unleashed passion. His hands roamed over her body, caressing her through the wispy lace bra and brief panties until Angelique wanted to tear them off so there would be no barrier to his hands.

"I never knew anyone could be so perfect." His fingertips slipped inside the lace bra to touch her tight nipples. When she pressed against his hand he liberated one bare breast and bent his head to circle the aching nipple with his warm, wet tongue.

Angelique's shaking hands pulled his shirt out of his slacks. "I need you so, Tristan," she whispered, kneading the smooth skin of his back.

"We need each other, sweetheart. I'm going to make you part of me in every way."

In one swift movement he removed her bra and panties, and lifted her onto the bed. After covering her face with kisses he moved down her body, trailing a path of excitement from her breasts to her knees. Angelique quivered with unashamed passion as he knelt over her and stroked the soft skin of her inner thighs. When he reached his goal she gasped and murmured his name over and over, holding out her arms wide to him.

Tristan threw off his clothes in a blur of movement, then returned to take her in his arms. The contact with his hard body was so exquisite that she pressed against him and felt an answering surge of passion. She wrapped her legs around his, filling with a desire so molten that it was driving her wild.

"Love me, Tristan. Please love me!"

"Yes, my darling. More than anyone has ever loved you before."

His weight pressed down on her heavily. Angelique felt her body melting into his, fused by the fierce heat he was generating. As Tristan completed their union she arched upward, welcoming his male challenge. He filled her with unbelievable joy that intensified in power with every unrestrained movement.

She clung to him in the storm they had built, anchoring her fingers in his thick hair while he took her on a wild ride that suddenly spun out of control. She was propelled into space, on a collision course with a far distant star. The impact was explosive. The tension that had gripped her suddenly burst in a throbbing conclusion that left an aftermath of pure pleasure. Angelique slowly relaxed in Tristan's arms. The glow that warmed her whole body was reflected by the blissful smile on her face.

He kissed her closed eyelids tenderly. "I always knew you'd be even more beautiful in the aftermath of love. Did I make you as happy as you look, sweetheart?"

"Happier than I've ever been." She touched his face with delicate fingertips, tracing the line of one high cheekbone.

Tristan lifted himself up on one elbow to search her face intently. "I didn't plan for this to happen."

"I know," she reassured him.

"Any regrets, Angel?" He needed to hear her say it.

She looked at him with eyes as clear as blue mountain lakes. "Not a one."

It was true. All of her soul searching was behind her. The consuming passion she had shared with Tristan was worth anything that came afterward. For as long as he wanted her she would stay. And when it was over, she would enjoy her memories without regret.

If chilled fingers touched her heart at the thought of life without him, she brushed them away. Nothing was going to spoil what she had right this minute. When Tristan rolled her into his arms again, his eyes darkening to molten gray, Angelique knew she was right.

Chapter Nine

That trip to Paris would always remain in Angelique's memory as an idyllic time, unclouded by what was to come afterward.

Tristan showed her all the famous landmarks of the city. They wandered for hours in the Louvre and strolled hand in hand through the Bois de Boulogne. He took her to charming little restaurants, and sometimes they went dancing afterward. Often though, their eyes would meet and they would cut the evening short.

The nights were filled with the kind of passion Angelique hadn't known existed. Tristan made love to her over and over, and each time it was new and wonderful. Every day when she awoke in his arms, she was flooded with joy.

One morning she woke to find Tristan gazing at her with an expression that sent a chill up her spine. There was tenderness and desire, but also sadness.

"What is it, Tristan? What's wrong?" She moved out of his arms in order to see his face more clearly.

He pulled her back against his quickening body. "I thought you were never going to wake up."

One hand wandered down from her back and over her hip, before starting the return journey to cup her breast. He nibbled delicately on her lower lip while his thumb rotated lazily over her sensitive nipple. It was difficult to resist such an onslaught. Her body's response was immediate, but Angelique had to know what was bothering him.

She grabbed for his disturbing hand. "Tell me why you were looking at me that way."

"Don't I look at you this way every morning?" he teased.

"No, it was different. You seemed...I don't know... sad."

His face sobered and he tilted her head onto his shoulder. "I guess I was thinking about this time we've had together. I hate to see it end."

Ice crystals began to form around Angelique's heart. She had known it wouldn't last, but was it going to be over so soon? Tears tightened her throat, sending her into a panic. Tristan must never know she was in love with him! He thought their mutual attraction was solely sexual, that when it was satisfied neither of them would be touched by it. If he knew how she felt he would be embarrassed, maybe even apologetic. It was too horrible even to think about!

She eased herself out of his arms. "All good things come to an end," she observed brightly. "There's nothing to be sad about."

"I know, but it won't be the same in Souveraine. I hate sharing you with other people."

"Wha—what are you talking about?"

"We have to go home tomorrow, honey. I really stole these extra days, but now things are starting to pile up."

She stared at him numbly. After thinking the gates of paradise had slammed shut in her face, it was hard to believe they were swinging open again. The ice around her heart melted in a blaze of joy.

He didn't seem to notice her silence. "I'm sorry, sweetheart, but we'll make this last day special. You haven't been to the couture houses yet, so I thought we'd do that today and go to the opera this evening. How does that sound?"

"Whatever you want!" She flung her arms around his neck and rained kisses all over his face.

After a surprised moment he wrapped his legs around hers and slid her body beneath him. "As long as you've given me a choice," he murmured in a husky voice. It was afternoon before they were out of the suite. Tristan had ordered a late breakfast in the room. They ate in their robes and looked through the morning paper leisurely.

Tristan glanced up from the sports section, smiling at the picture Angelique made. She was curled up on the couch with her bare feet tucked under the ruffled hem of a flower-sprigged peignoir. Her hair was tied on top of her head with a bright ribbon, and her clear skin was free of makeup.

"My, don't we look domestic?" he chuckled.

She lowered her section of the paper, gazing back at him. Her pulse quickened at the now familiar sight of his taut, lean body. Would she ever get enough of this man? It was almost frightening to feel such love. If only they *were* married, instead of just playing at it.

Angelique rose swiftly to her feet. "I think I'll go take a nice domestic bath," she said lightly.

"I'll join you in a minute," Tristan answered casually, going back to his paper.

After pouring bubble bath in the huge sunken tub, she turned on the taps. When the bubbles formed a thick layer of froth she tossed her robe over a chair and stepped in. Sitting on the little marble seat that projected from one side, Angelique leaned her head back against the sloping edge and closed her eyes. Conscious thought was washed from her mind as happiness took its place.

An upheaval in the water made her eyes fly open. Tristan was lowering himself in beside her. "What are you doing here?" she gasped.

"I told you I'd join you. I thought it would save time if we bathed together." His hand stroked the length of her thigh. "I can scrub your back for you."

"That isn't my back," she pointed out.

"I perform other services too."

"I'll just bet you do!"

"Shame on you," he said reprovingly. Grasping her by the waist he stood her up while he remained seated. He pulled her between his knees and picked up a large sponge. "This is what I meant."

He soaped her body in gentle circular strokes. Starting at her shoulders he glided over the round globes of her breasts to the flat plane of her stomach. When he went beyond, Angelique caught her breath. Her knees gave way and she sank into his lap, clasping her arms around his neck.

Tristan's mouth covered hers, warm and seeking. As his tongue plunged deeply, she ran her hands over the straining muscles of his back. Tristan's slick body was almost unbearably sensuous, moving against her sensitized flesh with the water lapping all around them.

"How is it possible that I want you night and day?" he muttered. His tongue explored the inner curve of her ear. "You're like a fever in my blood, angel mine."

"Tristan, Tristan." She whispered his name like a prayer. If only I could tell you how much I love you, she wished silently.

"I want you now, this minute!" Turning her in his lap, he staked the ultimate male claim.

The piercing wonder of him filled her with rapture as turbulent as the water churning around them. Angelique was rocked by the driving force of his hard body. She twisted in his arms, moving to the beat of wild music. It reached an explosive crescendo that faded gradually into throbbing pleasure. Her rigid body relaxed, and she kissed the hollow in Tristan's throat.

It was an unbelievable experience; their passion was spontaneous and irresistible. When it was sated he cradled her in his arms, whispering tender words in her ear.

It was afternoon before they finally got around to the couturiers, the famous dressmakers of Paris. Angelique didn't intend to buy anything, but she did want to see these fabled salons where the rich and celebrated bought their clothes. She had modeled them; now she wanted to see how her French counterparts did the same thing.

Tristan took her to the establishment of the most prestigious designer. It was located in a town house on a fashionable street. No sign outside gave the illustrious name. Regular customers knew the address, and anyone who didn't probably couldn't afford the prices anyway.

The large first floor salon might have been the living room in an elegant home. Thick white carpeting deadened their footsteps as they were shown into a room with crystal chandeliers hanging from a high ceiling. Everything was white and gold except for the mauve velvet love seats scattered about.

A stunning woman in a simple, but chic, black dress greeted them like honored guests. There was no chance of Tristan being plain Monsieur Charolais here. The receptionist recognized him immediately. Had he accompanied Natalie Caron to this place? And other women as well? Angelique decided not to spoil things by thinking about it.

The illusion of being guests was furthered when they were served coffee in delicate bone china cups. There were no dresses in evidence, or glass display cases. Finally, after some polite small talk, the receptionist summoned another elegant woman who asked if they were interested in any particular kind of gown.

Tristan looked questioningly at Angelique. When she answered vaguely that she wasn't sure, they were shown a whole spectrum of clothes. Graceful models with carefully blank faces glided by, giving them a private fashion show. There were tailored suits for daytime wear and softer versions for evening, silky afternoon dresses, and magnificent gowns for special occasions.

Every now and then Tristan would suggest that she consider a particular outfit, but Angelique always shook her head. She had come to enjoy the show, not to spend a month's salary on a dress. Nor did she intend to let Tristan buy her anything. He didn't seem to understand that it cheapened their relationship somehow. She had given her love freely, but of course he didn't know that's what it was.

One special dress tested Angelique's resolve. It was champagne-colored chiffon, with triple layers of crystal pleats flaring out from the dropped waistline. Rhinestones skimmed the V-neck and formed a band down the front. It looked like an updated version of something worn in the 1920s—designed to catch the eye.

"You can't say no to that one," Tristan declared.

"It's darling, but I really don't need it," she said tentatively, unable to take her eyes off the beguiling gown.

He smiled. "I'm sure you could find some use for it."

The saleslady added her discreet persuasion. "We can take your measurements and have it ready for a first fitting in two weeks."

"First fitting?" Angelique echoed.

"We require at least three."

Angelique shook her head. "Then that settles it. I'm leaving Paris tomorrow."

"No problem." Tristan dismissed her excuse. "We can fly back."

He seemed to take it for granted that she was staying in Souveraine indefinitely. It was a subject Angelique hadn't wanted to discuss, or even think about, but sooner or later she'd have to go home. In spite of her love for Tristan, she couldn't stay on in the ambiguous position of his mistress. Better to leave while his eyes still glowed with ardor. She would pretend that she was leaving because of her career. It wasn't something she could tell him at the moment, however.

"It seems like a lot of running up and back for a dress." She rose gracefully to her feet. "Perhaps some other time."

When they were out on the street Tristan looked at her incredulously. "I can't believe you didn't buy anything."

"I just wanted to see the place."

"It would have given us an excuse to come back to Paris," he reminded her.

"Maybe it's better not to," she answered slowly. "That way nothing can spoil the memory of this time we've had together."

He turned her toward him, gripping her shoulders hard. "Nothing ever will! But you sound as though this is all we're going to have."

"Life doesn't come with a guarantee," she answered soberly.

"Maybe life doesn't, but *I'll* give you one." His hands tightened. "I'll never let you go, Angel."

He must have felt that way about Natalie too, but it hadn't lasted. Maybe Tristan liked to pretend it would, though.

Angelique forced a smile. "If I'd known it was going to lead to all this I would have bought the dress."

"We're still here."

"No, we'd better start getting ready for this evening. I don't want to be late for the opera."

The dress she chose was a short, wine-colored silk with a portrait neckline. It was simply cut, without any frills. The addition of Tristan's diamond and ruby star made it outstanding.

Tristan crossed the room to stand in front of the mirror to tie his tie. Looking at her reflection he said, "I didn't know you'd brought that. Do you like it?"

"It's beautiful. Is it really a medal, Tristan?"

"Would you have accepted it if it weren't?"

"No, I think you knew that. Why did you give it to me?"

He linked his arms loosely around her neck and kissed the top of her head. "When you're in—" He started over. "When you're fond of someone, you want to give her gifts."

Angelique sat very still. Had Tristan been about to say he was in love with her? No, that didn't make sense. What reason would there be for him to hide it? Angelique's lashes drooped to mask her sadness. When would she stop clutching at false hopes?

The Chagall paintings on the ceiling of the Paris opera house were as magnificent as Angelique had always heard. The muted colors and floating figures the famous artist was noted for were breathtaking, especially when spread over such a broad area.

The opera was *Carmen*, one of Angelique's favorites. But she had never seen it performed like this before, with a troupe of live horses on the stage. The pageantry, combined with the rich costumes and beautiful voices, made it a truly memorable performance.

Angelique's eyes were still shining when they got back to the suite. "It's been such a wonderful evening, Tristan!"

"It isn't over yet," he murmured, taking her in his arms.

Their return to Souveraine brought an abrupt change in their lives. Tristan's work had piled up while he was gone, and he was busy all day. He started so early that Angelique didn't even see him at breakfast. They both looked forward to the evenings, but they hadn't counted on Alain.

He was so grateful to Angelique that he dogged her footsteps like a faithful puppy. It was all right during the day when she had nothing to do, but he carried it into the evening as well. Alain felt that he had an obligation to entertain Angelique. After he had shown her all the tourist attractions of Souveraine, he insisted that she swim and play tennis with Suzette and him. Then at night Alain arranged for the four of them to go out together. There was never a moment alone with Tristan.

Alain had been aware of the tension between his uncle and Angelique, and he was delighted that they had resolved it on the trip to Paris. He wanted the two people he loved the best to be friendly. The problem was that he didn't realize just how far they had progressed along those lines.

One night Tristan pulled Angelique into his arms desperately. "I never thought I'd have the urge to do away with my own nephew," he said passionately. They were waiting for Alain in the den before going out to dinner.

Angelique couldn't enjoy the stolen moment. Alain might join them at any second. She mentioned it to Tristan.

"I don't care! It's driving me out of my mind not being able to touch you! Besides, he must know how I feel about you."

"There are some things it's better for him not to know," she said delicately.

Tristan released her, but he scowled as he jammed his hands in his pockets. "You're right, but we can't go on like this. I'm coming to your room tonight."

"No, Tristan, you can't! Alain's rooms are right next to yours—he might hear you."

"You're being ridiculous, Angel." He looked at her sharply. "Don't you want to be with me?"

The expression on her face made his frown disappear. She touched his cheek gently. "More than you'll ever know," she murmured. "But not furtively, like a French farce with people sneaking in and out of bedrooms."

"I understand, sweetheart. I don't want that either." He rumpled his elegantly combed hair. "But what are we going to do?"

Before any solution could be found Alain joined them. "Sorry I'm late. Have you two been able to amuse yourselves without me?" he joked.

As Tristan grew more and more frustrated, Angelique grew increasingly tense. She didn't know what might have happened if Alain hadn't been chosen to be on the national junior tennis team. They were slated to play a match in Monaco, and he would be gone overnight.

"I can go, can't I, Tristan?" Alain asked eagerly.

"I don't see any reason why not."

"Gee thanks! You're the greatest!" Alain exclaimed.

Angelique frowned at Tristan with mock disapproval when they had a moment alone. "I hope you realize what a fraud you are. Letting Alain think you're doing him a big favor by letting him go."

Tristan laughed. "He doesn't know I'd underwrite the whole team's expenses personally if he asked me to."

She put her arms around his neck. "And I'd be happy to chip in."

But when Alain left, Angelique tried to postpone Tristan's ardor. "We can't both go to our rooms at ten o'clock in the morning. How will it look?"

"I don't give a damn! If you think I'm wasting one minute of our time together, you're badly mistaken." Determination was written all over his strong face as he clamped his hand around her wrist.

"Tristan, wait! Isn't there someplace more...how about your studio?" The thought occurred to her out of desperation. "Could we go there?"

He clapped a hand to his forehead. "Of course! Why didn't I think of that?"

"It just seems more...well...private."

"It is. No one is allowed to disturb me there for anything less than war being declared."

When they got to the studio Angelique felt unaccountably self-conscious. The spontaneity of their lovemaking in Paris seemed to be absent. Perhaps because this place had negative connotations for her. Was it a mistake to suggest it?

She braced herself as she looked around the large, untidy room. But all the canvases of Natalie were stacked with their faces to the wall. Angelique brightened. Tristan couldn't have done that for her benefit, since he didn't know they were coming here. She was just being foolish.

Tristan was watching her with expressionless gray eyes. "Would you like some coffee?" he asked quietly.

Angelique accepted quickly. "I'd love a cup."

"There are some croissants in the freezer." He led the way to the small, compact kitchen. "I sometimes feel like a snack in the afternoon if I've skipped lunch. It would only take a few minutes to warm them in the oven."

"No thanks, coffee will be fine." Her heart swelled with love at Tristan's sensitivity. He realized that she was a little hesitant, and he was giving her time to come to terms with it. "Would you like me to make it?" she asked.

"No, coffee is one of my specialties."

Angelique sat down at the small butcher-block table. "One of? What else do you make?"

He laughed. "Did you have to ask that? I'm afraid my only other specialty is chocolate milk."

"That's just milk with syrup in it," she pointed out.

"I hoped you wouldn't know that."

"I don't know a great deal more," she consoled him. "I'm no great shakes in the kitchen either."

Something flickered in his eyes. "I guess we'd have to hire a cook if we got married—either that or live on love."

"A cook sounds more practical." With her eyes downcast, her long lashes were feathering her cheeks so she didn't see Tristan's expression.

"Are you always practical, Angelique? Haven't you ever wanted to take a chance?"

The intensity of his voice made her look up. "Only when there's a possibility of success," she answered evenly.

"And you don't think there is for us?"

Angelique's heart started to race. What was he asking? It couldn't be what it sounded like; he hadn't even told her he loved her. But if there was even the remotest chance that he was serious, she had to find out. How, though, without making a fool of herself?

She stared into her cup as though it held the secrets of the universe. "Were you planning to come to New York?"

He was silent for so long that she glanced up, and her hopes died. The expression on Tristan's face was almost austere. What an idiot she had been! There wasn't even desire evident at the moment.

Then his mouth curved in a smile that didn't reach his eyes. "It's possible. Do you think you'd even remember me if I came to visit?"

Angelique gazed at his beloved face, memorizing the strong planes and angles, although they would never be erased from her heart. "I'll always remember you, Tristan," she answered quietly.

His expression softened swiftly. He knelt by her chair and put his arms around her waist. "Sweet angel mine, why are we worrying about what's going to happen next week or next year? Today is what matters. We have twenty-four wonderful hours. Why are we wasting them?"

He raised her to her feet and together they drifted into the bedroom, gazing wordlessly into each other's eyes. Excitement rose like sap in Angelique's veins as Tristan took her in his arms. Her mouth blossomed under his, opening in the way a flower reacts to the heat of the sun.

His movements quickened at her response and he plundered her mouth more deeply, his hands wandering restlessly over her back. She pressed closer to him, catching fire from the friction of their bodies. The sensation was almost unbearably arousing.

"It's been so long," Tristan groaned, burying his face in her neck. He trailed a line of tantalizing kisses up to her earlobe. "Do you know what torture it was to sit across the table last night and make polite conversation?"

"For me too," she murmured, twining slim fingers through his dark hair.

"Instead of complimenting you on your dress, I wanted to take it off." The tip of his tongue explored the inner cavities of her ear, making Angelique shiver deliciously.

"There's nothing to stop you now," she whispered, starting to unbutton his shirt with eager fingers.

"Nothing could." He framed her face in his palms, looking at her with burning eyes. "I'm going to possess you completely, my darling. I'm going to know every inch of your beautiful body, inside and out."

Angelique closed her eyes briefly as Tristan removed her clothes. But she opened them when he left her for a moment to remove his own. The sight of his virile male form was something she could never get enough of. The wide shoulders tapering to slim hips and a taut stomach, had the perfection of a statue sculpted in bronze. But Tristan's pulsing loins assured her that he was flesh and blood.

They made love in a frenzy of passion, and then they made love more slowly, drawing out the pleasure as long as possible. Angelique had never known such fulfillment, even in Paris. Tristan sought out every erotic spot on her body, caressing her with his mouth and hands until she was a throbbing mass of desire. Then he satisfied her.

They finally drifted off to sleep in each other's arms, totally relaxed. When Angelique awoke some time later, Tristan was looking at her thoughtfully. She was suddenly conscious of her tumbled hair and the fact that all her lipstick was surely gone.

"I must be a mess." She brushed ineffectually at the silken mass of her hair.

Tristan caught her hand and kissed the fingertips. "You're the most beautiful sight in the world—a woman satisfied by love." He sucked the tip of her little finger into his mouth. "You are satisfied, aren't you?"

"Is that an idle question, or are you leading up to something?"

"You're insatiable!" He rolled her over on top of him and wrapped his legs around hers.

"You must have found that out in Paris."

"It was a delightful surprise." He grinned. "Sometimes I have the feeling that I chased you until you caught me."

"Isn't that just like a man!" she cried indignantly. "You seduce me shamelessly and then imply that I led you on!"

His smile broadened. "I'm not complaining."

Angelique sighed. "What am I going to do with you?"

"Anything you like," he assured her. "Does that work both ways?"

She dropped her head to his shoulder, resting her lips against his tanned throat. "You know it does."

This man could ask anything of her and she would give it. He was as necessary to her as breathing or sleeping. A tiny glow of anticipation began to build as she waited for what would come next. Tristan surprised her, however.

He rolled her over on her back and leaned over her, propped on an elbow. "Will you pose for me?"

"Oh...Tristan, I don't know."

"Why do you have reservations, sweetheart?"

How could she tell him that it was because of Natalie? Tristan would protest that the other woman meant nothing to him, which was part of the problem. Angelique wanted to be more than the latest in a stream of changing loves. And if that was impossible, at least she didn't want to be captured for posterity, like a fading snapshot pasted in a scrapbook. Let Tristan search his memory if he wanted to remember her.

She moved out of his arms, pulling the sheet around her shoulders while she searched for an excuse he would accept. "I told you, I don't pose in the nude."

There was a glint of laughter in his eyes as he pulled the sheet down and cupped her breast lovingly in his hand. "I'm not advocating it—do it only for me."

"Please, Tristan!" She stilled his disruptive fingers. It was difficult to think when he was caressing her that way. "I know how you feel about the human body, but it would make me very uncomfortable to have anyone see me like that."

"I promised you no one ever would." He smiled ruefully. "I realize now that I was a little hard on my friend Claremonte. I don't want to share you with the world either."

"Then why do you want to paint me?"

Tristan's eyes wandered over her face. "You aren't the ideal model. I can't find a flaw anywhere." He traced her delicate features with a gentle forefinger. "I don't even know if I can get this perfection down on canvas, but I have to try. You'll be my masterpiece, my own private treasure that will enrich my life."

Angelique felt herself being carried along by the warm current of his voice. "If it means that much to you," she murmured.

He bent his head to kiss her lips. "You know the answer to that."

Before she could be swept under again, Angelique tried for a small concession. "You mentioned a...a scarf, or something."

Tristan laughed, folding her in his arms. "If you insist, my shy little darling. Although I warn you, it's going to be much more suggestive."

"I'll take my chances." Another problem occurred to her. "How long will this take, Tristan?"

A little smile played around his firm mouth. "Who knows? If I spin it out long enough, maybe the rest of your life."

"Are you trying to be the male counterpart of Scheherazade?" she asked lightly.

There was nothing light about Tristan's husky answer. "She only told her stories for a thousand and one nights. I want you for longer than that, Angel."

Would he? Angelique knew she couldn't count on it. Still, what she had now was enough. If only the time weren't so fleeting.

"Really, Tristan, how long do you expect the painting to take?"

"Why do you want to know?"

"Because I can't stay forever. I mean, I'm going to have to start thinking soon about going home."

He frowned. "I thought we'd settled all that."

It was clear that Tristan expected her to stay on as his mistress. Her passionate response could certainly be construed that way, Angelique conceded. But it was time to set the record straight.

"I have to be home by the first week in September at the latest. The new advertising campaign starts then," she explained.

He looked at her with controlled emotion. "You're going back for that?"

"I have to. I have a contract." Angelique was annoyed at the plea for understanding in her voice. Tristan had no right to expect her to stay merely to satisfy his whim of the moment.

"And you're at the peak of your career." The sarcasm she hated so much was back.

"That's right," she answered stiffly.

They stared at each other for a long, challenging moment. Then he swung his long legs out of bed. "Okay, come on."

"Where?" She looked at him blankly.

"If I have to work under a time limit, I'd better get started," he said grimly.

Angelique got up reluctantly. Tristan's switch in moods changed everything. Where was all the tender passion? Posing for him now was going to be like being examined under a microscope by a scientist. But it would only provoke an open argument if she tried to back out.

After hesitating for a moment, she went to the closet and took out a white silk robe of Tristan's. It trailed on the floor, and the sleeves covered her hands, but it was better than walking into the studio naked.

Tristan wasn't troubled by the same qualms. He was wandering around quite unself-consciously, selecting paints and brushes. When he turned around and saw her, a smile broke through his rather forbidding manner.

"That's a great deal more than a scarf," he observed.

"Well, I...I just thought until you..."

"It's okay, sweetheart, I understand." He kissed the top of her head. "Curl up on the couch, and I'll see what I can find to preserve your modesty."

He came back with a long filmy black scarf. "Take off the robe and lie down on your right side."

When she did as he instructed, Tristan tucked a pillow under her head and arranged one arm so it was resting along her side.

"No, that's no good," he muttered. "It hides the flowing curve of your body."

He rearranged her arms and legs, moving them impersonally, as though she were a wax doll with jointed limbs. Angelique was fascinated by his total absorption. For the first time she began to understand what Tristan's work meant to him.

After tilting her chin a final time he stood up. "There, that's perfect!"

She stopped him as he started to walk toward the easel. "My scarf?" she reminded him in a small voice.

"Oh, I forgot." He frowned slightly. "Do you really have to have it?" When she looked at him mutely, he sighed. "All right, but it's a crime to tamper with perfection."

Tristan knelt beside the couch once more. When he flung the scarf the length of her body Angelique felt better, but only for a moment. Then he began to drape it, starting with her breasts. Instead of covering them completely, he pulled the wispy chiffon down until her nipples were only partially veiled. Half of the pink circles peeked out above the edge. Angelique suffered as his fingers brushed against the sensitive points time and again before the position of the scarf was to his liking.

She breathed a sigh of relief when he was finally satisfied, but then he started to drape it over her body. His deft hands were everywhere, lighting bonfires without even being aware of it.

When he was finished Tristan looked at the total result. A subtle change came over him. He said, "I can't paint you like this."

Angelique didn't think she could go through the whole thing all over again. "Why not? What's wrong?" she cried.

"I told you that you'd look more erotic than if you were nude, but I didn't realize just how *much* more." One finger touched the hardened nub of her nipple, rotating over it until her breasts rose and fell rapidly. "How can I keep my mind on my work when you're a temptation no man with blood in his veins could ignore." His voice was smoky with desire.

"I can't go through with it, Tristan," she said with a sigh. "I never knew it would be like this."

"It wasn't supposed to be—it never has been." He rained feverish kisses over her face and neck before tearing aside the drapery and moving down her body. "Right now all I can think about is touching you, breathing the perfume of your skin, tasting you. I can't leave you alone."

Angelique shivered as he continued his fiery path, branding her with tiny stinging kisses. When his teeth nipped gently at the satiny skin of her closed thighs she moved her legs restlessly. He parted them and touched her intimately, sending a shock through Angelique's entire body.

Tristan gripped her hips while he rubbed his cheek over the tight muscles of her stomach. "You're so soft and smooth," he murmured. "Your skin is like creamy velvet."

Her fingers tangled in his hair and she pulled him up to her, reaching desperately for his lips. As his mouth closed over hers, Angelique arched her body into Tristan's, digging her nails into his firm buttocks. She had never felt so wild, so totally out of control.

The words she whispered in his ear made him clasp her tighter. Her name was like a prayer on his lips as he filled her with plunging rapture.

Spiraling circles of pleasure vibrated between them, increasing in intensity until their bodies were taut. The throbbing wonder of him drove her to dizzying heights. When the peak was reached, Angelique was bathed in a warm glow that dissolved all tension. She floated down weightlessly, clasped in Tristan's arms while her body pulsed with the aftermath of passion.

They remained curled together for a long time. Finally he stirred enough to kiss her temple. "Maybe next time you'll listen to me."

"What do you mean?" Angelique felt too languid to open her eyes.

"I told you that scarf would cause trouble."

Her mouth curved in a smile. "You didn't seem to feel that way a few minutes ago."

"Has anyone ever told you that you're a brazen little hussy?" Tristan laughed and bit her ear. "And I wouldn't have it any other way. But from now on we're going to dispense with the scarf, until after working hours anyway."

"You still want to paint me?"

"Of course. Why would I change my mind?"

"Well...you don't seem to have much willpower," she said mischievously.

"You're going to pay for that, young woman! Next time you'll beg me to make love to you."

"I did this time," she answered softly, stroking his cheek.

"You don't have to ask, sweetheart," he said huskily, turning his head to kiss her palm. "I'm yours whenever you want me."

He didn't know that would be for the rest of her life. But it no longer mattered. Angelique knew she wouldn't change a thing she'd done. The wonder she'd shared with Tristan was something most women never achieved in their entire lifetimes.

Chapter Ten

The days flowed by in a haze of pleasure. Angelique enjoyed each golden moment, managing to ignore the fact that September was approaching. Tristan never mentioned it either. It was a distant storm cloud on the horizon, but for the present, life was perfect.

They had the joy of seeing each other every day, and whenever Tristan could manage time away from his duties, they made beautiful, fulfilling love in his studio. All the tension between them was gone, including the frustration of never being alone together. Everyone accepted the fact that Tristan was doing a painting of Angelique. However, as the work progressed, he wouldn't let her see the partially done canvas.

"How do I know you're not giving me that extra eye you mentioned?" she complained.

He smiled warmly at her. "You don't need anything extra, you're perfect just the way you are. Now stop trying to distract me."

"How could I do that?" She gazed at him through long, flirty lashes. "I thought the nude form was supposed to inspire artists."

"In your case, a little too much." Tristan's eyes started to smolder as they swept over her bare body. He put his palette down. "I think we've done enough work for today."

By the time Angelique came down to breakfast each morning, Tristan was already hard at work. Although he begrudged the time and hated the paperwork, he was extremely conscientious. Sometimes she didn't see him all day, so Angelique stopped by his office to say good morning. It was a special ritual they both looked forward to.

One day she found several other people with him. As she started to leave Tristan stopped her. "Don't go, Angel."

"You're busy," she said. Chef Ducloix was one of the people, along with Mrs. Voisin, the housekeeper, and Tristan's secretary, Charles.

"Never too busy for you." Tristan never made any attempt to hide his feelings for her. "Besides, maybe you can help me with some of this stuff. You're good at parties."

"What's going on?" she asked cautiously.

"Victoire Day is coming up. Didn't I mention it?"

"No, this is the first I've heard of it."

"It's a national holiday, supposedly to celebrate the date back in the fifteen hundreds when the barbarians were driven out of Souveraine. But mostly it's just an excuse for a lot of festivities."

"You have a party?" Angelique asked.

Tristan sighed. "It's a little more than that."

"The palace is thrown open to the public," Charles explained. "They come to pay their respects to the prince."

"Also to eat and drink," Tristan commented dryly.

"In the evening there is a large formal reception," Charles continued unperturbed. "That, of course, is private."

"Sounds like fun, but a little out of my league," Angelique remarked. "I've never given a party on that scale."

"You just order more of everything," Tristan said. "Besides, I don't want you to do any of the work, just make decisions. I don't have time for that sort of thing."

"What kind of decisions?" Remembering her clash with Chef Ducloix, Angelique wasn't about to tangle with him again.

"The kind you can make better than I—which china to use, what kind of flowers to put where. How the devil would I know?" Tristan scowled. "What we need around here is a woman."

"It really would be helpful if you could handle some of the details for the duke, Miss Archer." The housekeeper was clearly eager to have her do it, probably because Tristan was more of a hindrance than a help, with his famous impatience. It had never occurred to Angelique that the palace really required a woman as well as a man to run it.

"I'd be happy to do anything I can," she told the woman.

The days that followed were very busy for Angelique. She enjoyed being occupied again after her long vacation. It was also fun to plan a party where both money and help were unlimited. She threw herself into the details so wholeheartedly that Tristan started to complain.

"Where were you all day?" he demanded when she didn't get home until late afternoon.

"I had to run to a million different places before I located our pattern in wineglasses. We're at least six dozen short for the party."

He regarded her with a mixture of amusement and annoyance. "You didn't have to do that. We call Monsieur Bonfils, and he sends them over."

"Except that they were out of stock, and it will take six weeks to get them. Honestly, Tristan, do you know how much breakage there's been that hasn't been replaced? Someone ought to keep an inventory so there isn't all this rush at the last minute."

"Well...uh...maybe Mrs. Voisin did mention it." He looked slightly sheepish.

"All you had to do was sign an authorization," Angelique scolded.

"It's probably buried under that mountain of papers on my desk."

"Well, don't worry, I took care of it."

"You also ruined my day. I worked like a galley slave so I could have the afternoon free. Your painting is almost done and I wanted to finish it."

"Oh, darling, I'm so sorry! I wish you'd told me."

He took her in his arms, burying his face in her neck. "That wasn't the only reason I was disappointed." Tristan's hands moved down her back, molding her lower body to his.

Angelique felt the familiar warm tide rising inside her. "If you're willing to skip dinner, maybe we can make up for lost time," she murmured.

"Just what I was thinking." They smiled into each other's eyes.

Much later, Angelique ran her nails lightly up and down Tristan's naked thigh. "Are you really almost finished with the painting?"

He matched her caress by stroking her breast with feathery fingertips. "Yes, I expect to finish it tonight if you aren't too tired."

She put her arms around his neck and rolled over on top of him. "Wouldn't tomorrow do just as well?"

Before his mouth closed over hers, Tristan said deeply, "Or whenever we get around to it."

It was actually the day before the festivities that he finally found the time. Tristan worked intently that day, scarcely hearing Angelique's occasional comments. After a while she lapsed into a contented silence, watching his supple movements and absorbed face. The companionship between them was very precious.

Angelique was surprised when Tristan stuck his brushes in a jar of turpentine and started to clean his hands on a rag. It was still early in the afternoon. "Are you quitting so soon?" she asked.

"It's finished." He was looking at the canvas with quiet satisfaction.

"Can I see it?" She jumped up and slipped into Tristan's silk robe.

"Yes, I'd like you to."

Angelique didn't know what she expected, but certainly nothing so overwhelming. The large painting on the easel was obviously done by someone with great talent. The flesh tones were extremely lifelike, also the impression of delicate bones under smooth skin. But it was the love shining from her face that appalled Angelique. It was there for the whole world to see! Tristan had captured not only her face and figure, but her inner feelings as well.

"It...it's very good," she faltered.

"It's more than just good." He tilted his head to one side, examining the canvas critically. "It's the best work I've ever done."

"I'm glad you think so," she said faintly.

"It isn't just my opinion. Anyone would tell you the same thing."

Angelique's blood ran cold. "You said no one would see it!"

"They won't." He took her in his arms. "You can relax, my modest little angel."

Tristan thought she was worried about being seen in the nude, when actually that was the least of her worries now. It seemed incredible that he didn't perceive what was so glaringly obvious to her. Perhaps because he was too involved with the actual mechanics of art. But a disinterested onlooker would spot it immediately. Angelique's soul would be as naked as her body!

"I know you'd like to exhibit it, Tristan, but I...I just wouldn't be comfortable about it."

"You're wrong, sweetheart." He tilted her chin up, gazing down at her with loving eyes. "This painting is for my pleasure alone. In my own way I've created you, and I want you to belong only to me."

"I always will," she whispered.

A fierce light of joy filled his face as he bent his head to kiss her, and Angelique knew Tristan had misunderstood. It was true that she would always belong to him, but it would shortly be in spirit only. Tristan had never said the words that would make her stay.

Victoire Day dawned bright and clear, which was a distinct blessing. Red and white striped refreshment tents had been set up on the lawn for the hundreds of people expected, but rain would have sent them all inside at once.

Angelique was dressed and downstairs early. She was wearing a thin white cotton dress with lace down the front. The sleeves were long and trimmed with lace, and the short skirt was gathered onto a peach-colored hip-band. Because of the amount of standing she would be doing, her shoes were low-heeled sandals.

Tristan started to chuckle when he saw her. "If you had a big bow under your chin you'd look like a little French schoolgirl."

"I thought I'd save the glamour for tonight, but if you think this dress isn't right I can go up and change."

"You look adorable." He put his arms around her and gave her a squeeze. "I want to thank you for all the work you did. Mrs. Voisin implied that you're much easier to work with than I," he admitted.

"I was glad to do it. Besides, you shouldn't be bothered with details like that. Your job is running the country."

"We make a good team, don't we?"

Angelique was dazzled by the thought of just how superb a team they could be. Had there been a deeper meaning behind his casual statement? Something special in his eyes? But Tristan was called away by one of the servants, leaving Angelique to answer her own question.

The afternoon was great fun. Angelique wandered among the crowds on the spacious lawns, talking to everyone. She found the people of Souveraine very friendly. She also eavesdropped shamelessly, finding the consensus of opinion was that the prince was charming, and the duke was gorgeous. Both opinions she agreed with heartily.

One conversation, however, made her sorry she had indulged in the innocent game. Two women on the other side of a hedge were talking about her.

"That Miss Archer is certainly beautiful, isn't she? It's no wonder the duke is infatuated with her."

"He does get the women," her friend answered. "Natalie Caron was stunning too."

"I like this one better. She's—oh, I don't know—softer somehow."

"It's too bad if she is. That's the kind that gets hurt."

"Well, maybe he'll marry this one. It's about time the duke settled down."

"Oh, Marie, don't be such a ninny! He's not going to marry her."

"Why not?" The other woman was defensive.

"For one thing, I don't think he's through sowing his wild oats. For another thing, she's an American. And besides that, I hear she's a model."

"So what? Princess Grace was a movie actress, and the people of Monaco loved her."

"That's true, but the duke just looks like he ought to be married to somebody royal."

"None of his girlfriends have been titled," Marie pointed out.

Her friend's snicker was cynical. "There's a big difference between romance and marriage."

Angelique had remained rooted to the spot, unable to move. When the women drifted off she found she was trembling. None of what they said was new to her, but it was painful to hear it put into words. One of those women was very astute. Angelique *was* the kind that got hurt.

Tristan joined her as soon as she moved into the crowd again. "Where have you been, Angel? I've been looking all over for you."

Angelique forced a bright smile. "I've been talking to everyone."

"Not everyone. There were a couple of people who wanted to meet you. They asked who that exquisite vision in white was, and I knew immediately who they meant." He took her hand, bringing it to his lips so he could kiss her fingertips.

It was late before the last reluctant guest left the palace grounds. There wasn't much time to get ready for the evening's event.

As Angelique took the yellow chiffon gown out of the closet, her hurried movements slowed. It brought back memories of her first night in Souveraine. She had been so outraged when Tristan inadvertently walked in on her. Would she ever have believed that she'd wind up posing in the nude for him? She was still smiling when Tristan stopped by her room.

"I just wanted a moment alone with you before the hordes descend on us again." He took her in his arms and buried his face in her hair. "I've hardly seen you all day."

"Be careful or you'll spoil my hairdo." She clasped her hands around his neck, not really caring.

"How about your makeup?" His lips barely grazed hers in a butterfly caress. "If I'm very gentle, can I kiss you?"

Angelique's lips opened softly as she lifted her head. "You can kiss me any way you like."

Tristan's tongue entered her mouth eagerly, staking a claim in the moist warmth. He parted the lapels of her robe and ran his hands over her body, groaning deep in his throat. "If only we had more time. It's torture to touch you and not be able to make love to you."

"I know, darling, but we have to be downstairs in just a few minutes." Angelique might not have been so practical if she'd known it would be her last chance to lie in Tristan's arms.

The palace looked lovely. Angelique never knew how the servants performed such quiet miracles, but all the downstairs rooms had been swept and dusted after the afternoon's invasion. Dozens of candles provided a soft counterpart to the glittering chandeliers, and masses of flowers perfumed the air. Background music from a string quartet was gently unobtrusive. A large orchestra would take over later in the evening.

By now Angelique knew a great many of the guests. The palace was also beginning to feel like home. New

York and her former life seemed light-years away. As she moved gracefully through the elegant rooms, stopping to chat with acquaintances, Angelique was filled with happiness. It came to an abrupt halt when she saw Tristan talking to a new arrival.

His dark head was bent over the sparkling face of a stunning redhead. Angelique recognized Natalie Caron immediately. The woman was as beautiful as her paintings, and just as sensual. Her low-cut satin dress showcased creamy white shoulders and full, swelling breasts. But it wasn't just her lush figure. Some women radiated sexuality the way a flower gave off perfume.

Angelique hated the jealousy that rose like a choking lump in her throat. She was about to turn away when Tristan's eyes caught hers across the room. He started toward her immediately, bringing Natalie with him. There was no way to avoid the meeting.

After the introductions had been made, Natalie remarked, "I just returned from your country. It's quite fascinating."

"Was it your first visit?" Angelique asked politely.

"Yes, but certainly not the last. Your city of New York is utterly marvelous—the theater, the simply divine shopping."

"Better than Paris?" Tristan was amused at her superlatives.

"Ah well, there is only one Paris."

The smile she gave him was like a stab in Angelique's midsection. Had Tristan taken Natalie there too? Was it a little bonus he gave to all his mistresses?

"Do you agree?" There was a special look in Tristan's eyes as he turned to Angelique, a secret reminder of their recent trip.

She was outraged. How dare he remind her of the passion they'd shared, when his former girlfriend was standing there recalling the same experience! "I don't mean to sound chauvinistic, but I prefer to buy my clothes in New York,'' she told Natalie, refusing to look at Tristan.

The other woman gazed admiringly at her dress. "If you found that gown there, I don't blame you."

Angelique was infuriated when Tristan grinned broadly. If he told Natalie the truth she would never forgive him! When he didn't say anything, Angelique answered vaguely, "I don't spend a lot of time shopping."

"My husband wishes I could say the same thing." Natalie laughed.

"Angelique is a career girl," Tristan said.

"Really? What do you do?" Natalie asked.

"I'm a photographic model."

"This is America's Dream Girl." Tristan's mockery was thinly veiled.

Natalie looked puzzled for a moment, then her brow cleared. "Of course! I thought your face looked familiar. You advertise that shampoo, don't you? I've seen your picture in magazines." She regarded Angelique critically. "You must have to be very careful of your hair to keep it in such glorious condition."

"Thank you, but I don't do anything special."

All the mockery was gone as Tristan touched Angelique's curls gently. "She was born beautiful."

Natalie's eyes narrowed as she began to understand the relationship between them. "How very fortunate for you, Miss Archer," she remarked dryly. "The rest of us have to spend hours over our appearance."

Tristan laughed. "Stop fishing for compliments, Natalie. You're a married woman with a very jealous husband."

She batted her lashes at him. "Even married women like to be told they're attractive."

"I'm sure your husband does that regularly."

"It isn't the same."

For just an instant there was a naked expression of
hunger in Natalie's eyes. It was gone in a second, but
Angelique was appalled. This woman still wanted Tristan. Their affair was over long ago, and she had made a
new life for herself, yet he still owned part of her heart.
It must be galling to meet his new mistress. The most
chilling thing was the way Tristan treated Natalie with
casual affection, like a favorite cousin. Angelique knew
she was looking into the face of the future.

"I...if you'll excuse me." She made a mumbled excuse and walked away.

Nothing could salvage the evening after that. Angelique longed for it to be over, but the worst was yet to
come. She tried to put them out of her mind, yet in the
middle of a conversation her eyes would sweep the room,
looking for a tall dark man with a stunning redhead.

Angelique saw Natalie leave by the French doors to the
terrace. A short time later she saw Tristan follow her.

It was useless to tell herself that he wasn't in love with
Natalie anymore. She was a beautiful, desirable woman,
and he was a virile man, one who had once enjoyed her
thoroughly. It was more than coincidence that they both
felt the need for a breath of air. There was something
furtive in the way they left separately. Angelique hated
herself for what she was going to do but she had to find
out.

There were voices coming from Tristan's studio, as she
had known there would be. Angelique's heart was en-
cased in a band of ice so freezing that her whole chest felt
constricted. How could he bring Natalie here after what
they had shared in this idyllic place? The cold voice of
reason reminded her that he had shared the same thing
with Natalie.

The pain deepened when she looked through the open
window and saw them standing in front of the painting
of her that he had finished only the previous day. So

much for Tristan's promises! Angelique was about to return to the palace when the final blow fell.

Natalie was staring at the canvas somberly. "The girl's in love with you, Tristan."

"Love has never been mentioned," he replied grimly.

"No, I suppose not. In your own way you play fair."

"You don't understand. Angelique didn't even want to pose for me."

"I can just imagine how you persuaded her" was the cynical response.

"No, you can't! This isn't what you're thinking," Tristan insisted. At least he was trying to save her reputation.

"I see a girl with love shining in her eyes, a vulnerable girl who's going to get hurt." Natalie turned her head. "And I see a man who doesn't want to admit it."

Angelique turned and fled back to the palace, her degradation complete. Would Tristan believe Natalie? It was vital to convince him that she was wrong, but nothing could be the same now. Nothing could change the fact that he had allowed Natalie, of all people, to see her painting.

Angelique was part of a group when Tristan returned. Her face was frozen in a fixed smile, and she wasn't following a word of the conversation. He took her arm and led her away unobtrusively.

"Keep a stiff upper lip, honey. They have to leave sometime." His eyes gleamed with amusement.

"I'm enjoying myself," she said coldly. "And I should think you would be too. It must be nice to see old friends again."

His amusement faded as he noticed her rigid expression. "You mean Natalie. I didn't know she would be here tonight. I haven't seen her in months."

"Is that why you picked the studio for your reunion?" Angelique was taut with anger.

Comprehension was evident in Tristan's expression. "I'm sorry about that, Angel. I had no idea she would go there. When I realized, and went after her, it was too late. She had already seen your painting."

"You don't honestly expect me to believe that?" Angelique asked scornfully.

"It just happens to be the truth." Lines formed around his firm mouth. "What reason would I have to lie?"

"Possibly because you think I'd care. I do consider it a little tacky to...renew old acquaintances...with her husband here. But, of course, I'm not one of the nobility!"

"I ought to put you over my knee and whack some sense into at least one end of you." Tristan's nostrils flared in anger.

"Don't worry, I'm not about to tell him," Angelique said defiantly, although she felt sick inside.

He stared at her in frustration for a long moment before grabbing her wrist in a viselike grip. "Come with me, I want to talk to you in private."

She was dragged along against her will, not wanting to hear his excuses. There was nothing Tristan could say that would lessen the hurt.

The entry hall was already occupied by another couple having an argument. A distinguished-looking older man was confronting Natalie furiously. He was obviously her husband.

"I should have known better than to bring you here!" His voice quivered with emotion.

"This jealousy of yours has gotten out of hand, Phillipe," Natalie answered impatiently. "You suspect me of carrying on with every man I even smile at."

"Not *every* man—just the one who knew you before I did. It was stupid to think you could stay away from him!"

"Oh, for—" Her annoyed exclamation was broken off as she noticed Tristan. He had paused in the doorway when he saw the other couple quarreling.

Phillipe Claremonte followed her gaze. "Well, if it isn't the grand duke himself! It was good of you to bring my wife back to me, even if she didn't want to come."

"Will you please tell this madman that we didn't leave the party together?" Natalie demanded of Tristan.

"I've never accused you of being obvious, my dear," her husband said sarcastically.

"Too bad she can't say the same about you." Tristan's eyes glittered with cold anger.

"You're scarcely in any position to give lessons in behavior," Phillipe replied furiously.

"Will you two stop it?" Natalie stormed. "Tell Phillipe the reason you came to the studio after me, that you didn't want me to see—" She stopped abruptly, suddenly aware of Angelique's presence.

When they had first stumbled onto the other couple, Angelique was embarrassed. She kept trying to back away, but Tristan wouldn't release her wrist. Now she stood perfectly still.

After an awkward moment Natalie gave a tiny laugh. "Tristan doesn't allow anyone into his studio unless they're invited. He doesn't like people to see his work before it's finished."

"Surely you can do better than that," her husband mocked.

Natalie's patience came to a swift end. "I really feel sorry for you, Phillipe, but that doesn't mean I intend to put up with your paranoia." She turned her back on him. "Believe me, Tristan, this will never happen again."

As she swept out with her beautiful head held high, Phillipe's expression changed to alarm. He hurried after his wife, calling her name.

There was a pulsing silence after they left. Angelique was busy trying to adjust to what she had just heard. Tristan had told the truth! He hadn't arranged to meet Natalie at the studio. It was her own insecurity that had led her to believe such a thing. Was there any way she could make amends? A quick look at his grim face wasn't reassuring.

"I guess I was as guilty as Lord Claremonte of jumping to conclusions," she said haltingly.

"What makes you sure you weren't right?" His sardonic answer told her that Tristan wasn't going to forgive easily.

"Anyone might have thought the same thing under the circumstances." Her voice was muted.

"Anyone who had lain in my arms only yesterday, experiencing everything a man and a woman can share?"

"Please, Tristan." Angelique's lashes veiled her eyes.

He forced her chin up roughly. "Don't pretend to be shy with me. I've seen you flame in my arms and beg me to make love to you."

Angelique met his angry eyes squarely. "I'm not the only woman who's done that. Can't you understand how I would feel if I thought that you and Natalie..."

"You couldn't possibly think that!"

"She was an important part of your life." It was painful but it had to be said. "You can't be totally indifferent to her."

"That was before I ever met you. It's been over for both of us for a long time."

Did he really believe that? "Why did she go to your studio?"

"You still think we met by arrangement?" He looked at her incredulously.

"No, I know you didn't," Angelique said hastily. "I...I just wondered why she went there alone, in the middle of a party."

"A whim." He dismissed it with a shrug. "She wanted to see the paintings of herself again. Natalie knew I wouldn't discard them. They were some of the best things I'd done, until yours. I saw Natalie leave, but I thought she had just gone outside for some air. When she didn't come back, I guessed where she'd gone, and I went after her." He looked somberly at Angelique for a moment. "I'm not surprised at Claremonte's interpretation, but I don't deserve yours."

"What a lovely party, Tristan!" A woman's voice broke the tense silence between them. "You've really outdone yourself this year."

"Yes, everyone is commenting on it." A second woman who had accompanied the first added her praise.

After a flash of irritation at the interruption, Tristan managed a polite smile. "I'm glad you're enjoying yourselves."

"You must tell us where you got that charming string quartet."

Angelique used the diversion to slip away. She needed some time alone to sort out her chaotic thoughts. Every instinct urged her to accept Tristan's explanation, to gloss over the unpleasantness. After all, he *had* told her the truth. But Angelique couldn't let it go at that. In a dark corner of the terrace she faced what she had become—an insecure, clinging mistress, with no claim on the man she loved.

When she thought of the shrewish way she had accused Tristan of being unfaithful, Angelique shriveled inside. It wasn't true in this case, but there would come a time when his interest would start to wane. He wouldn't be furious at an accusation of infidelity, he'd be bored by her jealousy. The expression of distaste on his face tonight was a portent of what was to come.

If she could make the kind of scene she'd made this evening, what would happen when Tristan told her it was over? Angelique shuddered in the protective darkness. It was time to end it herself before their memories on both sides were marred by tears and recriminations.

Once the decision had been made Angelique knew it had to be acted on immediately. She would go home the next day. Tristan couldn't help but know that it was all tied up with Natalie and the painting, but maybe she could use it to her advantage. The crucial thing was to strike just the right note. It would be devastating if he ever guessed her true reason for leaving!

The evening dragged on until Angelique's nerves were at the breaking point. When the last guest had been shown out she said to Tristan, "For once I agree with you. I thought they'd never leave."

"No one could ever tell," Alain commented. The three of them had gathered in the den. "You were the perfect hostess. Just what we've been needing around here, right, Tristan?"

Tristan's eyes rested broodingly on Angelique. There was still a coolness present, which told her that all wasn't forgiven, nor forgotten. Perhaps that would make it easier.

"Angelique did a lot of work even before the party," Tristan remarked, not really answering Alain's question.

"You can consider it payment for my room and board," she said flippantly.

"We're not in the habit of charging guests." Tristan's frown showed his displeasure.

"Anyone who stays as long as I have, can't be considered a guest anymore," she answered, laying the groundwork.

"You have a permanent invitation," Alain assured her. He stood up and stretched. "I think I'll turn in. Suzette and I are playing tennis early in the morning."

"The energy of youth." Tristan smiled as he watched his nephew leave the room. The smile faded when he turned back to Angelique and noticed her strained expression. "You'd better go to bed too. You look tired."

"Maybe a little," she admitted.

"Stay in bed tomorrow; I'll have your breakfast sent up. There's no reason for you to get up early."

"I'm leaving tomorrow, Tristan," she said quietly.

"Leaving?" His eyes narrowed. "When did you decide that?"

"I told you I had to go home," she evaded.

"But why so suddenly? Why tomorrow?"

"Well, I...it's as good a day as any."

"It's Natalie, isn't it? You still think there's something between us." A muscle jerked at the point of his strong jaw.

"No, I'm sure there isn't."

"Then what other reason would you have for making up your mind without even telling me."

"I'm telling you now."

There was leashed anger in his powerful body as he rose to stand over her. "Don't fence with me, Angelique. Something's happened, and I want to know what. If it isn't Natalie, then what's bothering you?"

"In a way you were right the first time." Angelique looked down at her hands. This was the tricky part. "I *was* upset when I thought you had asked Natalie to meet you in the studio. In fact I...I was furious. The studio had become special to me. I felt almost as though no one else had a right to be there but us."

Tristan dropped to one knee and put his arms around her waist. "Darling, don't you know—"

"No, wait! Let me finish." She put her palms against his chest to hold him off. "When I calmed down and started to think about it, I realized I was turning into something I detest—a possessive woman."

"Is that so bad?" His voice dropped to a husky register as his hands caressed her back. "We've belonged to each other completely."

Angelique shook her head. "We've made love with no strings attached because that's what we both wanted. We're very good together sexually."

He stared at her. "Are you saying that what we've shared has been the mere gratification of a mutual urge?"

She sighed. "Men are really more romantic than women. You like to pretend every affair is a grand passion that will never end, but there comes a time to be practical."

He stood up, looking down at her with gathering anger. "And you're always practical, aren't you, Angelique?"

"Not always. I let myself get a little more involved this time than I usually do." She was amazed at how calm her voice remained while her heart was breaking wide open.

"So you're running away before you get in any deeper," he said contemptuously.

"I wouldn't call it that. I told you I had to go home."

"In September," he reminded her.

"Well, it's almost that now, and I really should get in touch with my agent ahead of time. It takes ages to negotiate a new contract, and I want to be sure he asks for more money."

Tristan's cynical gaze swept over her face and figure, lingering on the small, rounded breasts. "You're certainly worth it." He made it sound like an insult.

She wanted to wrap her arms around her body for protection. Instead, she made herself relax against the back of the chair. "Well, nothing is forever. You have to get it while you can."

"That's what I always say." His smile was mocking.

Angelique felt swift color flood her cheeks. She sprang to her feet. "You don't have to be crude! That really wasn't worthy of you."

He shrugged. "I thought you believed in telling it like it is. You were being rather frank yourself."

"I'm sorry if your feelings are hurt because I refuse to pretend we meant more to each other," she said stiffly. "If you were as honest you'd admit it."

His eyes were like an impenetrable gray curtain as he gazed at her. "I suppose you're right—about everything. I guess I do like to think I've found the perfect woman, the one I want to spend the rest of my life with. It hasn't worked out that way though." He raised a derisive eyebrow. "I guess I'm just annoyed that you made me face the fact before I was quite ready to give you up."

Angelique felt she had taken as much as she could stand. There wasn't any reason to prolong the misery anyway. She held out her hand. "Well, goodbye, Tristan, and thanks for everything."

He looked mockingly at her hand. "A formal handshake? That really is a little absurd, Angel, under the circumstances. I think a goodbye kiss is in order, at the very least."

Before she could back away he took her in his arms. She went rigid and pushed against his shoulders, but he held her easily. His mouth covered hers when she opened it to protest, and his tongue slipped inside to probe sensuously.

It was what Angelique had feared the most. How could she keep up the fiction of indifference when every inch of her longed for him? She held her body taut, trying to avoid contact with his. But Tristan was bent on extracting every ounce of revenge. He drew her inexorably closer until she was molded to the full, wondrous length of him. His hard chest dug into her breasts while his thighs joined hers in a remembered union. In spite of all her efforts,

Angelique's hands moved caressingly over his shoulders, tracing their width before her fingers plunged into his thick hair.

Tristan's mouth was burning its brand on her, reinforcing his ownership. How could she leave him? Was she making a mistake? Suppose Tristan felt more than passion for her? Angelique's willpower was slipping rapidly. If he asked her to stay...

When he finally released her, Tristan seemed shaken, but he recovered swiftly. "You were right about another thing, Angel, although you understated it woefully. We're dynamite together as man and woman."

She needn't have worried about Tristan asking her to stay, Angelique reflected bitterly. Once he started being honest, he admitted to his only interest in her.

Chapter Eleven

Angelique was packing when Alain arrived at her room. "One of the servants told me you were leaving." He looked upset.

"Yes, I have to go home." She finished folding a sweater and put it in her suitcase.

"There's nothing wrong, is there? I mean, this is kind of unexpected."

"Not really. I spoke to Tristan about it some time ago. I guess I never mentioned it to you."

"He didn't say anything either. Why doesn't anyone ever tell me anything?" Alain complained.

"I wouldn't have left without saying goodbye."

"Well, I should hope not! Do you really have to go, Angelique? I'm going to miss you terribly."

She stopped packing to look at him fondly. Tears weren't far away. "I'm going to miss you, too, Alain dear, but we'll keep in touch."

"That's for sure, but it won't be the same. Having you here has changed my whole life," he said earnestly.

"I'm glad if I helped, but you don't need me anymore."

"That's not so. Tristan and I both need you."

Angelique went back to her packing. "Your uncle is the most self-sufficient man I know."

"Not really. He's bored and miserable in this job. The time he spent with you was the only relaxation he's had lately. Tristan's been like a different man since you've been here."

"I can scarcely stay on just to amuse him," she said sharply. "I do have a career of my own."

"I know." Alain looked pensive. "It's hard to remember when you were just a picture in a magazine, and I wrote you all those dumb letters. You must have thought I was a real flake."

"No, I thought you were a very lonely person," she answered gently. "But that's all over with."

"You knew I was in love with you, didn't you?" he asked soberly.

"You weren't really. We both knew that."

"It took me a while to figure it out." He gave her a shamefaced smile. "I really was a pain in the ankle, wasn't I? It sounds crazy now, but I thought Tristan was trying to take you away from me just to break us up. I should have realized how he felt about you right from the start."

"Tristan was only doing what he thought was best for you," Angelique said matter-of-factly. "He was just too impatient to be subtle about it."

Alain shook his head. "I might have acted like a kid when I thought I was in love with you, but I'm not blind, Angelique."

She wasn't stupid enough to let herself hope again. "Your uncle and I enjoyed each other's company, but that's all there was to it," she said firmly.

"Not for Tristan. I've seen him with other women, and I've seen him with you. There's a big difference. I can't believe he'd let you go without a struggle."

"There's your answer," Angelique said tartly.

"What did he say when you told him?"

"He just kissed me goodbye." Angelique's voice was calm, but her hands crumpled the blouse she was folding into a wrinkled mess.

Alain frowned. "I don't understand it. I know him so well."

"You're just an incurable romantic," she said lightly, trying to smooth out the blouse.

"Don't you care anything at all about him?" Alain asked searchingly.

"I think he's a very interesting man. Now if you don't mind, Alain, I really have to finish packing. My plane leaves in two hours."

Alain's young face was concerned as he went to look for his uncle. He found Tristan at the stable.

"Why didn't you tell me Angelique was leaving?" he demanded.

Tristan's expression wasn't welcoming. "I just found out last night."

"She said she told you some time ago."

A look of outrage was immediately replaced by indifference. "Perhaps she did. I don't remember." He turned away to throw a saddle over the big black horse that was tossing his head restlessly.

"Don't hand me that, Tristan! None of this adds up. Did you two have an argument or something?"

Tristan smiled sardonically. "I'll give you a little tip. Never argue with a woman—you can't win."

"You *did* quarrel then!"

"Don't be ridiculous. Angelique is going home to resume her career, which is the most important thing in her life," he muttered grimly.

"Did you ask her to stay?"

"Why on earth would I do that?"

"Because I think you're in love with her," Alain stated confidently.

Tristan's eyes narrowed dangerously, but he kept his voice even. "You're imagining things."

"Don't let her get away," Alain urged. "She's someone special."

"My dear nephew, when you grow up a little more you'll discover that the world is full of beautiful women." The sardonic smile was back. "All of them special in their own way."

He put one foot in the stirrup and vaulted onto the horse's back. As Alain watched silently, Tristan spurred the spirited stallion into a restless gallop.

The stores were full of fall fashions when Angelique returned to New York, although the late August days were still uncomfortably hot. She missed the cooling breezes of Souveraine and the smell of flowers instead of exhaust fumes. Actually Angelique missed a great deal more than that, but she tried not to think about it.

Forgetfulness became a way of life. She plunged into a frantic social whirl, accepting every invitation that came along. It wasn't her usual life-style, yet it helped her to keep busy. She was so tired when she went to bed in the early hours of the morning that she fell asleep immediately. Then the dreams began.

Angelique could block Tristan out of her thoughts during her waking hours, but the nights were filled with him. He invaded her bed and her body, making love to her with such exquisite tenderness that she cried out his name in her sleep. Each remembered caress was repeated in her dreams. Tristan's passionate kisses on every secret part of her drove Angelique to such heights that she begged for fulfillment. The rapture would die when she awoke to find herself achingly alone.

She looked forward to going back to work, hoping that would break the cycle of pointless days and agonizing nights. Once she was back in the familiar routine, Souveraine and everything connected with it would fade from her memory. Or if that was too much to expect, at least it wouldn't always be uppermost in her mind.

Phil Nestor greeted her with a bear hug and a kiss on the cheek. "Boy am I glad to see your beautiful face again. All I've been doing this past month is photographing jocks with beer cans in their fists."

"What's the matter, wouldn't they share with you?" she teased.

"It almost did drive me to drink, trying to deal with their egos. Not like you, Angel. Let me look at you." Phil's smile faded as he examined her face. "What have you been doing to yourself?"

"I had a nice long vacation," she answered brightly, purposely misunderstanding his question. Angelique was well aware that the disturbed nights had taken their toll.

"A vacation? You look as though you haven't slept in weeks."

"Well, I guess I have been living it up recently." She avoided his eyes.

"Too many late nights aren't good." Phil frowned disapprovingly. "The camera picks up every tiny line."

Angelique was relieved when he turned his attention to setting up the giant flood lights. For the next hour Phil was too absorbed in his work to ask any inconvenient questions. During a break in the shooting, however, he asked how she had spent the summer.

"I went to Europe on the spur of the moment." She shrugged, dismissing it as nothing special. "Just a whim."

"Pretty expensive whim. Where did you go?"

"Oh...Paris...and some other places."

"Isn't that little country over there somewhere, the one your rich boyfriend comes from? You should have stopped in to see him."

Angelique debated how much to tell Phil. She didn't like to deny visiting Souveraine. It had been her life for so many weeks that she was bound to refer to it inadvertently. But she didn't want to pique Phil's curiosity either. How could she tell part of the truth without incurring painful questions?

"I did spend some time in Souveraine," she said reluctantly.

"No fooling! And you kept it to yourself all this time? Did you see the old geezer? What was he like?"

"Claude Dumont? Oh, he...he was a disappointment."

"He made a pass at you just like I said." Phil grinned. "You should have listened to me, kid. They're never too old."

"No, it was nothing like that. He turned out to be a schoolteacher—a very dull one."

"How could that be? They must pay teachers pretty well over there if he could afford all those flowers."

"Oh, well, he...actually, he had connections with the royal family."

"You mean he has a title?"

"No, Claude was Alain's tutor—Alain de Marchal, the crown prince of Souveraine."

Phil whistled. "You got on a first name basis with a prince?"

"Don't get any ideas, Alain is only sixteen," Angelique said sharply. She pushed her hair back from her forehead. "Those bright lights have given me a terrible headache. I don't think I can pose anymore today."

"Sure, Angel. We can pick up where we left off tomorrow. Why don't you go home and get a good night's sleep?" He stared after her with a thoughtful frown on his face.

If Angelique had entertained any hopes of following Phil's advice, Alain's phone call put an end to them. His familiar voice brought a flood of memories.

After telling her all the news about himself and Suzette, Alain said, "We miss you, Angelique. How's New York?"

"About the same—hot and sticky, with a thunder shower now and then that washes away the top layers of grime."

"Sounds grim. Why don't you come back to Souveraine?"

Angelique was belatedly sorry for sounding so negative. "Actually, New York is very exciting at this time of year. The theater season is beginning, and my advertising campaign has just started. I'm enjoying every minute."

"Well, I'm glad about that. I'll call you again next week."

"Alain, wait!" She stopped him just before he could hang up. Alain hadn't said a word about Tristan. "Has...has school started yet?" she asked for something to say.

"Next week. I passed all my entrance exams, incidentally."

"I knew you would." After a slight hesitation, she said, "I suppose your uncle was pleased."

Alain laughed. "You know Tristan. He would have come down on me hard if I hadn't."

"It's only because he cares about you. Is...how is he?"

"I guess he's fine. He isn't here right now."

"Where is he?" Angelique could have screamed with frustration. Why was Alain making her drag every detail out of him? She didn't know if she was angrier at him for not volunteering news of Tristan, or herself for having to know.

"Paris, I think. At least that's what he was planning. Shall I say hello for you?"

"Sure, why not," she answered bitterly. It hadn't taken Tristan long to get back on the pleasure trail. Who was his companion this time, she wondered. "Tell him I wish I'd taken snapshots when *we* were in Paris. I've almost forgotten the whole trip." Angelique was sorry the minute the words were out of her mouth, but telling Alain to forget them would only make it worse. "It's been great talking to you, but I have to go," she said hurriedly. "My date will be here any minute."

Alain wore a thoughtful look when he hung up. He told Suzette about the phone call a short time later.

"I knew I was right about those two. She's as unhappy as he is."

"How can you tell? You barely talked about your uncle."

"That's just the point! I didn't even mention Tristan—she was the one who asked about him."

Suzette looked doubtful. "That's not much to go on. What if she was just being polite?"

Alain shook his head. "How about the message she gave me? I'll bet you she wants Tristan to think he didn't mean anything to her. Maybe she hopes it will make him as miserable as she is. I could have told her he already is." Alain bunched his hands in his pockets and paced the floor, scowling ferociously. "The trick is to get her back here. I know they'd make up if they just saw each other again."

"It's possible, but I don't see how you can do it."

Alain's youthful face looked suddenly mature. "Tristan is all the family I have, and I love Angelique like a sister. They've both done more for me than anyone else in the world. They straightened out my life, and now I'm going to return the favor."

"How?" Suzette asked helplessly.

"There has to be a way. What would get her to come back?"

"Maybe if you could get your uncle to apologize for whatever he did."

"I don't know *what* he did, or if it was something *she* did. Anyway, Tristan would never apologize. He has that stiff-necked de Marchal pride." Alain made a disgusted sound. "He'd rather work until he's ready to drop, and then go riding alone on Diavolo. That's his only relaxation except for shutting himself up in his studio half the night—if you can call that fun."

"He isn't going out at all?"

"No, and that ought to tell you something. When Angelique first left he took out one girl after another, but now he's not seeing anyone."

Suzette looked thoughtful. "But suppose she thought he was."

"What do you mean?"

"If Angelique is as crazy about him as you think, she's not going to be very happy about Tristan being back in circulation. Perhaps she's been playing hard to get because she thought he'd be the one to weaken and beg her to come back. If she thought he was romancing someone else, she might rush back to put a stop to it."

A big smile broke out on Alain's face. "That's it! Suzette, you're a genius! I'll call her up and start spreading the word."

Angelique was fixing a salad for her dinner when Alain's phone call came. She had stopped accepting dates when she started to work again. Phil's criticism of late nights gave her a good excuse to get off the social merry-go-round which bored her excessively. It hadn't even served its purpose. Tristan still dominated her thoughts, waking or sleeping.

She was looking at a head of lettuce and a can of tuna with mild distaste. Preparing even a simple meal for herself seemed more bother than it was worth. The telephone was a welcome interruption.

This time Alain didn't wait for Angelique to ask about Tristan. After the briefest mention of his own activities he remarked, "By the way, Tristan said to be sure and say hello next time I talked to you. I gave him your message and he laughed. He said that trip to Paris seemed like ancient history to him too. Of course he's been there several times since you left."

Angelique couldn't speak until the sharp pain in her midsection eased. When she finally answered, her voice was strained. "I didn't realize Souveraine had such close ties with France."

"I guess there are always trade agreements to hammer out. Although, personally I think Tristan is seeing someone in Paris." Alain sounded admiring. "I don't know where he gets the energy at his age. For a while after you left he was out just about every night with a different girl."

"I wouldn't worry about him. I gather he's been that way all his life." She fought to keep the bitterness out of her voice. "Tristan will never change."

"I'm not so sure. Sometimes I get the feeling that he'd like to settle down. There's one girl who seems to have the edge. It's possible that Tristan is getting serious about her."

"Anything is possible," Angelique observed with determined brightness.

"Right now it could go either way." Alain hesitated. "I hope she's right for him. I'd hate to see him make a mistake after waiting all this time."

"I'm sure your uncle knows exactly what he's doing," she answered grimly.

"I wish I shared your confidence. She seems to really go for him, but she wouldn't be the first woman who would do anything for a title. Not like you, Angelique," Alain said fondly. Then as though he had just thought of it, "Hey, I've got a great idea! Why don't you come over here and check her out? A woman can always judge another one better than a man."

"That's the most ridiculous thing I ever heard!" The very thought of watching Tristan romance someone else made Angelique feel ill. "How can you even ask such a thing?"

"I thought you'd be willing to do it for Tristan." Alain managed to sound hurt. "The three of us got to be almost like a family while you were here. We both look on you as a sister."

Angelique's misery deepened. "That's very flattering, but you'll have to solve your own problems. Just tell me when the wedding is and I'll send a gift."

Her nerves wound tighter and tighter as Alain continued to urge her to change her mind. It was typical of him that he expected her to drop everything and come when he called, just like Tristan. But Tristan had never called. In a secret part of her heart Angelique had expected him too. Or maybe hoped was a better word. She should have known that women were expendable to him.

Could he have found someone he considered different? Angelique shriveled inside as she faced the possibility. It was a death blow to any dreams that might have lingered.

Angelique thought she had hit bottom the night of Alain's phone call. She didn't know it was going to get

worse. He began calling every few days with bulletins on
the progress of Tristan's affair. It was impossible to get
him off the subject. Angelique suffered as she was forced
to listen to all the details. Did she think it was significant
that Tristan brought his girlfriend to the palace for dinner? Was the woman sincere when she said that she
would rather stay home with Tristan than go out to the
most glamorous party with someone else?

Finally Angelique called a halt. "I love hearing from
you, Alain, but I'm not interested in your uncle. I don't
want to sound rude, but I wish you wouldn't call me unless you have something else to talk about."

It was a relief to know that she wouldn't have to hear
Tristan's name again, but Alain's phone call had the
usual effect of pouring salt in an open wound. Angelique spent another sleepless night, which wasn't any
worse than dreaming of Tristan.

When she went to the studio the next morning, Phil
took one look at her and exploded. "What are you trying
to do to yourself? You look like hell," he said bluntly.

Angelique was in no mood for criticism. "I don't have
my makeup on yet," she answered coldly.

"Makeup isn't going to hide those shadows under your
eyes, or the hollows in your cheeks. Pretty soon I'll have
to shoot you through gauze the way I do aging movie
stars."

A wave of self-pity swept over Angelique. "I wish
you'd get off my back! You've been finding fault with me
ever since we started this new campaign, and I'm getting
tired of it."

It was so totally unlike her that Phil just stared. This
taut, driven woman wasn't the Angelique he knew. "I'm
just concerned about you, Angel," he said slowly. "You
evidently don't realize you're jeopardizing your career."

"Am I supposed to give up my whole life for it?" she
demanded.

"What's gotten into you? All I want you to do is get out of the fast lane for a while. Your contract is coming up for renewal. If you don't slow down you aren't going to be Vendome's Dream Girl anymore."

The prospect left her unmoved. She'd never expected to hold the job forever. She was at the top of the heap now, but Angelique wasn't foolish enough to think she would remain there indefinitely. Younger women would come along to take her place. Time was the enemy in the modeling business, which was all the more reason to make it while she was able. Angelique realized that Phil was simply being a good friend.

"I'm sorry I snapped at you. I know you're just trying to give me good advice," she said quietly. "I didn't sleep well last night, and I have a rotten headache, but that's no reason to take it out on you."

"Is anything wrong, Angel?" He looked at her searchingly. "You can tell me. You know I'd do anything to help."

She managed a wavering smile. "Don't worry about me, Phil, I'll be okay. I played in a game where the stakes were too high, and now I'm paying for it. But at least it taught me a lesson."

Alain was sitting beside Suzette's swimming pool, giving her a progress report.

"There was only one thing wrong with your jealousy theory—I convinced Angelique that Tristan is in love with someone else, and now she won't even let me mention his name."

"You weren't supposed to be so specific," Suzette scolded. "The idea was to make her think he was dating *lots* of women. Did it really upset her?"

"She was so unhappy that I felt like a rat," Alain answered soberly. "It didn't even do any good. Angelique wouldn't come back now if it meant an end to world-wide inflation!"

"Then you'll just have to get your uncle to make the first move."

Alain sighed. "I'd rather work on the problem of inflation."

When Tristan wasn't in his office, Alain went to look for him at the stable. Tristan had just returned from riding Diavolo—a hard ride judging by the stallion's appearance.

"I wish I'd known you were going riding. I would have gone with you," Alain said, knowing Tristan hadn't wanted him along.

"I thought you were at Suzette's."

"I was." Alain followed his uncle up the gravel path to the palace, planning his strategy. "Suzette's a fantastic girl," he remarked innocently. "I feel as though I've known her all my life."

Tristan smiled faintly. "You have, just about. Since you were a toddler anyway."

"You know what I mean. I won't ever get over being grateful to Angelique for bringing us together." When Tristan didn't comment, Alain continued, "Suzette reminds me of Angelique. They're both blue eyed and blond for one thing, although nobody's hair is quite the color of Angelique's. Remember how it used to sort of glow, like a gold coin?"

Tristan lengthened his stride without answering, but Alain kept pace, pretending not to notice. "I really miss her, and I think she misses us too," he remarked.

That got a rise out of Tristan. "Angelique is too busy with her career to think about anything else," he stated grimly.

"I know she misses Souveraine—she told me so."

Tristan smiled sardonically. "And you're still young enough to believe that women mean what they say."

"There's one way to prove it." Alain was elaborately casual. "Ask her back here for a visit."

"Don't be ridiculous!" Tristan said explosively.

"I'll bet she'd come."

Tristan checked his pace to glare at his nephew. "Listen to me, young man! There will be no repeat of the childish behavior that started this whole thing. You are not to invite Angelique to Souveraine, either now or at any time in the future. In fact, I want you to stop calling her. I don't wish you to have any contact with her whatsoever. That includes letters, Christmas cards, the works. Is that clear?"

"I don't see why—"

"The matter is not open for discussion," Tristan interrupted. "You will do as I say. I don't ever want to hear Angelique Archer's name mentioned again, and that's final!"

Alain still looked shaken when he described the scene to Suzette a short time later. "I've never seen Tristan so angry—at least not at me."

"It shows you were right about how much he cares," Suzette consoled him.

"A fat lot of good it does. Neither of them will budge an inch. I'm a fine cupid," he said disgustedly.

"Well, at least you tried. There's nothing more you can do."

"It's so downright stupid!" He ruffled his hair in frustration. "Angelique sounds as though she's lost her last friend, and Tristan barks out orders like Genghis Khan. I think the reason he goes riding so often is that it gives him something to kick."

Suzette tried to cheer him up. "He'd better be careful. That wild horse will kick him back," she joked.

"Maybe it might knock some sense into his thick head," Alain muttered. "And hers too. I wonder how Angelique would feel if she was the cause of Tristan breaking his neck." Alain's dark scowl suddenly vanished. "That's it!" he cried jubilantly. "If Angelique thought Tristan was seriously hurt—maybe dying—she'd come flying over here on the first plane. All I have to do is call and tell her he had an accident."

"You're cracking up! What's going to happen when she gets here and finds out he's fine? She'll hold you down while your uncle skins you alive!"

Alain grinned. "At least they'll finally be doing something together." His laughter died as he said slowly, "If I'm wrong, things could get pretty sticky, but I'm willing to take the chance. They're both so miserable right now that I think one glimpse of each other is all it's going to take."

Suzette looked worried. "Have you really thought about what you're getting yourself into if things don't go according to plan?"

Alain's cheerful grin was back. "Tristan will probably oil the lock on that old dungeon in the cellar. If you don't see me for five or six months, that's where I'll be." He pulled her to her feet. "Come on, let's go call Angelique."

Angelique's face was white and strained as she refused the flight attendant's offer of breakfast. Her body was taut against the restraining seat belt, and her hands were icy.

Her entire world had been shattered by Alain's phone call the night before. At first she thought it was a horrible practical joke. How could anything happen to Tristan? He was so vitally alive, so in charge of his own life and everyone else's. Hadn't he dominated hers from thousands of miles away? Angelique couldn't imagine a world without Tristan in it.

It was almost as incredible that he had called for her when he was injured. Had Tristan really cared for her after all? Could she have spared them both this agony if she'd stayed? Her eyes closed in pain. If only she wasn't too late. Tristan just couldn't die!

Alain's face was so sober when he met her at the airport that Angelique's heart turned over. She clutched at his arm. "He isn't—"

"No, he's fine. I mean he's holding his own," Alain corrected himself hastily.

He seemed reluctant to talk about Tristan's accident, which was understandable. But Angelique had to know all the details.

"I don't understand it," she said helplessly. "Tristan is such a superb rider. It's almost unbelievable."

Alain pressed down on the accelerator, sending the car shooting up the twisting mountain road. "He isn't invincible. He's just a man, Angelique, a very lonely one. All the purpose went out of his life when you left, and I'm betting that your life wasn't any better." He looked sideways at her. "That's what you have to remember when you see Tristan again."

Before she could answer they arrived at the palace, and everything else was driven out of her mind. Instead of stopping at the front door, Alain drove around to the back.

When she looked at him questioningly he said, "Tristan is in the studio. They took him there because it was the closest place, and then he couldn't be moved. Don't knock, in case he's sleeping, just walk in." As she started to get out of the car Alain caught her hand. "Remember what I told you, Angelique—and good luck."

She was in too much of a daze to pay any attention to his cryptic words. Tristan was just a few steps away. Could she bear to see him helpless and in pain? No matter what condition he was in she had to tell him she loved him. It might be her last chance. Taking a deep breath, she opened the door softly.

Tristan was lying on the couch with his arms folded over his chest, staring at her painting which still stood on the easel. He had on jeans and a navy T-shirt. Outside of appearing thinner than she remembered, he looked exactly the same as the picture she carried in her heart.

For a moment they just stared at each other. Tristan got slowly to his feet, like a man in a trance. "What are you doing here?" His voice sounded hoarse.

"You aren't hurt!" Her dazzled eyes roamed over him, taking in every detail of his beloved body. He was as big and powerful as ever. It was like a miracle!

A scowl marred his classic features. "What do you mean I'm not hurt? How the devil would you know?"

"Alain told me. He said you'd been thrown from a horse. He said—" Her breathless rush of words came to a halt as she realized that Alain had lied to her.

Angelique's first reaction was overwhelming relief. Then the full impact of it struck her. If he lied about Tristan's accident, then the rest of Alain's story was false too. Tristan hadn't called for her on his deathbed where people reveal their true feelings. He wasn't even glad to see her! Misery and embarrassment washed over Angelique.

Tristan was looking at her with incredulity. "You came back because you thought I'd been hurt?"

"Alain made it sound so serious," she said haltingly. "I thought you were dying."

"That must have meant you cared." He walked slowly toward her.

"Of course I did! We were...we were friends."

"That isn't the word I'd use." He touched her cheek gently, as though to convince himself that she was real. "Do you know how much I've missed you? Life hasn't been worth living since you left."

That reminded Angelique of how Tristan had been spending his time. "Did your latest romance go sour too?" she asked bitterly.

"The only romance I've had is with your painting." He examined her features with a kind of wonder. "I stay up half the night staring at it, remembering how you felt in my arms."

"Don't lie to me, Tristan! At least you were honest before." Her voice was tortured. "Alain told me you've been seeing someone else."

All the lines were magically erased from his face. "Alain has been a very busy boy. I don't know whether to punish him, or raise his allowance. As I understand it, he's been phoning you with detailed bulletins about my love life."

Angelique's long lashes fell. "He was concerned about you. He wanted me to...he wanted my opinion."

"Which I gather you declined to give. So Alain told you I'd been thrown from a horse." Tristan shook his head admiringly. "That young man has a real talent for intrigue."

Tristan thought it was all a big joke! He had no idea of the suffering she had gone through. Angelique's eyes filled with tears. "I'll never forgive him. It was a cruel, heartless thing to do."

Tristan was watching her with growing excitement. "I'll admit it went beyond the bounds of a boyish prank, but cruel, Angel? That would only be true if you were in love with me." He moved very close. "*Are* you in love with me?" Before she could answer, he put his fingers gently over her lips. "No, wait. Let me tell you how I felt when I saw you standing in the doorway with the sun turning your hair to a golden halo. I thought I'd died and gone to heaven because it's been hell on earth without you."

He took her in his arms then, crushing her so tightly that she could hardly breathe. There was a kind of desperation in his kiss, a pent-up longing that expressed his emotion better than any words. His hands caressed her almost roughly, kneading her back, tangling in her hair, urging her hips against his.

She was completely enveloped by him. This was what she had dreamed about for so long, but the reality was much more wonderful than her fantasies. Tristan's plundering tongue was a torch that set her on fire, and his hard body sent the flames higher. Waves of pure sensation washed over Angelique as she strained against him, her desperation matching Tristan's.

When he finally dragged his mouth away it was only to groan deeply, "I'll never let you go again. Tell me you've come back to stay."

"For as long as you want me," she assured him.

There was no question of leaving him. Without Tristan there was no joy in life. She would take whatever he would give her. Angelique knew she would even share him if she had to.

"How about for the rest of our lives?" he murmured.

Before his magic could complete its spell, she said what needed to be said. "You don't have to make any promises, I know there's someone else. Just let me be part of your life, Tristan, please!"

"My dearest love. There's never been anyone else since I first laid eyes on your beautiful face."

"But Alain said—"

"He has more sense than both of us, Angel. I guess there's a lot of John Alden in me after all. I had to have a sixteen-year-old boy ask the woman I love to marry me."

"Is that what he—" Angelique stared at him incredulously. Surely she was imagining these words she longed so desperately to hear. "But you never even said you loved me!"

He stroked her cheek with gentle fingers. "You must have known that. How much plainer could I have made it? But every time I hoped that you were beginning to care about me too, you told me how important your career was."

"Oh, Tristan, we've been such idiots! That was just a defense mechanism. I thought *you* were only interested in...well...making love to me."

A little smile played around his firm mouth as he unfastened the top button of her blouse. "That's a pretty true statement if you leave out the word 'only.'" He bent his head to kiss the cleft between her breasts. "I dreamed about your beautiful body every night since you left. Did you ever think about how wonderful it was when we made love?"

Angelique slid her hands under his T-shirt, running her palms over his smooth warm back. "Only every night since I left," she echoed.

He crushed her tightly against his chest, kissing her almost as though he wanted to devour her. There was urgency in the way he swung her into his arms and started for the bedroom. "It's been so long, my love."

Angelique trembled with anticipation as Tristan removed her blouse. It built in intensity as his teeth nipped at her hardened nipples through the thin lace bra before he removed it and took each pink bud in his mouth. While she gasped with pleasure he unzipped her skirt. As it slid to the floor he knelt in front of her, his mouth gliding down her body. His tongue circled her navel before continuing its molten path. He explored every inch of her with slow, arousing kisses. Angelique moaned at the feathery caresses on her thighs and fiery flames licking at her midsection.

She anchored her fingers in his thick hair, murmuring faintly, "I love you, Tristan."

"And I love you, my dearest one—now and forever."

He stood up, stripping off his T-shirt and jeans in one swift movement. Her dazzled eyes feasted on him in the moment before he clasped her bare body against his, scorching her with the pulsing heat of his hardened loins. Their bodies fit like two pieces of a puzzle that only needed to be connected.

Tristan lowered her onto the bed without letting her out of his arms. He covered her body with his, fitting himself between her parted legs. Angelique drew in her breath at the remembered entry. She melted against him, becoming such a complete part of him that his ecstasy became hers. They traveled the path to fulfillment, their bodies radiating with waves of sensation that built and then burst in a fiery blaze. Tiny sparks died slowly as Angelique clung trustingly to the man she loved so dearly.

A long time later he raised her chin tenderly. "You will marry me, won't you, darling? I won't ask you to give up your career. Just live here part time, and I'll come to New York every chance I get. All I want is to know that you belong to me."

She trailed a finger down his straight nose. "I don't think long distance marriages work out very well." When apprehension started to darken his face, Angelique smiled enchantingly. "Besides, being a Dream Girl isn't much fun anymore. I'd rather be a real live duchess. It has more job security."

Incredulous joy shone in Tristan's eyes. "I guarantee you'll have that job for the rest of your life, my love—including fringe benefits."

His mouth covered Angelique's with male determination as he wound his legs around hers.

AMERICAN TRIBUTE

Where a man's dreams count for more than his parentage...

Look for these upcoming titles under the Special Edition American Tribute banner.

LOVE'S HAUNTING REFRAIN
Ada Steward #289—February 1986
For thirty years a deep dark secret kept them apart—King Stockton made his millions while his wife, Amelia, held everything together. Now could they tell their secret, could they admit their love?

THIS LONG WINTER PAST
Jeanne Stephens #295—March 1986
Detective Cody Wakefield checked out Assistant District Attorney Liann McDowell, but only in his leisure time. For it was the danger of Cody's job that caused Liann to shy away.

AMERICAN TRIBUTE

RIGHT BEHIND THE RAIN
Elaine Camp #301—April 1986
The difficulty of coping with her brother's
death brought reporter Raleigh Torrence
to the office of Evan Younger, a police
psychologist. He helped her to deal with
her feelings and emotions, including love.

CHEROKEE FIRE
Gena Dalton #307—May 1986
It was Sabrina Dante's silver spoon that
Cherokee cowboy Jarod Redfeather couldn't
trust. The two lovers came from opposite
worlds, but Jarod's Indian heritage taught
them to overcome their differences.

NOBODY'S FOOL
Renee Roszel #313—June 1986
Everyone bet that Martin Dante and Cara
Torrence would get together. But Martin
wasn't putting any money down, and Cara
was out to prove that she was nobody's fool.

MISTY MORNINGS, MAGIC NIGHTS
Ada Steward #319—July 1986
The last thing Carole Stockton wanted was to
fall in love with another politician, especially
Donnelly Wakefield. But under a blanket of
secrecy, far from the campaign spotlights,
their love became a powerful force.

COMING NEXT MONTH

LOVE'S HAUNTING REFRAIN—Ada Steward
Amelia had left the East Coast to join King on his Oklahoma ranch.
Theirs was a marriage of love and passion, yet it was threatened by
the secret that King dared not reveal.

MY HEART'S UNDOING—Phyllis Halldorson
Colleen's love for Erik had grown from a schoolgirl crush into the
passions of a woman. Erik had loved before.... Could he forget the
woman who'd broken his heart, or would she haunt their future?

SURPRISE OFFENSE—Carole Halston
Football superstar Rocky Players had a reputation as a womanizer,
so why was he treating Dana like one of the boys? Dana was
definitely a woman, as Rocky was soon to find out.

BIRD IN FLIGHT—Sondra Stanford
When Andie and Bill met by chance in London, they were each
flooded with memories. Had a three-year separation taught them
enough to overcome their differences and rediscover their love?

TRANSFER OF LOYALTIES—Roslyn MacDonald
Adrienne was a dedicated employee who thought of little but her
career, until Jared Hawks came along and showed her the truth in the
old adage "all work and no play..."

AS TIME GOES BY—Brooke Hastings
Sarah needed the funds that Jonathan Hailey controlled in order to
continue her underwater exploration, but slowly her need for funds
was overridden by her need for Jonathan.

AVAILABLE NOW:

RETURN TO PARADISE
Jennifer West

REFLECTIONS OF YESTERDAY
Debbie Macomber

VEIN OF GOLD
Elaine Camp

SUMMER WINE
Freda Vasilos

DREAM GIRL
Tracy Sinclair

SECOND NATURE
Nora Roberts